Praise for

"Readers everywhere will devour the hilarious, action-packed adventures of Ronald Zupan. In this dazzling debut, Steve Bramucci takes us on the ride of a lifetime. Warning: devilish traps and ferocious pirates ahead!"
—**Matt de la Peña**, Newbery Award–winning author of *Last Stop on Market Street*

"I've closed the book, but I'm still wearing my adventure hat. I want to be ready when Ronald Zupan and his friends set off on their next courageous journey."
—**Cassie Beasley**, *New York Times* bestselling author of *Circus Mirandus*

"A fast-paced, comic update of a classic swashbuckler!"
—**Mac Barnett**, *New York Times* bestselling coauthor of *The Terrible Two*

"Adventure, suspense, humor, and heart! I loved reading about Ronald and his brave friends, and I know you will, too! Watch out, evildoers—you don't stand a chance against the unflappable Ronald Zupan!" —**Varian Johnson**, author of *The Great Greene Heist* and *To Catch a Cheat*

BOOKS BY STEPHEN BRAMUCCI AND ARREE CHUNG

The Danger Gang and the Pirates of Borneo!
The Danger Gang and the Isle of Feral Beasts!

THE DANGER GANG
AND THE PIRATES OF BORNEO!

STEPHEN BRAMUCCI

ILLUSTRATED BY ARREE CHUNG

BLOOMSBURY
CHILDREN'S BOOKS

NEW YORK   LONDON   OXFORD   NEW DELHI   SYDNEY

BLOOMSBURY CHILDREN'S BOOKS
Bloomsbury Publishing Inc., part of Bloomsbury Publishing Plc
1385 Broadway, New York, NY 10018

BLOOMSBURY, BLOOMSBURY CHILDREN'S BOOKS, and the Diana logo are
trademarks of Bloomsbury Publishing Plc

First published in the United States of America in August 2017
by Bloomsbury Children's Books
Paperback edition published in October 2018

Text copyright © 2017 by Stephen Bramucci
Illustrations copyright © 2017 by Arree Chung

Bloomsbury books may be purchased for business or promotional use. For information on bulk
purchases please contact Macmillan Corporate and Premium Sales Department at
specialmarkets@macmillan.com

ISBN 978-1-68119-434-9 (paperback)

The Library of Congress has cataloged the hardcover edition as follows:
Names: Bramucci, Stephen, author. | Chung, Arree, illustrator.
Title: The Danger Gang and the Pirates of Borneo! / by Stephen Bramucci ;
illustrated by Arree Chung.
Description: New York : Bloomsbury, 2017.
Summary: When Ronald Zupan's parents are kidnapped on his 11th birthday, he
teams up with his trusty butler, Jeeves, his fencing nemesis, Julianne Sato, and his
pet cobra, Carter, to face pirates and other dangers in the jungle of Borneo.
Identifiers: LCCN 2016037881 (print) • LCCN 2016049775 (e-book)
ISBN 978-1-61963-692-7 (hardcover) • ISBN 978-1-61963-693-4 (e-book)
Subjects: | CYAC: Adventure and adventurers—Fiction. | Kidnapping—Fiction. |
Pirates—Fiction. | Jungles—Fiction. | Borneo—Fiction. | BISAC: JUVENILE FICTION /
Action & Adventure / Pirates. | JUVENILE FICTION / Humorous Stories. |
JUVENILE FICTION / Social Issues / Friendship.
Classification: LCC PZ7.1.B7513 Dan 2017 (print) | LCC PZ7.1.B7513 (e-book) |
DCC [Fic]—dc23
LC record available at https://lccn.loc.gov/2016037881

Book design by Jessie Gang
Typeset by Westchester Publishing Services
Printed and bound in the U.S.A. by Berryville Graphics Inc., Berryville, Virginia
2 4 6 8 10 9 7 5 3 1

All papers used by Bloomsbury Publishing Plc are natural, recyclable products
made from wood grown in well-managed forests. The manufacturing processes
conform to the environmental regulations of the country of origin.

To find out more about our authors and books visit www.bloomsbury.com
and sign up for our newsletters.

For the mom who taught me to love stories, the girl who laughed at this one, and the adventure partner who helped me turn it into a real live book

1

Thrilling Entrances!

Hello friend,

Are you ready for a dazzling tale of grand adventure?

A tale of swordfights and disguises?

Of pirates and stolen relics?

If not, you should scramble up the moss-covered rocks of a towering waterfall and fling this book into a piranha-infested river.

Ronald Zupan won't allow a single unadventurous spirit to touch these pages.

I mean that.

Just feast your eyes on my swashbuckling mustache—isn't this the look of an eleven-year-old who demands to be taken seriously?

I am **Ronald Zupan**, the only son of Francisco and Helen Zupan, and from the moment I was born, I've been nothing short of spectacular.

Want proof? When I was just one year old, a seven-foot-long king cobra slithered across my bedroom floor and wound his way into my crib.

FACT: The king cobra is the most venomous snake known to man.

Luckily, even back then, I knew the number one rule for avoiding snake attacks: BITE FIRST AND BITE OFTEN! I clamped my gums onto the cobra's scaly body and held tight. He swiveled his head and shot at me like a dart, but the strike barely even fazed me. **Ronald Zupan** was born immune to poisons of all varieties.

We wrestled until my crib toppled over and sent us both sprawling across the floor, but by the time my parents came to investigate, the battle was over and the snake and I were napping side by side on the carpet. As I grew older, I tamed the beast and named him Carter.

Need more evidence of my derring-do?

At the tender age of five, I crept inside the Zupan Library and devoured my first book, *The Collected Plays of William Shakespeare*. As my mother, Helen Zupan, once said, "The most adventurous people are carnivorous readers." She was right, it was a feast of language.

Speaking of digesting the classics, hopefully by now you've deduced that you're holding the first part of my extraordinary autobiography. **Ronald Zupan**'s life is sure to be filled with far too many heart-stopping exploits to collect in a single volume, so consider this part one . . . of **INFINITY**!

Let's see Shakespeare top that!

Did the bard have his loyal butler, Jeeves, on hand to magnify his breathtaking adventures? I doubt it. And even though Jeeves's writing might not shine quite like my own, his notes at the end of each chapter will surely cast my bold deeds in a new light.

The past is prologue. Now, friends, we venture into the vast unknown!

Oh dear.

Did Ronald just say that I'd "magnify" his adventures? I'm afraid that's not quite true. I'm actually here to correct mistakes, add new details, and fill in bits of the story that Ronald leaves out. For example:

Errors in the Chapter "Thrilling Entrances!"

1. The king cobra is not the most venomous snake known to man; it's actually the third most venomous. But that hardly matters because the snake that slipped into Ronald's crib isn't deadly at all. His fangs and venom glands were removed ages ago.

2. "Bite first and bite often" is absolutely NOT the number one rule for preventing a snake attack. I'm sure there are all sorts of

better options. Personally, I think "Shriek and run away" would work just fine.

3. I want to make it clear that young Ronald was *LITERALLY* eating Shakespeare's Collected Plays until his mother caught him and explained that "carnivorous reading" meant reading eagerly, not swallowing an entire book page by page. Helen Zupan loves wordplay.

4. My name is not Jeeves. Ronald calls me that because I'm a butler from England and he's dead set that all butlers from England ought to be called Jeeves. My real name is Thomas Halladay, though I prefer the simple: Tom.

2
Mysterious Disappearances!

The morning I turned eleven, I sprang out of bed and pulled back the window curtains. The sun hovered above the peaked rooftops of our fair city—lurking behind the fog like the yolk of a poached egg in a bowl of dragon-fruit soup.

"My parents are in grave danger," I said aloud.

Francisco and Helen Zupan had been gone for more than a week—perfectly normal for two world-famous adventurers dealing in ancient relics. But the fact that they hadn't come to wake me up on my birthday was a very bad sign.

Seven years earlier, my mother had knelt beside my bed, twirled her slender fingers through my hair, and said, "Nothing could keep us from singing to our son as the sun rises on his birthday."

"If we ever aren't here," my father added, "you'll know we are in danger." He leveled his dark eyes at me. "*Grave danger.*"

My father must have misunderstood the brave look on my face, because he ruffled my hair, winked, and said, "Nothing to worry about just yet."

Then he handed me a package wrapped in hand-dyed paper that smelled like sandalwood. My parents watched excitedly as I peeled it open. Inside was a leather diary they'd bought from a spice trader. My first adventure journal!

Ever since that day, my birthdays had started with a song—long ballads that told of exotic lands and mysterious strangers.

This year there was no song, and I knew my father's warning had finally come to pass. I bounded across the room, dove into my clothes, stuffed my adventure journal into my pocket, applied my very realistic-looking mustache, and threw open the door. I was immediately hit with the fragrant scents of vanilla and melted butter. The smells trailed me as I hurried toward my parents' room.

I peeked inside and spied the gold death mask of an ancient Pharaoh, a stuffed woolly mammoth, and the first piggy bank in recorded history. But Helen and Francisco Zupan were nowhere to be found.

I rushed downstairs to tell Jeeves. He was in the kitchen, wearing an apron around his waist that read, MY NAME IS NOT JEEVES.

"Jeeves, we've got trouble," I said.

"Read the apron," Jeeves replied, using a spatula to peek under the edge of a buttermilk pancake.

"This is no time for games," I said. "My parents are in grave danger."

Jeeves glanced up from the griddle. "I doubt that. Probably just delayed. It's a long trip home from . . . where are they this time? Burma? Bengal?"

"Borneo," I said. "They kept talking about some highly charming gentleman they wanted to find."

There were eight pancakes on the griddle, and Jeeves flipped them one by one.

"If they had only accepted my application to join their team, I could have helped them," I said. "Now look, catastrophe strikes!"

Jeeves clicked off the stove and slipped the pancakes onto two plates. "Ronald, I'm sure there's nothing to fear. They probably just had to negotiate a flight out of the jungle with a one-eyed bush pilot or swim down class-five rapids."

I rushed to get the silverware. Jeeves set a pat of butter on top of my pancakes and it slowly slid down the side of the stack.

"Don't you see?" I asked, pouring each of us a glass of lychee juice. "Francisco and Helen promised to *always* come home before sunrise on my birthday. If they aren't here, it means they're in trouble. It's like a signal, or a secret code."

Jeeves pondered it as he chewed. "Sounds more like a misunderstanding. Your parents are very busy."

"Too busy to keep the promise they made to their only son?"

Jeeves set down his fork and his face tightened. "I'm sure they'll be here any minute. Now, about this matter of your birthday—"

"We're going to have to spend it searching for them," I interrupted. "We should make a list of all the enemies my parents have near Borneo. Any ideas?"

Jeeves looked at me for a long moment, then sighed. "Oh, I don't know . . . have you tried looking in the atlas?"

He was talking about a giant atlas that my father keeps in his private collection.

I remember asking once, "Dad, can I have some chocolate?"

"Look inside the atlas," he replied, stroking his beard.

I figured he wanted me to look at a map of Switzerland, where the very first cacao beans were grown—to satisfy my hunger with knowledge rather than sweets. I rushed off to do exactly that, but before I could get to the Zupan Library, I remembered that I had four squares of a Carroll's Caramel Crunch stashed under my bed. So I skipped the atlas that day.

Another time, I wanted to practice throwing playing cards—a perfect self-defense skill for any adventurer trying to escape a smoky gambling den—so I asked for a deck to borrow.

"Look inside the atlas," my father said. I was sure he wanted me to study the geography of Italy, where playing cards were invented. But I borrowed my mother's Scorpion Poker deck instead.

"So," Jeeves said, rousing me from my memories, "have you looked in the atlas?"

"The atlas?" I asked. "You think perhaps looking at the map of Borneo will help me discover a clue?"

The good butler's eyebrows pinched together. "Ronald, look *inside* the atlas. That's where your father keeps all his—"

He was interrupted by a heavy knock at the door and glided off to answer it. I followed at the heels of his perfectly shined shoes.

"Forget it," Jeeves said, setting his hand on the doorknob. "This is probably them now. Maybe they just lost their key."

FROM THE DESK OF
Thomas Halladay

Errors in the Chapter "Mysterious Disappearances!"

1. The costume facial hair that Ronald often wears glued to his upper lip is not "very realistic." Not even a little bit. The real truth is, pencil-thin mustaches look absolutely absurd on eleven-year-old boys.

2. When he tells the story of his father's atlas, Ronald claims that cacao beans were first grown in Switzerland. He's not quite right—they actually come from Mexico.

3. Similarly, playing cards were invented in China not Italy. Of course, Francisco wanted his son to look in the atlas for a totally different reason, but somehow Ronald managed to miss that simple clue for years.

3

Strange Houseguests!

When Jeeves swung the door wide, we found a man in a black suit waiting on the porch. The stranger's hair was clipped close to his head and he wore aviator sunglasses, even though it was foggy.

"Four niner one niner," he said, flipping open a badge one second and snapping it shut the next. "This house is now part of an active investigation."

"Pardon?" Jeeves asked, peering past the officer.

"Stand aside. We're coming in."

I leaped out from behind Jeeves like a crab-eating mongoose. "Not. So. Fast!"

The officer scowled down at me. "What's with the mustache, kid?"

"All master adventurers have stylish facial hair," I said. "What do you mean 'we're coming in'?"

"As you may know, your parents were scheduled to return to the city late last night."

"Of course. For my birthday."

"Sure," the officer said, "your birthday. Anyway, when their plane didn't land, the FIB was notified."

"The FIB?" Jeeves asked. "Don't you mean—"

"The Foreign Item Battalion," the man interrupted. "The Zupans hired us to secure the house so that no one could steal the Lion of Lyros if they ever go missing."

"So they *are* missing?" I said. "We have to find them!"

The officer leaned close to me. "My orders are to find the Lion of Lyros. You two should vamoose."

The Lion of Lyros is my parents' most famous artifact. It's a three-and-a-half-inch-tall sculpture of a human, kneeling upright, with bulging muscles much like my own. The only difference is that the statue has the head of a lion and I have the head of a brave explorer with a very convincing mustache.

"Foreign Item Battalion?" Jeeves said, arching an eyebrow. "I've never heard the Zupans talk about your agency. Do you have paperwork?"

He was studying the officer's scuffed shoes, and I deduced that he, too, smelled the suspicious odor coming off this stranger. The man threw open his suit jacket. A chrome pistol rested in a leather holster near his armpit.

"This is my paperwork. Understand, *butler*?"

Jeeves stiffened. "Ronald . . . I think we had better be leaving."

"Not without Carter!"

I ran back into the entryway and bolted up the stairs, two at a time. The officer yelled for Jeeves to get me out of the house.

"The boy is going to collect his pet cobra," I heard Jeeves say, "but if you prefer, I would happily leave the dreaded animal here to roam. I'll warn you though: it bites."

I searched under my bed, then in the closet, but didn't see Carter anywhere. I finally found him in the library, coiled on my father's famous atlas, which sat closed on a wooden pedestal near the radiator. I reached for him, but Carter hates being moved away from warm places, especially on foggy mornings.

FACT: Even if you're immune to poison of all varieties, it's no fun to start your birthday with a cobra bite.

I picked up the atlas, cobra and all, and rushed back downstairs. In the entryway, more men in suits flooded into the house, brushing past me, knocking down paintings and turning over couch cushions.

The first man yelled, "Hey, you can't take that!"

He grabbed my shoulder and spun me halfway around. Carter flared his hooded neck, and the officer shriveled like a Portuguese jellyfish in the Sahara.

"Well done, trusty beast," I whispered.

I jammed my feet into my expedition boots and clambered outside. By the time I made it to the driveway, Jeeves had wheeled his old motorbike out of the garage and was busy fastening his helmet. I jumped into the sidecar with Carter and the atlas, but before we could go anywhere, six bulky officers hustled to block our path.

"Stand down," I shouted. "The sooner we find my parents, the sooner we can sort this all out."

A female officer flicked a cigarette onto the driveway and ground it into the concrete with her boot heel.

"We've reconsidered," the man in the sunglasses said. "We think you'd better stay here until we find the lion . . . y'know . . . *for your safety*."

"What on earth does that mean?" Jeeves asked.

Without answering, the entire swarm of officers closed in on all sides.

"Jeeves," I said under my breath, "there's no time to waste. Hit the gas!"

But before he had the chance, a hulking brute lunged at us, wrapped his meaty hands around me, and yanked me out of the sidecar. I ordered Carter to strike the scoundrel, but the snake refused to budge. He prefers to strike when it's least expected, like when I'm just stepping out of the bath.

"Unhand **Ronald Zupan**!" I yelled, kicking wildly.

"Who?" the rogue grunted as he dragged me up the steps toward the front door.

I tried to shake free from the officer's grasp as the man in the sunglasses rattled off our rights. "You have the right to do what we say. You have the right to remain silent, unless you know where the lion is—"

He lifted his sunglasses and stared directly into my eyes.

"Do you, kid?" he rumbled. "Do you know where the lion is?"

His breath reeked of raw garlic and boiled beef tongue.

"Absolutely not," I snapped, elbowing the man who held me tight. I wasn't lying, either—my parents had never told me where they hid the statue.

The officer in the sunglasses sneered, showing dark lines of plaque between his teeth. "Fine. Then go back to remaining silent. *Capisce?*"

"I do say, there's no need to be so rough!"

I craned my neck to see Jeeves getting hauled away by two more men.

"Let him go!" I yelled. "Unhand my butler!"

The officers forced us both back to the house, leaving Carter alone in the motorcycle sidecar, coiled on the atlas. They herded us upstairs and into my parents' bedroom, shoving us inside Helen's walk-in closet. The man with the sunglasses said, "Don't move a muscle!" then slammed the door. Jeeves and I could hear him block us in with my mother's dressing table before clomping away.

"I suppose we'll just have to wait," Jeeves said, breathing heavily. "If we stay in here, no harm will come to us."

I pulled aside my mother's clothes, hoping to find a secret passageway.

"Jeeves," I said, knocking on the wall for hollow spots, "I have a good hunch that the Foreign Item Battalion is a pack of frauds, here to steal the Lion of Lyros for themselves."

Jeeves winced. "Is this like your last hunch?"

FACT: Jeeves was probably thinking of the time I'd had a hunch that his bed held a secret scroll in one of its legs . . . so I used a hacksaw to investigate.

"This is different," I said. "This is a *good* hunch."

"I'd prefer proof," Jeeves said.

I stepped close to him. "Would *real* investigators lock an eleven-year-old and his butler inside a closet?"

Jeeves opened his mouth to speak, then hesitated.

"*Exactly!* They're scalawags! But they'll never find the lion; my parents are too smart for that."

I could see that Jeeves's mind was spinning. I leveled my eyes at him. "It's our duty to escape and investigate my parents' mysterious disappearance. When we find them, they'll be in awe of our derring-do and invite us along on all their adventures."

Jeeves frowned. "Can't we just wait a few hours? I really do think they'll show up soon."

"We can't risk it," I told him. "A chance for greatness has been thrust upon us, and there's not a second to spare."

Jeeves paused for a moment, then sighed heavily—which was his way of saying that it was a dazzling speech.

"I suppose it wouldn't hurt to do some poking around," he said. "But there doesn't seem to be any safe way out of this closet."

"That all depends on how you define 'safe,'" I said.

FROM THE DESK OF
Thomas Halladay

Errors in the Chapter "Strange Houseguests!"

1. The Lion of Lyros is indeed one of the most famous artifacts in existence—but it doesn't resemble Ronald any more than I resemble a llama. It was unearthed by Helen Zupan on an archaeological expedition through the Arabian Desert.

2. Ronald writes that I could smell a "suspicious odor wafting" off the officer. Which isn't exactly true, though there was definitely a stench. The fact is, I was busy wondering why the Zupans would hire the FIB to protect the Lion of Lyros without telling their butler.

3. How I define "safe"? What a question! Here goes: safe does NOT mean dangling out of a window. How's that for starters?

4

Daring Escapes!

The closet was built into the southern corner of the house, with one small keyhole window at the far end. I opened it, stepped on top of the radiator, and peered down.

"Oh no," said Jeeves from behind me. "We're quite high, and jumping from this height will surely lead to severe injuries. Possibly death. Besides—"

I glanced over my shoulder. "Fear not, Jeeves. We're not going to jump."

He exhaled. "Thank goodness."

"Instead, we'll rappel, like canyoneers lowering themselves into an underground abyss."

Jeeves's eyes went wide and he leaned out the window, frowning down at his prized vegetable garden three stories below.

"This is going to end with us—"

"Being heroes," I said, finishing for him. "Now first, let's tie Helen's dresses together to make a rope."

I grabbed a yellow evening gown, pulled it off its hanger, and tied it to a blood-colored outback cape. When he saw what I was doing, Jeeves reached for a flowered sundress, which he hitched to the sleeve of a cashmere sweater.

"Ronald," he said, as both of our ropes grew longer, "have you considered that these fine bits of fabric might not hold us?"

"Fear not," I said, throwing him a dashing wink.

Jeeves cocked his head, curiously. "Is that your big finish?" he finally asked. "'Fear not?' And that was supposed to convince me that I'm safe on a rope made of dresses?"

"I also winked."

When the ropes were done, I tied them together and fastened one end to the bottom of the radiator. Next, I crawled over the windowsill and began lowering myself toward the ground, hand over hand.

Jeeves peered down at me. "Have I never mentioned how much I dislike heights?"

There was a clattering inside the house that seemed to change the good butler's mind. In another second, he'd twisted out the window and started inching his way down after me.

When I passed the billiards room on the second floor, I

realized that the officers were fortune's fools—in their search for the lion, they'd pulled all the curtains shut and couldn't see us. As for our rope, it held up excellently until my feet gently touched the ground.

"The perfect escape!" I yelled, just as the dresses frayed and ripped to shreds.

Jeeves plummeted the last few feet, but I was wisely positioned right below him and did a superb job of softening his landing.

"No time to spend ripening on the vine," I said, with my face mashed against a tomato vine.

Jeeves rolled off me, staggered to his feet, and shot a glance at the front door of the house. As we ducked across the lawn toward the driveway, he fished the motorbike key out of his vest pocket and we climbed aboard. I piled Carter and the atlas on my lap.

The second the engine roared to life, Jeeves hit the throttle. I spun around to watch the house, but no one chased after us.

If it had been one of my parents' harrowing tales, I'm sure the vicious gang would've followed us through a crowded bazaar. The way it happened was probably for the best, though—there are no crowded bazaars on our street, and the top speed of Jeeves's motorcycle is about eight miles per hour. We crawled around the corner and Zupan Manor slid out of sight.

"Where to?" Jeeves asked over the clunking of the engine.

I thought of something my mother always says: "If you don't want to get bowled over by your enemies, make sure you have a few bold adventurers by your side." I glanced over at Jeeves, who still had a piece of basil stuck to his forehead. Clearly, I needed someone I could count on when the going got tough.

I opened my adventure notebook and found the page titled Potential Adventure Sidekicks:

"Here we go!" I said, flicking the notebook with my finger. "107 Oak, and step on it!"

ster
curer
ld
wait
most
atic
nt to
clue.

POTENTIAL ADVENTURE SIDEKICKS

NAME	RELATIONSHIP	LAST KNOWN LOCATION
Jeeves	Butler	The room down the hall.
Carter	Snake	Wrapped around Jeeves's ankle.
Julianne S		
Julianne Sato?	Fencing Opponent	107 Oak Street

FROM THE DESK OF
Thomas Halladay

Errors in the Chapter "Daring Escapes!"

1. Just because a dress is lovely, doesn't mean it makes a good rope. Trust me, I found out the hard way.

2. In case it's not clear: when the rope split, I fell onto Ronald and we collapsed into my award-winning tomato plants. I was briefly caught in a heap of Helen's clothes before finally extracting myself near the herbs. All in all, it had been a rough morning.

3. I'll have you know that my motorbike tops out at a respectable twenty-five miles per hour, thank you very much.

5
A Vital Clue!

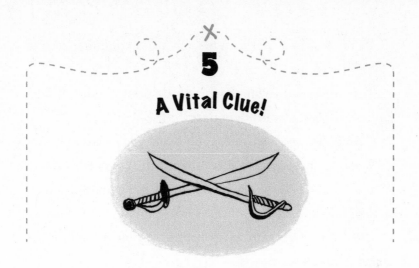

The house at 107 Oak was on a small lot with a pepper tree out front. Bougainvillea climbed the windowsills, and the door was painted fire-engine red. The whole neighborhood smelled like cut grass.

"Why are we stopping here?" Jeeves asked as the motorbike rattled to a halt.

"In the words of Francisco Zupan," I said, "'the key to any daring rescue is to gather a team of savvy specialists with a thirst for the unknown—and to avoid hornets at all costs.'"

Jeeves adjusted the cuffs of his shirt. "I'm not sure I—"

"Jeeves, as you're well aware, two years ago I won the city saber fencing championship. The next year I won a second time, becoming the first repeat champion in city history."

I waited for applause, but Jeeves missed his cue.

"This season I had to settle for a disappointing second place," I went on. "Remember? Of course you do."

Like a forest-dwelling bushbuck, I sprang from the sidecar and dashed toward the house.

"Wait!" Jeeves called after me. "What you're saying is . . ."

I was halfway across the yard before I turned around. "Jeeves, what I'm saying is that I lost my title to a fencer named Julianne Sato. And *this* is her home."

"Ronald," Jeeves groaned, brushing some mulch off his jacket, "this all seems so . . ."

"I know what you're thinking," I said. "Why would **Ronald Zupan** ever need help? He's a master adventurer! He has a stunning mustache! But I assure you, Julianne Sato will be an excellent addition to my crew."

I bounded up the steps and rapped three times on the door. When no one answered, I tried to peek inside, but the blinds were drawn.

"Seems like no one's home," Jeeves called from the street. "Come back and we'll talk this whole thing through."

I went to knock again, but before I could, the door swung open. I found myself facing an elderly Japanese man whom I recognized from fencing practices as Julianne's grandfather.

"Hello, sir," I said, bowing deeply. "**Ronald Zupan** is here for a word with your granddaughter."

"Ronald Zupan?" the old man asked, peering across the lawn toward Jeeves. "Is that him on the motorbike?"

"*I'm* him," I said, straightening up.

The elder Sato turned his gaze on me, sniffing the air. "*You* smell like a salad."

"Excellent deduction," I said. "I was just rolling around in a vegetable garden, wrapped in my mother's dresses."

Mr. Sato drew a set of reading glasses from his shirt pocket and settled them on his nose. "I know you. You're the boy who lost to Julianne in saber fencing."

I looked down at my boots. "Yes, well . . . I hadn't gotten much sleep the night before . . . my arms were sore, and—"

"She won fifteen to two, right?" he asked. "Really walloped you, is what I'm saying."

FACT: **Ronald Zupan** had still won the city championship two of the past three years, but there was no point in bickering.

When I looked at Mr. Sato again, I saw his eyes twinkling. "Come in, come in," he said. "She's in the back."

I motioned to Jeeves that I would only be a minute, then followed the old man as he shuffled through the house. It was small but neatly kept. Instead of invaluable vases and Egyptian artifacts, there were picture frames lining the mantel and tables.

Mr. Sato led me through the kitchen and out to the backyard, where I found Julianne with her cheeks puffed out. She was holding her breath and staring at the sweeping hand of a stopwatch.

Half a minute ticked off before she gasped for air. "What are *you* doing here?" Her voice had crisp edges and she was watching me like a great horned owl.

"You invited me," I said. "Remember, after the fencing tournament?"

Julianne frowned. "That was eight months ago. Also, I didn't give you my address."

I winked at her. "I uncovered it through deductive genius, shrewd investigation, and—"

"Tell me how you found out where I live or this conversation is over."

This girl had grit. She was feisty. A perfect fit for our mission.

"You're in the fencing academy phone book," I said. "I wrote your address in my adventure journal."

Julianne's face softened. She took one small step across the lawn. "Adventure journal? Like a notebook?"

"Exactly," I said.

She took another step toward me. "One that you keep with you at all times? Even when you sleep?"

"You never know when you might need tips on wrestling a yak," I replied.

Julianne's face hinted at a smile. "Mine is waterproof," she said, tapping her pants pocket.

"India ink?" I asked.

She nodded. Now it was my turn to take a step closer. "Sato, I've come to you for a favor."

"Whatever it is, you'll have to convince me." She held up her stopwatch and clicked the button. "And you've got exactly one minute."

I didn't waste a second. "Early this morning, I discovered that my parents, Helen and Francisco Zupan, are missing. A short time later, a ragtag bunch of rogues calling themselves the FIB locked me in a closet with my loyal butler, Jeeves. These charlatans were looking for the Lion of Lyros, my parents' most famous artifact."

"I know the Lion of Lyros," Julianne said. "I went to see it when it was on loan at the Museum of Ancient Civilizations. Made of crystalline limestone, five thousand years old, and—"

"The FIB *said* they were there to protect it," I interrupted, "but I think they were trying to steal it. Now it's up to us to untangle the mystery. Where are my parents? Where is the lion? And what does the FIB have to do with any of it?"

"Why did you come to me?" Julianne asked.

"I need someone skilled with a blade, which you most certainly are. The rest of the team is assembled and ready to risk their very lives to bring my parents home safely."

I heard a soft cough behind me and turned around. Jeeves had found us and wore a look on his face like he'd swallowed an eggplant.

"So your parents are missing?" Julianne asked, arching an eyebrow.

"Indeed."

"Missing parents is a worthy cause," she said. "But how do you expect me to trust someone in a fake mustache?"

"Fair question," Jeeves said under his breath.

I straightened up. "What do you mean? My mustache is dashing and very realistic! It says so right on the package!"

Julianne marched over, peeled the mustache off my upper lip, and slapped it in the palm of my hand. "Seriously?"

FACT: I decided I could go without my mustache for a little while.

"So," I said, "will you join us?"

Julianne thought for a moment. "We're probably going to battle devious villains?"

"Very likely," I grumbled, trying to massage feeling back into my lip.

"And have to avoid getting attacked by deadly animals?"

"There's a king cobra waiting outside for you to avoid getting attacked by at this very instant!"

I scanned my brain for anything else that might help convince her.

"I might just add," Jeeves said from behind me, "that since I, for one, still think this is a mix-up, it'll probably all be sorted out soon and we'll have tea and Ronald's birthday cake by evening. I ordered triple-decker chocolate."

Julianne's eyes flicked to Jeeves, then back to me. She clicked the stopwatch. "So it's a birthday thing, is that what you're saying?"

"That's how I knew my parents were in danger," I said with a nod. "They always promised to come home for my birthday."

Julianne stepped so close that I detected the scent of lemongrass soap and could see golden speckles mixed into her brown irises. "I'll come. But you have to promise me something: no open water."

"No open water?" I asked.

Julianne nodded. "If there's a swimming pool, that's fine. But if you expect me to swim in a river or a lake or"—she shuddered—"the *ocean*, then I'm out. Understand?"

"Agreed. No open water."

Julianne brushed past me and led the way back inside. We

found Mr. Sato in the kitchen, dipping three oatmeal cookies into a glass of milk. You had to admire the old man's style.

"Ojii-chan, this is Ronald Zupan," Julianne said. "It's his birthday and he needs my help with . . . a project."

Mr. Sato bit through the whole cookie stack at once and chewed slowly, studying his granddaughter. "What sort of project?"

"Oh, I think it's a simple mix-up," Jeeves said, leaning forward. "I really do. You see, Ronald's parents are missing and we thought—or he thought—that perhaps Julianne might help us . . . *locate* them. But . . ."

Mr. Sato breathed deeply. "You smell like a salad too. You *both* smell like salads."

"Ojii-chan," Julianne said, "about the project . . ."

Mr. Sato faced Jeeves and me. "Gentlemen, could you give us a moment?"

We stepped into the living room and the kitchen door swung shut behind us. I paced the carpet. Jeeves settled into a leather recliner and drummed his fingers against the faded armrest. After a few minutes of tense silence, he spoke.

"Ronald, what agency did the officer this morning say he was with?"

"The Foreign Item Battalion," I replied, biting my pinkie nail. "Why?"

"That's what I remember too," Jeeves muttered. "Hmm . . . F-I-B."

"Out with it," I said. "What are you thinking?"

"Well . . ." Jeeves glanced at the kitchen door. "Who is your parents' greatest enemy?"

It was the easiest question he could have asked. "The Liars' Club, of course."

The Liars' Club is a massive collective of thieves that spans the globe. Certain members are world-famous, while others lurk in the shadows of far-off lands.

"Exactly," Jeeves said. "And what is the Liars' Club known for?"

This one was simple too. "Body odor. I've heard that some Liars' Club members don't shower for months."

"Sure," Jeeves agreed, "but what else?"

"Toenail fungus?"

"I mean what are they known for *as criminals*."

"Right," I said. "Hmmm . . . stealing things?"

"And when they steal things, what do they always do?"

I studied Jeeves. I couldn't quite tell where he was going with these questions.

"They leave a clue," Jeeves finished. "They *always* leave a clue. At least they always did, back when I was first hired by your father and he told me everything about his adventures."

"But what does that have to do with the Foreign Item Battalion?" I asked. "Do you think they're part of the Liars' Club?"

"I'm starting to," Jeeves said. "The initials are FIB—that seems like a clue, doesn't it?"

"FIB," I said. "Foreign . . . Item . . ."

Jeeves was smiling like a drunken sea lion. "Fib. It means to tell a lie. A lie—like *Liars'* Club."

I sprang to my feet. "That's the clue! FIB . . . Fib . . . *Fib!*" I paced through the room. "You're exactly right. The FIB are frauds, just as I thought. You remember I said that? Worse yet, they're part of the Liars' Club—that rotten nest of dastardly villains! I can't believe they thought we wouldn't decipher the clue!"

"Technically, *I* deciphered—"

He stopped when Julianne stuck her head out the kitchen door. "I heard yelling. Everything okay?"

"Sato," I said, "we've just discovered a major key to cracking the case. There's not a second to lose!"

A Note on the Liars' Club

So it turns out this wasn't just part of a
complicated surprise birthday party planned by
the Zupans. It was looking more and more real by the
minute, and my spirits were sinking fast. Once I
figured out what "FIB" meant and realized that we
might get tangled up with the Liars' Club, a sense
of dread washed over me.

The gang's motto has always been "The Best of
the Worst," and they've gone to great lengths to
prove it.

6

The Chase Begins!

Julianne wanted a few more minutes to convince her grandfather to let her come.

"And I'll probably have to promise him some of that triple-chocolate cake," she added.

She disappeared back into the kitchen to smooth out the details.

I spun toward Jeeves. "If the Liars' Club is at the house, they probably kidnapped my parents too. Clearly, some unbathed rogue spotted Francisco and Helen in Borneo and spread the word. Or maybe someone lured them there. A trap! A double-cross! A *triple*-cross!"

"Now slow down," Jeeves said. "We need something solid. The FIB was after the lion. They might be totally unrelated to why your parents haven't shown up."

I pushed a wicker footstool toward the fireplace, climbed on top, and rested my elbow on the mantel gracefully. "Jeeves, that's too big of a coincidence. I think the only reason the FIB came to the house is that they *knew* my parents wouldn't be there. So the question is, did the Liars' Club capture Francisco and Helen here, or were they kidnapped before they could ever leave Borneo?"

My dizzying logic left Jeeves massaging his forehead. "Let's think this through . . . Even if there is some sort of conspiracy, we shouldn't just make wild guesses."

"Wild *deductions*," I corrected.

Julianne bolted out the kitchen door and straight up the stairs. A minute later, she rushed back down with a purple scarf looped around her neck, a violin case in one hand and a toothbrush in the other.

"Should be just one more second," she promised, disappearing into the kitchen a third time.

I hopped down from the footstool and went back to pacing.

"We need to find who's behind it all," I said. "Who put the FIB up to the heist?"

Jeeves pressed the heels of his palms into his eye sockets. "None of the evidence is solid. We need to—"

The kitchen door swung open and a splash of color catapulted into the room. It was Julianne, turning handsprings across the carpet. She launched herself head over heels all the way to where Jeeves sat and stopped on a dime. Her grandfather tottered in after her.

"See," she said, "*that's* what I'll do if anything goes wrong."

The old man folded his arms. "What about—"

"Ojii-chan, you gave me a trick question. The two trains would *never* collide. They're running on separate tracks."

Mr. Sato took in a long breath through his nose and exhaled with a sigh. It was a sigh I'd heard from Jeeves hundreds of times, and I could tell things were looking up.

"Promise me you'll put your violin to good use," the old man said. "You have a recital next week."

"I will," Julianne agreed, "but you should know that I'm thinking of taking up the six-stringed zither. Or maybe the oboe."

Mr. Sato turned to Jeeves, looking him up and down. "And you're going to be the adult supervision for this birthday excursion?"

Jeeves glanced at me, then back to old Sato. "Actually, sir, a new bit of information has come to light, and I'm a tad concerned that the situation might be more dire than I first imagined."

"Yes, yes," Mr. Sato said, peering at Jeeves over the top of his glasses. "A *very* serious situation. Julianne told me all about it." He leaned closer. "Listen, if there's a piñata at this birthday party and she gets candy, make sure she brings some home for me."

"Sir," Jeeves said, "I'm afraid I haven't made myself clear . . . Did Julianne tell you that Helen and Francisco Zupan are missing? Have you heard of the Lion of—"

"*Yes*," Mr. Sato insisted. "Birthday adventure hunt, sounds like fun. Just remember about sending her home with candy. And I believe there was talk of cake?"

Without waiting for Jeeves to say anything else, Julianne rushed to kiss her grandfather on the cheek and swore she'd call him the next morning. Mr. Sato ushered us out onto the porch, waved once, and then clicked the door shut.

Jeeves drifted toward the motorbike like a panda that had just stepped off a Tilt-a-Whirl. "Ronald, I think now would be a good time to look in the atlas."

"There's your appetite for adventure beginning to roar," I cheered, slapping him on the back.

"There might be a clue," Jeeves said, still looking dazed, "*inside* the atlas."

Julianne hopped aboard the motorbike behind Jeeves. I tried to hand Carter off to her so that I could open up the book, but she jerked backward.

"He's perfectly tame," I explained. "I trained him

myself. He's called Carter, after my favorite Egyptologist, who—"

FACT: Luckily, Julianne is also immune to the cobra's venomous bite!

This discovery came as a relief, because a king cobra is a handy thing to have on an adventure. In the words of Helen Zupan, "When facing villains, bring a venomous reptile. They'll pray not to become his prey!"

Jeeves was trying to kick-start the motorbike, without any luck. He grunted as the engine made the sound of a snoring rhinoceros and puttered out.

"Who do you think kidnapped your parents?" Julianne asked as I tried to pry Carter off her shoulder.

"A soulless villain," I said. "A dastardly dog, a spineless rogue, a—"

"So, no idea then?"

"Not yet," I said as Carter finally let go of our newest expedition member. "But we do know that it's probably a member of the Liars' Club."

"Next question," Julianne said. "What's the motive?"

"The Liar's Club must be after the Lion of Lyros," I answered just as the motorbike coughed out a huge cloud of black smoke and finally started up. "The FIB asked about it when they raided our house."

"That's not enough to go on," Jeeves said over the clunking of the engine. "We need hard evidence. We don't know if Francisco and Helen landed here or if they're still in Borneo."

"Then we go to Zupan Hangar," I said. "If my parents landed, their plane will be there."

Jeeves brightened a little. "Well . . . that's the first reasonable thing I've heard all day."

Julianne nodded her agreement. "Makes sense."

The motorbike swung left, and we rumbled toward Zupan Hangar.

"One more question," Julianne began. "Why does this motorbike go so slowly?"

"Just like the Lion of Lyros, it's extremely old," I told her, "and from the sound of it, there's a chinchilla caught in the tailpipe."

From the corner of my eye, I could see Julianne smirk at my witty line, while Jeeves chose to show his amusement by gritting his teeth and scowling.

We were on our way!

FROM THE DESK OF
Thomas Halladay

Errors in the Chapter "The Chase Begins!"

1. I should never have taken Julianne with us, but I suppose I still held a little shred of hope that the day would end happily. Besides, I could always bring her back home if the situation became dangerous . . . at least that's what I told myself.

2. I can assure you that, just like Ronald and myself, Julianne is *not* immune to poisons of all varieties. Not even a little bit.

3. I'd also like to note that I was not in agreement that a cobra is a handy thing to have on an adventure. Even a defanged cobra is bound to lead to trouble.

4. LOOK INSIDE THE ATLAS! LOOK INSIDE THE ATLAS! How many times did I have to say it?

7
Something Solid!

Jeeves revved the throttle and we floored it toward the hangar. On the way, I told Julianne that I'd have to tie her scarf around her eyes—to keep the location hidden. As Francisco Zupan always says, "You can never be too safe with hiding your secrets . . . or hiding from blister beetles."

"Sato, I'm sorry to scramble your internal compass like this," I said, cinching the scarf as the motorbike bumped over a set of train tracks, "but I always follow my dad's advice."

We were holding up a long line of cars, and their blaring horns made it hard to talk. After a few miles, Jeeves hung a left toward the waterfront, buzzing past the famous Millers-burg Bread Factory. We cut between old warehouses until Jeeves finally parked his motorbike in front of the hangar.

Julianne sniffed the air. "Ronald . . ."

"Yes?" I asked.

"I don't want to spoil the secret of your hangar's hidden location but . . ."

"What is it?"

"Well, my skin feels clammy, so I can tell we're near the waterfront. That part's easy." She gave the air another sniff. "It also smells like baking bread, which makes me wonder if we aren't close to the bread factory. They're doing sourdough today, I think. We crossed the train tracks so we must be on the east side of the factory. And of course, Francisco Zupan is known to have strong ties to Argentina, whose national flag is blue and white. He would probably feel drawn to the faded blue and white paint covering the old Dockside Shipping Exchange." She paused and gathered herself up. "By any chance are we at the Dockside Shipping building?"

There was a long silence as I gazed up at the side of Zupan Hangar. I'd never noticed its blue and white paint before.

I turned to Julianne and whipped off her blindfold. "Sato, you've just aced my famous 'Where are we?' test!"

She arched an eyebrow. "Was that really a test?"

"Indeed! Congratulations!"

I led the way through the double doors of the hangar. For as long as I can remember the building has been run by Elexander Davidson, the wily master mechanic who taught me how to fly. The moment he saw us, he shot up from his oak workbench like he'd been jolted with electricity.

"Have you heard from your parents?" he asked. "No, I can see you haven't, and neither have I! Tell me everything you know."

"This morning the house was raided by a gang of bandits," I said. "They called themselves the FIB and they were looking for the Lion of Lyros."

"FIB!" Davidson said with a sneer. "They're a bunch of Liars' Club lackeys! Someone must have ordered them to go to Zupan Manor."

"So where *are* the Zupans if they aren't here?" Julianne asked. "Still in Borneo?"

Elexander seemed to notice her for the first time, so I stepped in to make introductions.

"Elexander Davidson," I said, "meet my trusty assistant . . ."

Julianne gave me a long look and a slow shake of the head. "You serious?"

"I mean . . . my second-in-command."

"Keep trying," she said.

"My . . . *backup*?"

Julianne stepped toward Elexander's desk with her arm outstretched.

"I'm Julianne Sato, Ronald's new partner in dazzling schemes and grand adventures."

Elexander shook her hand. "Good to meet you, Sato."

"Except, **Ronald Zupan** doesn't need partners," I said. "He's spectacular all on his own."

Julianne leveled her eyes at me. "*Partners*. It'll grow on you."

Elexander stepped out from behind his desk. Carter was slithering across the concrete floor, and the old mechanic watched him for a moment before waving us toward the main hangar.

"This way," he said.

The hangar was packed with all sorts of dirigibles, flying machines, and helicopters. The spot where my parents' two-person plane was usually parked stood empty.

"See!" I called over my shoulder. "My parents swore never to miss my birthday, and their plane is still gone. This means we have no choice but to—"

"Call the police," Jeeves interrupted. I turned to face him. He took a breath and drew himself up to his full height.

"This is all getting out of hand, and they'll be better at gathering solid evidence."

For a long minute, no one said a word. My eyes were locked on Jeeves, and my face had gone hot. I could feel Julianne and Elexander watching me.

"Jeeves," I said, speaking slowly, "Francisco Zupan has a saying: 'Doubtful friends are worse than enemies, and fire ants are the worst of all.'"

"I'm not trying to hurt you," Jeeves said, "but the only proof you have that your parents are in trouble is the fact that they didn't come home for your birthday. It's not hard evidence. On the other hand, we're *sure* that the FIB is at the house. We need to contact the authorities. And for God's sake, could we look in the atlas?'"

I glanced to my right, where Elexander stood. "Do you agree with him?"

"I think the police can handle the FIB," Elexander said. My face fell, but he held up a hand to show he wasn't finished. "While you and your team fly to Borneo to rescue Francisco and Helen."

Without any more explanation, he turned around and started weaving through a row of single-person flying machines.

"*WHAT?*" Jeeves called from the back of the group. "No one is flying us to Borneo until we have hard evidence. We need to find something solid!"

At that exact moment, Jeeves finally *did* find something solid—the wing of my mother's pedal-powered cliff glider. He ran into it headfirst, gave one tiny grunt, and crumpled to the floor like a Nepalese fainting goat.

Words No One Said Before I Was Knocked Out Cold

1. "Careful"

2. "Watch"

3. "Your"

4. "Head"

8

Web of Intrigue!

I ran to help Jeeves and found him breathing but completely lost to the world. Julianne knelt beside me on the concrete floor. She forced open the butler's eyelids to inspect his pupils.

"They're dilated," she reported. "Looks like a concussion. I have a page on head trauma in my adventure journal."

Elexander crouched beside us. He lifted one of Jeeves's arms and let it fall to the ground with a thud. "He's got a thick skull, I'm sure he'll be fine. Now, before we get the plane ready, there's something you'd better see first."

He tottered toward a dark corner of the hangar, where Francisco's gyrocopter sat collecting dust. I followed him, leaving Carter coiled on Jeeves's chest to keep watch. As everyone knows, there's nothing quite like a cobra to help perk up an injured adventurer.

The pounded-aluminum body of the gyrocopter was touched off by four sets of propeller blades—one on top, one on each wing, and one at the tail. Elexander opened the cockpit door and motioned us in.

Julianne and I exchanged a nervous glance, then climbed three metal steps up to the door. Each of the steps was slightly bowed from years of use. Elexander closed the door and we stood in silent darkness for a long moment before he found a short chain dangling from a lone lightbulb.

The bulb hummed and came to life, swinging gently and scattering light around the gyrocopter.

"Wow," Julianne said.

"I concur," I murmured.

The inside of the gyrocopter was nothing like its dusty shell. The instrument panel had been torn out and the windows painted black. Only the two leather pilots' chairs remained.

One side of the hull was crowded with filing cabinets. The other had a massive map of the world. Hundreds of spots on the map had been marked with metal rivets shot straight into the body of the copter. At least one piece of red yarn was tied to each rivet, creating an intricate web.

Above the map, where the ceiling curved, the words "LIARS' CLUB LAIRS" were painted in bloodred block letters.

"Elexander," I said, "how long has this spectacular research station been here?"

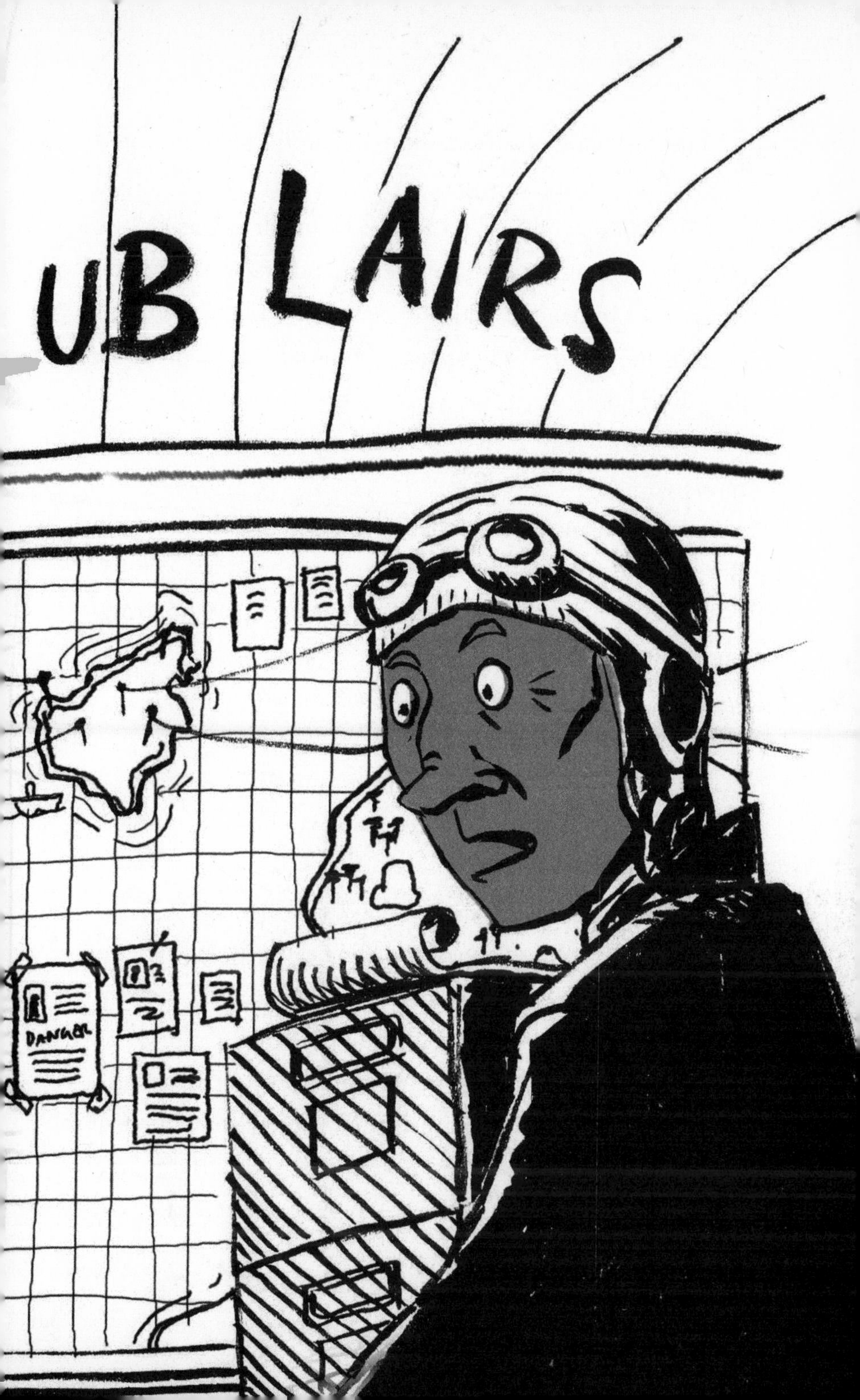
UB LAIRS
DANGER

The mechanic grabbed the base of the lightbulb and angled it so it cast a warm glow on the map.

"Your parents have had this secret nook for years," he said. "Sometimes they use it more than others. It depends on where they're headed and how active the Liars' Club has been in those parts. These last few months, it seemed like they lived here."

"So *that's* where they've been spending all their time," I muttered.

Julianne turned to me. "Do you know why they were in Borneo?"

"Probably an artifact," I replied, staring up at the strings on the wall. "They didn't really say."

"Not an artifact, a boat," Elexander corrected.

"A boat?" I asked.

"A fake pirate ship," Elexander said. "It's owned by a famous movie star, and he hired your parents to get it back. Guess who stole it?"

"The Liars' Club," Julianne and I said together.

Elexander went to one of the filing cabinets, brought out a newspaper clipping, and handed it to me. Julianne read the article over my shoulder.

"I've seen this!" Julianne exclaimed. "Josh Brigand is my favorite actor. He plays this charming gentleman of fortune who sails the seven seas. He's handsome and funny—"

Production Halts on Brigand's Adventure Flick, *Buccaneers of the South Seas*

FILMING FOR JOSH Brigand's latest Capstone blockbuster, on location in Borneo, was put on hold this week. The break comes after the film's second unit suffered a major theft at the hands of pirates. The studio is reporting "significant" losses, including props, costumes, equipment, 5,000 trained bees, and even Brigand's beloved ship.

Brigand, who rose to stardom in such films as *Sea Devils off the Starboard Bow, Cannon Fire on the Spanish Main,* and *No Quarter Given,* was at his wit's end over the loss of his prized vessel. "The fact that these . . . these . . . freebooters stole my ship on the high seas is an outrage!" the actor said.

The hive of bees was slated for a cameo in the film's grand finale—the writing team is now at a loss for how to move forward. Meanwhile, Brigand's plans to travel to Borneo for filming have been canceled.

"I've never even heard of this Jason Brickhouse," I said.

Julianne shot me a look. "*Josh Brigand.* And he's probably the most famous actor alive."

I turned back to the crisscrossing red threads strung across the map. Each rivet marked a different Liars' Club hideout, safe house, or crime scene. Some had names—Snidewater Industrial, the School of Thieves, Isla sin Nombre—while others simply had coordinates scribbled beside them.

"There's a pattern to these," Julianne said, taking a step back. "Look how many of these strings cross in the same place."

"You're right," I said. "They all meet in Borneo."

"Exactly," Elexander agreed. "The spot you're pointing to is home to a pirate named Zeetan Z. He's the head of the Liars' Club. It was *him* who stole the movie star's ship."

"So a *real* pirate stole the ship from a fake pirate movie?" I asked.

Elexander nodded. "Sounds like he took everything from the film set, even the trained bees. He usually goes for artifacts, though. He's taken hundreds of treasures over the years. The plan was that Francisco and Helen would capture the pirate, take back the ship, and come home as heroes."

I felt my face get flushed and turned to Julianne. "So we go after this Zeetan Z, right?"

Julianne looked worried for the first time. She rolled her bottom lip between her teeth and didn't say anything.

Elexander put his hand on my shoulder. "You should know that Zeetan Z is the most dangerous pirate alive."

I scoffed. "If he's so dangerous, how could a master adventurer like **Ronald Zupan** not know about him?"

"You haven't heard of him," Elexander said, "because he doesn't leave many people around to tell the tale."

A Few Things I Might Have Mentioned If I Weren't Knocked Out

To Ronald: "No, a seven-foot-long king cobra coiled on my chest will not make me feel better. In fact, I think quite the opposite."

To Elexander: "Why would Helen and Francisco tell you and not me about their hidden Liars' Club research station? Why do *you* know so much about their plans?"

To Julianne: "It's time we get you home; this has all gotten quite out of hand. I'll phone your grandfather and tell him where he can pick you up."

But of course I didn't have the chance to say any of these things, because I was knocked out, with a seven-foot-long king cobra coiled on my chest.

9

Dashing Departures!

I leaned close to the map again, tracing the crisscrossing threads with my fingers, then spun around. "Elexander, chart a course for Borneo! If Zeetan Z is as dangerous as you say, we can't waste a moment!"

Julianne grabbed my elbow. "Ronald, it was really the whole 'birthday' thing that convinced my grandfather to let me come. He thinks I'm going to be home tomorrow."

"It also explains why he was so set on you coming back with candy," I said.

I could see that she needed to think about the situation, but it was time for **Ronald Zupan** to snap into action. I pointed at the two oversized filing cabinets inside the gyrocopter. "Elexander, these are my parents' files?"

"Everything they have on Zeetan Z and the Liars' Club is in there," he replied.

"Let's bring them," I said. "Along with all the standard adventure gear: food, water, tents . . . do you have dynamite on hand? A good adventure needs dynamite."

Julianne and Elexander helped me wrestle the filing cabinets out of the gyrocopter and slide them across the polished concrete floor. Halfway to my parents' biggest plane, the Rome, we came to Jeeves, sprawled out as flat as a manta ray.

"We'll load him onto the plane too," I said. "If I know Jeeves, he won't want to miss an adventure like this."

"Really?" Julianne asked, kneeling down and touching the kumquat-sized bump on Jeeves's head. "Because right before he was knocked out, he seemed like he *specifically* wanted to miss an adventure like this."

"If he woke up and I wasn't there, it would be very hard for him," I explained. "We've been together almost every day since I was born."

We slid the filing cabinets and the concussed butler toward the Rome. Elexander slowly rolled open the two giant doors of the hangar, and sunlight poured into the building. The plane's chrome body and twin propellers glinted in the bright light. Her red-tipped nose aimed toward the runway strip, and her cargo ramp hung back like a tail.

"Careful now," I grunted as the three of us carried Jeeves up the ramp into the hold of the plane, easing him down into a hammock.

As Elexander headed to the cockpit, I ran outside to the front of the hangar and hopped aboard the motorbike. I drove it back through the open doors and straight up the cargo ramp, into the plane. Having his beloved vehicle would surely make Jeeves feel more comfortable in the untamed wilds of Borneo. Finally, Julianne and I used a winch to hoist the two filing cabinets aboard.

When the cargo door was closed, I headed toward the cockpit. Julianne was in the main cargo hold with Jeeves, checking his vital signs. Elexander was in the captain's chair, dialing in the flight equipment.

I sat down beside him. The excitement of the morning was wearing off and a new set of feelings had taken over. What if we didn't get to Borneo soon enough? What if we couldn't help my parents? What if it was already too late?

It felt like a belt was being cinched tighter and tighter around my chest. I reached into my pocket for my dashing mustache and stroked it a few times—but it wasn't as comforting, not being on my lip. Julianne stepped into the cockpit, and I swiveled my seat to face her.

"He's going to be fine," she announced. I could tell she wanted to say something else but was holding back.

"I have to save my parents," I said. "I'll understand if you don't want to come."

"Jeeves said it might still be a mix-up," Julianne said. "I mean it *does* seem like they're gone a lot."

I let the words soak in for a second. Elexander watched me out of the corner of his eye but didn't speak.

"They swore they'd always come home for my birthday," I said. "And I trust them."

Julianne nodded slowly, taking in what I'd said. "Then I'm coming with you."

"Are you sure, Sato?"

"What kind of adventure partner would I be if I let you go alone?"

I opened my mouth to remind her that she wasn't so much a partner as a savvy specialist, then decided we could discuss it later.

Elexander looked up from the control panel. "Listen," he said, making a few final adjustments, "the jungle that you're flying into is nothing like the rest of the country. It's a rogue's gallery, where it's nearly impossible to tell the difference between friend and foe. Be careful."

He opened the cockpit door and climbed down the boarding ladder.

"Wait, you're not coming?" Julianne asked.

Elexander shook his head. "You're in good hands. I taught Ronald myself."

FACT: I wasn't *technically* certified to fly the Rome. But desperate times call for eleven-year-olds to fly giant cargo planes to Borneo.

"Don't worry," Elexander said, "the autopilot is set. Even Jeeves could fly the plane now and he's concussed. I need to go to the Zupan house and handle these FIB rascals."

"Can you get a message to my grandfather?" Julianne asked.

Elexander nodded, and she scribbled a note in her adventure journal, tore out the page, and passed it to him.

I took over the captain's chair, latched the cockpit door, and pressed the ignition button. The Rome's propellers started to hum. The volume swelled until it was all we could hear.

"Parting is such sweet sorrow!" I yelled to Elexander through the thick glass.

We began speeding down the runway. Carter rested heavily on my lap, basking in the glow of the midday sun. Julianne settled into the copilot's chair with a pair of flight goggles over her eyes.

"Next stop, Borneo," I announced. "Expect an easy flight and a landing as soft as the belly of a Mexican walking fish."

FROM THE DESK OF
Thomas Halladay

On Second Thought

Maybe it's better I was unconscious. I never would have agreed to fly to Borneo with two children and a cobra. I would have sent Julianne back to her grandfather and called the police.

Take a journey halfway around the world with a boy who started the day in a fake mustache? It makes me shudder just to write the words.

10

An Easy Flight!

As soon as the Rome's wheels left the runway, I explained the autopilot to Julianne. Then we took turns watching over the controls and reading the files on Zeetan Z. It was important that no clue went unstudied.

"It says here that he once captured three yachts on the same afternoon," I told Julianne as we flew over the vast Pacific Ocean.

She nodded and chewed on the corner of a fingernail.

"Look at this," I added a few minutes later. "Zeetan Z became a pirate because he didn't get a part in the school play."

When we started to feel hungry, I cracked open a food crate and Julianne made sandwiches with dry salami and aged cheese. Later, I explored the hold of the plane and found a box filled with Francisco Zupan's collection of adventure hats. Julianne picked out a felt bowler.

"Nice hat," I said.

"Nice hat yourself," she replied, as I settled a pith helmet on my head.

All this time, Jeeves continued to sleep, perchance to dream. At least that's what I think it's called when you have a concussion and don't wake up except to groggily mumble gibberish. When he did finally fight through a full sentence, it was, "Are we in an airplane?"

"There's the fog lifting!" I cheered, just as the autopilot banked two degrees to the east. "We thought it would be easier to get to Borneo in a plane than in a zeppelin or a glider. Make yourself at home back there."

I was in the cockpit with Carter coiled on my lap and glanced over my shoulder just as Jeeves's eyes fluttered shut again.

"Mmmm, *home*, that's nice," he said. "For a moment there I thought you said Borneo."

"I *did* say Borneo," I announced, using the intercom to be sure he heard me this time. "It's home to the nefarious pirate—"

Jeeves sat up. "Now wait just one minute—"

"Here's the quick version," Julianne said. "We think the Zupans were captured by a Malaysian pirate who's the head of the Liars' Club and likes historical artifacts." She held up a file full of Zeetan Z's victims. "Francisco and Helen have been studying him for years."

Jeeves massaged his temples and took ten slow breaths. "We're in a plane?"

We nodded.

"Headed to Borneo?"

Julianne offered an encouraging thumbs-up.

"To chase a pirate named . . . ?"

"Zeetan Z," I said, turning halfway around to face him again. "After you were brutally attacked by the wing of the hang glider, Elexander led us to a hidden office built inside of Francisco's gyrocopter. The walls were lined with red yarn that crisscrossed between Liars' Club hideouts. The threads of this web of intrigue all came together at the same spot. Right where my parents landed."

"And Elexander told us that Zeetan Z is known to hide nearby . . . but no one knows exactly where," Julianne added. "He just robbed the set of an old-fashioned pirate movie last month. Elexander said that's why the Zupans were in Borneo—to recover the ship of—"

"I know that bit," Jeeves groaned. "I heard Josh Brigand talking about it at a party."

"*You* know Josh Brigand?" Julianne asked, practically bouncing out of her seat.

Jeeves was making a strange face, like he was queasy. "I met him at a retirement celebration for his butler, Wiggins—who happens to be an old friend. Strange that the Zupans didn't tell *me* they were trying to get his ship back."

"Strange that you never told *me* about being friends with Jasper Brackface," I replied.

I checked the gauges and adjusted our altitude. Jeeves ignored the jab and wobbled to his feet long enough to grab Zeetan Z's file from Julianne. He took it back to the hammock and collapsed again.

"This pirate Zeetan Z seems absolutely vicious," he said after a long silence. "I can only find one man who's ever escaped from him."

He held up a yellowing piece of paper and Julianne and I spun around to look. "Diamond Jack Roberts," Jeeves read, "attacked on his yacht the *Luciana*."

Julianne ran back to examine the paper for herself. "He's right! There's a note on the page that says, '*Whereabouts unknown . . . reportedly calls himself Three-Fingered Jack.*'"

"Dashing news!" I said. "If this Three-Fingered Jack fellow escaped Zeetan Z, how hard could it be?"

Jeeves didn't answer, just closed the file and lay back down. For a few minutes, the only sound was the rapid-fire *whomp*s of the propellers. Finally, he forced himself up again.

"Sorry, Ronald, but I must know: Have you ever landed a plane like the Rome?"

I raised the nose of the plane and we broke through a cloudbank. The sun was setting way out ahead of us. "Well, that depends on how you look at it. I have landed a plane before and it was *like* the Rome in that it flies . . . but never a plane quite so big."

Jeeves didn't answer, just turned to face the wall and curled up without another word.

"The concussion is probably making him cranky," Julianne said under her breath.

"Get your rest, friend," I called over my shoulder. "We've got to find Zeetan Z, rescue my parents, take back the pirate ship, and get home in time for Julianne's violin recital. It's going to be a busy few days."

Jeeves must have agreed, because he put a pillow over his head and didn't speak another word for the next two hours. Julianne decided to snatch some shut-eye of her own on a bunk that sat across from the hammock. She jammed twisted-up napkins in her ears to block out the sound of the propellers.

A few hours later, I found myself staring down at Borneo's dense rainforests. The jungle looked like a bright green carpet spread across the mountains, with a few muddy rivers threading through.

I switched off the autopilot and slowly decreased the plane's altitude, circling for somewhere to land. This was a tricky maneuver—the trees grew as thick as the fur of a polar bear, and the Rome was a very big plane.

"Hmmm," I said aloud, "that's quite unfortunate."

"*What* is quite unfortunate?" Jeeves asked, sitting up and rubbing his eyes. He cracked an ice pack and pressed it to his head.

I leaned close to the windshield so that I could look directly below us. "Well . . . there doesn't seem to be any place to land."

"Come again?"

"It's only minor danger," I promised. "Just look at Julianne Sato; she's perfectly relaxed."

Jeeves glanced over at Julianne, who was still fast asleep on the bunk across from him. "She's sleeping. She has no idea what's happening."

"And I admire her approach," I said. "As for the matter at hand, this might be the perfect time to take a look in the atlas. Atlases, as you know, are full of maps. Maybe one of them shows a spot in the jungles of Borneo that's not quite so . . . *jungley*."

"Ronald," Jeeves said, giving me a puzzled look, "you *have* opened your father's atlas before, right? You *do* know what's inside, don't you?"

"Maps?"

He started to say something, but the droning of a siren cut him off.

"BREER-EEEPP-BREER-EEEPP-BREER-EEEPP!"

"Now, what is that racket?"

I checked the dials and realized that the plane was almost completely out of fuel.

"That's just . . . the alarm I set to wake me up for landing," I said, trying to sound calm.

"Can't you turn it off then?" Jeeves asked. "I've got a throbbing headache."

Sweat began to bead across my forehead. "Sure . . . just . . . one second."

Jeeves plopped down in his hammock, pressing two pillows tightly against his head to block out the siren. A few feet away, Julianne slept on, with the napkins still in her ears. Which explains why I was the only one to notice when the engines sputtered to a halt.

What I Was Thinking After Waking Up in an Airplane

As I said before, I'd heard Josh Brigand talk about
his missing ship at the retirement party he threw
for his butler, Wiggins. Still, the pirate ship
news wasn't the strangest thing I heard at the
retirement party. Mr. Brigand followed it up by
saying something far more surprising: he offered
me the chance to be his new butler.

When I folded a pillow over my head, I didn't
fall asleep, not for a second. I was thinking about
the acceptance letter I'd written, which was in my
jacket pocket at that very moment. I'd been on the
fence about sending it, but being dragged onto an
airplane while I was unconscious felt like the final
straw.

I decided I'd mail the letter as soon as I got
home . . . *if* I got home.

11
Dramatic Landings!

As the propellers of the Rome stopped spinning, I glanced over at Carter, who was now coiled on the cocaptain's seat. His tongue flitted in and out of his mouth, but he didn't seem to have any advice for what to do.

With the sirens droning on, I angled the wings upward to keep us as high as I could, searching desperately for a runway. The Rome was losing altitude and the brilliant green jungles of Borneo were coming up fast. Below us, I saw a village, a river, and smoke twisting lazily up from a fire.

What I *didn't* spot was any open space big enough to land a cargo plane.

"BREER-EEEPP-BREER-EEEPP-BREER-EEEPP!"

"*Enough!*" Jeeves yelled.

I jerked my head around to see him stomp toward the back of the plane, with his hands still covering his ears.

"*No!*" I screamed. But it was too late.

Jeeves slammed his elbow against the large red button that controlled the cargo doors. He must have thought it would turn off the alarm. Instead, the doors at the back of the plane started to open. I looked toward the ground again—we were falling like a sack of coconut crabs.

The ruckus was enough to finally wake Julianne. She sat up, taking the twisted napkins out of her ears.

"So," she yelled over the blaring sirens, "did I miss anything?"

"Sato," I said, with sweat running into my eyes, "I think you should know that we're completely out of fuel. As a result, we'll be crash-landing very shortly."

"What?" Jeeves screamed. "Three minutes ago you said everything was fine!"

"The situation has taken a nosedive," I replied.

The cargo door was almost finished opening and raging winds began to tear through the Rome. Julianne shot to her feet and dashed into the cockpit. "Is it a water landing? Are we landing in the open sea?"

"Too risky," I told her. "We'll have to crash in the jungle."

"Well, that's something." She put on her bowler hat and flight goggles and grabbed her violin case. "I'll take jungle over an ocean any day."

"But we'll be killed!" Jeeves cried.

"That issue is still up in the air," I insisted, flipping the switch for the landing gears.

"Not for long!" Julianne yelled. The wind rushed through the cockpit as she peered down at the rapidly approaching treetops.

Jeeves staggered into the cockpit and slammed himself down in the cocaptain's chair. Almost immediately, he screamed and jumped back up, with Carter's jaws latched firmly to the seat of his pants.

FACT: King cobras don't take kindly to being sat on mid-plane wreck.

"*Get. It. Off!*" Jeeves yelled.

Julianne rushed to calm him down. "Please, Jeeves, your concussion!"

The butler tried to get Carter off him—twisting in circles, bumping dials, and knocking into switches—but the snake held tight.

"Sit down!" I hissed. "You're endangering an endangered species. And a concussed butler!"

"Look!" Julianne jabbed her finger at the windshield. "Can you land on that dirt road?"

"Buckle in," I said. "We'll have to try."

Jeeves desperately fought to get the seatbelt latched with Carter still clamped onto him. Julianne strapped herself into the jump seat behind my chair.

I had just enough altitude to steer toward the muddy path, and we all braced ourselves for impact. At the last second, I jerked the controls toward my chest, and the nose of the plane snapped up one final time. Our landing gear slammed down on the red clay, and the wings of the Rome chopped through trees that lined the road. The plane fishtailed wildly, wrenching our bodies against our seatbelts.

All I could do was hang on to the controls and try to keep us from smashing into the jungle. The landing gears broke with a horrible crack, and the nose of

the Rome dug into the dirt, spraying a curtain of mud across the windshield.

"*This is the end!*" Jeeves screamed.

I held our path steady as the tail of the plane swung back and forth. It felt like being shaken by a silverback gorilla. The pallet of our supplies broke loose and skidded across the floor toward the cockpit, ready to smash us all. Then, at the last possible moment, the plane came to a stop.

The droning siren weakened and died out. For just a second or two, the only sound was our ragged breathing.

"Evacuate!" I yelled.

I snatched my adventure hat off the cockpit floor. We squeezed between the pallet and the wall of the fuselage, with Carter still gripping Jeeves in his jaws. Once everyone had made it to safety, we stood in a row watching the Rome from fifty feet away, wondering what would happen next.

"Look," Julianne gasped, pointing in front of us.

Just beyond the wreckage, an old man, skinny and hunched, sat on a wooden cart harnessed to a water buffalo. The back of the cart was loaded with ripe papayas and mangoes. The man stared at us with wild eyes.

"Those papayas look good," I said. "I'd kill for a piece of ripe fruit."

"You almost just did," Julianne said.

A fire broke out in the plane. Circuits popped and wires sizzled. In seconds, we heard the cockpit window shatter. A black cloud that smelled like burning rubber drifted toward us. Then, strangely, music filled the air.

Jeeves and I both turned toward Julianne, who was dramatically slicing the bow of her violin across its strings.

"What are you *doing*?" Jeeves asked.

Julianne hardly glanced up. "Fiddling while the Rome burns. I thought it might help calm your nerves."

As she played, the three of us watched the fire crackle through the plane.

"Question, Ronald Zupan," Julianne asked, mid-sonata, "do you think the plane will explode?"

"Impossible," I promised. "There's absolutely no—"

The rest of my sentence was drowned out as the plane erupted into an enormous fireball. A wave of shredded metal rocketed toward us. I didn't know I was airborne until I saw the earth pass far below me. I soared up, up, up—then slammed down into the muddy road.

All sound was lost except for a shrill ringing in my ears and the thrumming of my heart. *Whom-pum, whom-pum, whom-pum.*

A flaming seat cushion landed inches from my head with a muffled thud. I looked up at the wreckage with my chin resting in the crook of my elbow.

"On second thought," I said, "maybe it *will* explode after all."

As my hearing slowly came back, I managed to locate Julianne. Her face was covered in ash, but her eyes were as alert as ever. She'd already crawled over to inspect the seat cushion.

"This floats, right?" she asked. "I know just what to use it for."

"What will we do without our plane?" Jeeves moaned. He was kneeling in a puddle beside the road. Mud ran down his suit in tiny streams.

"Don't worry about that," I said, standing up. "You should never return home from an adventure the same way you left."

Jeeves pulled on the lapels of his jacket and snorted his agreement.

When the flames stopped climbing, I saw the old man and his water buffalo still sitting in the distance. The fruit farmer's face was covered in soot, and his hair was blown back. I couldn't say for sure, but it also looked like his eyebrows had been singed off.

After staring at us for a full minute, he turned the cart, ever so slowly, and headed back the way he'd come.

"Congratulations to us!" I announced to my companions. "The first stage of the journey was a success."

"Fantastic," Jeeves said, standing up and rubbing the spot where Carter had bitten him. "We crashed in the jungle, we were almost killed, and our plane exploded with our supplies inside."

I winced as I pulled a sliver of shrapnel out of my arm. "Jeeves, even in the face of peril you should never forget to see the bright side. We have our health and Carter has *clearly* bonded with you. Besides, we're that much closer to rescuing my parents."

Jeeves used two fingers to swipe away a layer of soot from above his eyelids, spun on his heels, and walked away. Carter slithered along behind him.

A few pieces of half-burned paper swirled around my feet. I stepped on one and stooped to pick it up.

It was an application I'd written for one of Francisco and Helen's bold adventures. I'd told them all about my exploits with Jeeves, and my dashing facial hair. Reading it over, I couldn't believe that they'd rejected my plea to go on their excavation.

Had Francisco been worried about how long it took me to escape a constrictor knot? Was he worried about my deduction skills? Or had I simply not used enough exclamation points? It was a riddle without an answer.

Julianne peeked over my shoulder. "What's that?"

"Just an old adventure application," I said. "It must've been in the filing cabinet."

There was another small explosion over at the plane, and

we both flinched. I jammed the charred application into my pocket.

"You apply for your parents' expeditions?"

"Every single one," I said, wiping dust from my forehead. "How else am I going to be selected?"

Julianne frowned. "Wait, are you saying you've never been on one of Francisco and Helen's trips?"

"Sato, we have bigger things to worry about. We've got to locate Zeetan Z. And get your hero Jackie Brickhead's ship back. And, most of all, we have to find my parents."

"*Josh. Brigand*," Julianne said, reaching down to grab her bowler hat. "Anyway, you're right, there are bigger fish to fry. I guess I just always imagined that you'd gone with your parents dozens of times."

"That would be your first incorrect deduction of the day."

I crumpled the adventure application into a tight ball inside my pocket, picked up my pith helmet from the dust, and started following Jeeves down the path. Julianne tipped her hat and put her violin back in its case. We walked side by side, with Julianne dragging the smoldering seat cushion.

"Sorry, Jeeves," I said when we caught up to him, "we should have grabbed you an adventure hat. There was a whole box of them."

"Nice hats too," Julianne added.

Jeeves didn't say anything, just kicked a dirt clod into the undergrowth.

We slogged forward without another word. Our mission stretched out before us, but there was no clear path. I hadn't quite decided how we would go about finding the treacherous Zeetan Z and his band of pirates, but I knew that we needed a plan and fast.

As my father once said, "A true master adventurer chooses the perfect plan just as easily as a tik-tik fly chooses the perfect spot on the earlobe to bite."

All at once, Jeeves froze in his tracks.

"What's wrong?" I asked him. I'd been getting more and more worried about him by the minute. "Are you dizzy? Nauseous?"

He spun toward us, wearing his first smile of the day. "Finally some luck! She must have slid right out of the cargo doors before we crashed!"

About fifty feet ahead, tangled in bright green vines on the side of the road, rested the butler's beloved motorcycle. And, for a vehicle that had recently fallen from the back of an airplane, it didn't look half bad.

FROM THE DESK OF
Thomas Halladay

Errors in the Chapter "Dramatic Landings!"

1. Ronald said that I was "endangering an endangered species" when I tried to shake Carter off me, but this isn't true. There are *plenty* of king cobras roaming around India, and after Ronald's pet bit me, I was of the mind that the world could do with one less.

2. Smooth landing? HA! Successful journey? DOUBLE HA!

3. Ronald kept trying to insist that things weren't so bad. I beg to differ. We had no leads, no information, and the files and supplies had all burned up. No wonder I was overjoyed when we stumbled upon my motorbike—it was the only bright spot in an otherwise catastrophic day. For the briefest of moments I thought, "Perhaps everything

will work out. It's not like someone is going
to try to poison me this afternoon or I'll be
attacked by an angry giant before
suppertime . . . right?"

12

Francisco's Secrets!

Jeeves loped ahead to the motorcycle, happy as a howler monkey in springtime. The key was still in the ignition, and the engine fired on the first try.

I clasped my hands together behind my head as I walked toward him. "I will admit: it's a sturdy vehicle."

We clambered down into the gully, peeled away the vines, and leaned our shoulders into the motorbike as Jeeves steered it up onto the road. When we reached level ground, something in the sidecar caught my eye. It was Francisco's famous atlas—open, revealing a hidden compartment hollowed out from inside the pages.

"That sly fox," I said. "The atlas was a fake all along!"

Jeeves spun to face me. "*Please*, tell me you knew the atlas was a false book."

I was too busy inspecting where the middle section of the book had been carefully cut away to bother with an answer.

"Why do you think your father kept telling you to look in the atlas?" he asked. "*In* the atlas."

I glanced at the items spilled across the seat. "Well . . ."

Jeeves paused to study me. "Oh, *I* see . . . This is about devouring Shakespeare, isn't it?"

I didn't like the direction things were headed. "Jeeves," I replied, "I'd rather not—"

"What about Shakespeare?" Julianne asked.

I kept my focus on the odd items hidden in the book's pages. When I spotted a bar of chocolate and a deck of playing cards, everything made sense. For years Francisco had been leaving things for me inside the atlas. Like a code!

"Tell Julianne about Shakespeare," Jeeves said, with a twinkle in his eye. "There's no need to be embarrassed."

"Go on," Julianne urged.

When he could see I wasn't about to say anything, Jeeves cleared his throat. "Ronald's mother, Helen, loves words that sound the same but have different meanings."

"Homophones," Julianne said.

"Exactly." Jeeves stepped away from the motorbike and took off his jacket. "And homonyms. And regular words that can mean different things at different times."

"She's razor sharp," I cut in. "Now let's go rescue her."

I leaned into the sidecar to pick up a blood-colored

candle shaped like a grapefruit, which must have dropped from inside the atlas and rolled under the seat.

"Anyway," Jeeves went on, shoving up his sleeves, "when Ronald was five, Helen bought him a few picture books and told him that 'the most adventurous people are carnivorous readers.'"

I set the candle back down and kicked the front tire of the motorbike. "Jeeves, does this look flat to you?"

"He misunderstood," Jeeves continued, ignoring my attempts to distract him. "Helen meant people who read a lot, but Ronald pictured a starved beast of some sort."

"What about the handlebars?" I asked, wobbling them back and forth. "Are they as you like it?"

Jeeves kept going. "The next day, Helen found her son wolfing down an exceptionally rare first volume of Shakespeare's plays. He'd gotten through most of the comedies and the whole scene quickly turned into a tragedy."

A laugh burst from Julianne. "That's a hard story to swallow. I bet you had quite a tempest in your stomach."

"At the time, the book was valued at six million British pounds," Jeeves finished. "So it wasn't much ado about nothing."

I turned to Julianne. "There you have it, Sato. I've always had an appetite for great literature. And since the only other book we owned worth so much money was the atlas, I never actually opened it."

"Because . . . ," Julianne said.

My face went hot. "I thought maybe the reason they never brought me along was because I ate the Shakespeare. If something happened to the atlas, I'd *never* get to have an adventure."

I kept my eyes on the motorbike instead of my companions.

After a long pause, Jeeves shrugged. "Well, you're on an expedition now, aren't you? And luckily we brought the atlas too. So all's well that ends well."

I glanced over at him. He was smiling slyly at me and I couldn't help but grin back.

Items Inside the Atlas!

✔ One bar of milk chocolate
✔ One deck of playing cards
✔ One book of waterproof matches
✔ One large, round, blood-colored candle
✔ One envelope, addressed: *To **Ronald** Only to be read in a case of IMPENDING MUTINY!*

I tucked the envelope away in my pocket. Julianne inspected the inside of the false book and drew out a small piece of paper that had been stuck in the corner.

It read:

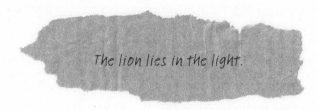

The lion lies in the light.

"What could *that* mean?" Julianne wondered. She drummed her fingers against the body of the sidecar.

I started a few different theories, but none of them seemed strong enough to finish.

"Well . . . ," Jeeves said after a minute, "it's obviously a clue of some sort. And assuming that Elexander steered you right about the crisscrossing yarn—"

"Web of intrigue," Julianne and I corrected.

"Very well, web of intrigue," Jeeves said, "then hopefully we can figure out the meaning and track down Zeetan Z before it's too late. This fellow they call Three-Fingered Jack may be able to help us too. He might know something."

"Then we'll drive until we hit a village," I said. "The chase is afoot!"

The three of us leaped dramatically aboard the motorbike. Jeeves manned the controls and I sat behind him. Julianne was in the sidecar, perched on top of the atlas, with the charred airplane seat cushion and Carter piled on her lap. The revving motor sounded like a dying hedgehog.

"Runs as smoothly as ever!" Jeeves said to Julianne and me, beaming.

"The old man with the oxcart turned around when he saw us," Julianne said over the burping engine. "Let's catch up to him."

The engine revved louder.

"Julianne, you are possibly the sharpest sidekick that I've ever met," I said.

"That's because I'm not a sidekick," she called over the noise. "I'm your partner!"

We spun around and headed toward the ruins of the plane. When we passed the wreckage, we saw an unrecognizable smoldering heap where the mighty Rome had fallen. No one said a word.

While Jeeves piloted the motorbike, Julianne and I gazed up at the giant, craggy hills, shrouded in smoky fog and covered in tropical rainforest. Massive boulders stood wrapped in brilliant green tangles of moss and vine.

One hill rose higher than the rest, with a lush valley beneath it. It was rounded on top, which made it look like a giant, jungle-covered skull. I imagined that from the top of that hill, you'd be able to see for miles in every direction.

We drove on, with the sun warming our backs, until we came upon a muddy outpost carved into the jungle. The road was lined with houses built from wood and tin. In certain places the undergrowth washed across the shacks and swallowed the buildings whole.

We didn't see anyone. Jeeves drove for another mile, until we spotted a tumbledown building with a tin roof and a painted wooden sign that read: The Rakus Saloon.

It was packed to the gills. People crowded shoulder to shoulder and spilled out onto the wooden porch. The swinging batwing doors were pressed open by the mass of bodies. We got off the motorbike, climbed three wooden stairs, and headed inside. Julianne carried Carter slung across her shoulders.

At the first sight of us, the crowd fell silent and parted down the middle. The old farmer who'd watched our plane explode was holding court. He looked angry. Or maybe surprised. Happy, perhaps? Just as I feared, his eyebrows had been scorched off by the explosion, so it was impossible to tell.

"Hello, friend," I said, offering a wave.

The man leaped to his feet and jabbed a finger at us.

"*Itulah merekah! Merekah gila!*" he yelled, springing up onto the bar, sprinting down its length, and diving headlong out the window.

The whole bar watched him go, then turned back to see what we'd do.

"Well," Julianne said with a shrug, "we can't blame him for that."

"Not a bit," Jeeves said as he sidled up to the bar.

The crowd filled in from all sides, mashing us tight. Dust seemed to hang in the air, catching in the sunlight. The room smelled of stale sweat. A woman standing to my right smiled, revealing a toothless mouth.

Jeeves motioned for the bartender, who crossed toward us. "What'll you have?"

"You speak English," I said excitedly. "Maybe you can help us."

The man's eyes drilled into me. "I wouldn't count on it."

His skin was weathered and cracked, and he had faded tattoos running up and down his arms. His long, jet-black hair was tied in a ponytail. He noticed Julianne and eyed the cobra pulsing along her shoulders.

"I usually kill snakes when I catch 'em in here, missy."

"That is a highly trained pet," I informed him.

Carter flared his hood and clamped onto Julianne's bun.

"Case in point," Julianne said.

"Let me guess," the bartender grunted, "you three came looking for something, eh?"

"A water with ice would be a start," Jeeves replied, tapping the bar. "Are you Australian?"

The bartender swiveled toward him, sneering. "Don't you worry, mate. I got just the thing for a limey."

He fished under the bar and came up with a glass jar filled with milky liquid. When I looked closely, I saw a pickled viper coiled at the bottom. Julianne lifted her hand to shield Carter's beady eyes. The bartender gave the jar a good shake, then unscrewed the lid and poured a glassful for Jeeves.

"That should do ya, *gov'nor*," he said with a yellow-toothed smile. "Tell me how it slides down the old gullet."

Jeeves hesitated. The voices around the room became hushed whispers. The woman next to me gripped my arm and squeezed until her fingernails dug into my skin.

Everyone was waiting to see what Jeeves would do next.

FROM THE DESK OF
Thomas Halladay

A Note on Snake Wine

Venom and poison aren't the same thing, even though
Ronald sometimes gets confused about that. Venom
has to be delivered straight to the bloodstream,
which is why snakes have fangs. This means that if
you drink venom—that has been pickled in a bottle
for quite some time—you should be just fine.*

*Please do take care, however. Nothing is fail-
safe. It's a bit of craziness only worth attempting
if you've just been insulted by an Australian
barkeep in Borneo.

13
Strange Invitations!

Jeeves sized up the bartender with a long look. Then, in one quick move, he swallowed the wine in a single gulp and slammed the empty glass back on the countertop.

"Jolly good stuff," he said. "Could I have another?"

The bartender hesitated for just a moment, then poured a second tumbler full of the strange brew. "Let's talk in a few minutes, Pommy, 'cause that drink is sure to be rough on yer delicate British guts."

"No problem there," I assured the crowd. "The whole team is immune to poisons of all varieties."

"Fair dinkum?" the bartender asked, cracking open a bottle with his teeth. "Well bully for you, eh? Now, I reckon it's time you told me what you three are doing in Borneo—besides landing planes in the middle of our roads, that is."

"We're on a mission," I told him.

"Yeah?" the man asked, sipping his drink. "What sort?"

"We're looking for the dastardly pirate Zeetan BrrrGGGmmmBBBldabrsen—"

Before I could get the last words out, the bartender had dropped his beer, lunged across the bar, and slapped his hand over my mouth. In a mad dash, most of the crowd rushed for the door. The bar was almost empty in seconds.

"*Don't*," the bartender said, with his eyes roving wildly around the room. "Don't you ever say that name unless you trust every soul in earshot."

He pulled his hand away slowly. Julianne, Jeeves, and I surveyed the motley few left inside. They were covered in scars, tattoos, and threadbare clothes. Not a single one looked trustable.

The man kept his glassy eyes leveled at me.

"What did you say your name was?" he asked.

"My name is—"

"Not important right now," Julianne interrupted.

The bartender's eyes darted to her, and his nostrils flared. He scratched at his stubbly chin.

"All right, love, have it your way. Listen up, in a few minutes I'll give this whole mob the boot. Then I'll break three glasses on the porch. One. Two. Three. When you hear that, you'll know it's safe to come inside. Climb down to the cellar and we'll have a yarn. Maybe I can help you find the man you're looking for."

FACT: This plan sounded extremely dangerous and ill-advised.

"We accept," I said.

We promised to make ourselves scarce until the bartender gave the signal and started for the door. On our way out, a bleary-eyed scalawag sitting by the window forced his head up from a crooked table.

"This island will swallow you up!" he yelled. "Through its maw and down to its belly!"

The man let his mouth fall slowly open, then swallowed like he was gulping us down. A crust of dried blood lined the creases of his lips.

"Senyap," the bartender snapped coldly.

At once, the man's vacant eyes began to wobble. He collapsed forward onto his table, gave a single hiccup, and went dead silent.

The three of us pushed past the swinging doors and headed back to the motorbike. Jeeves drove us a little way down a small path and parked within earshot of the saloon. For the next hour or so, we rested fitfully while Carter basked in the afternoon sun. Every time a glass shattered in the bar we jumped to our feet, but three glasses never broke right in a row.

There were birds cawing away in the jungle, and the smells of smoke and overripe fruit swirled around us. I glanced at Julianne. She was turning her wrists, admiring the pattern on her skin made by long shafts of sun filtering through the trees. I watched her through fluttering eyelids . . . and then . . .

The next thing I knew, Jeeves was kneeling beside me, shaking me awake. I sat up, out of breath, eyes darting into the jungle.

"You were having a nightmare," he explained.

"I doubt that," I said, once I'd finally collected myself. "**Ronald Zupan** sleeps as soundly as a three-toed sloth."

"You were yelling," Julianne said.

"Cries of derring-do," I insisted. "Besides, what would I be having a nightmare about? My parents getting tortured by a monstrous pirate? Stepping into battle with this sea dog, only to fail as Francisco and Helen watch helplessly?"

Julianne gave a slight shrug. "Well . . . *yeah.*"

"Don't underestimate the Zupans," I said. "It's quite possible that they've already outsmarted Zeetan Z, just like they outsmarted the False Sheik of Zanzibar. Or outfought him, like they outfought the Parisian Legion of Diamond Thieves. Isn't that right Jeeves?"

I looked over at him.

"Either way," Jeeves said, "we need a plan."

I shifted my weight and the dried banana leaves beneath me rustled. "Well, what do we think of this strange bartender?"

"Why should he have to close the saloon just to talk to us?" Julianne asked. "It doesn't feel right."

"Which begs the question," Jeeves said, "why are we going at all?"

"Remember what Helen Zupan says," I reminded him. "'Don't allow danger to faze you at any phase of your journey.' If it *is* a trap, then it could also be a clue. It might mean the man at the bar knows something."

"He's right," Julianne agreed. "But we can't give up too much information. Stay quiet. And if the bartender says anything about the Lion of Lyros, we play dumb and get out of there, agreed?"

Crash! A glass shattered in the distance. *Crash! Crash!*

Jeeves rose to his feet, his long legs wobbling slightly. His face was drawn and serious. "Trap or not, we'll know soon enough."

A Conversation Between Julianne Sato and Tom Halladay

As Ronald slept, I chatted with Julianne while she ripped up small pieces of the cushion and stuffed them inside the sound holes of her violin.

Me: Do you mind if I ask what you're doing?
Julianne: Putting this violin to good use by turning it into a life preserver. The foam floats, so now the violin will float . . . Borneo is known to have flash floods.
Me: But then the violin will never quite sound the same, will it?
Julianne: Probably not, but I'm actually thinking of taking up the oboe. Or the didgeridoo.

She finished her first task, then pulled down three thin vines from a nearby tree and began to weave them into a rope. Her mind seemed to work at a dizzying speed.

Julianne: Question, Jeeves. Do you like being Ronald's butler?

Me: That's complicated . . . I've done so for his entire life. I'm sure Ronald wishes he had someone else. In fact, I'd bet that if I took a different job, he'd be quite happy.

Julianne: You think so? I remember at fencing practice he was always looking over to see if you were watching.

Me: Really?

Julianne: Yes, really.

14
Shadowy Meetings!

We started back toward town on foot, leaving Carter in the sidecar of the motorbike to keep watch. Our long shadows slanted across the sunbaked road as we strode toward the Rakus Saloon.

"Remember the man who escaped Zeetan Z, from my parents' files?" I asked as we walked. "Three-Fingered Jack? Maybe *he's* the bartender?"

Jeeves glanced at me. "To tell the truth, I didn't look at his fingers. Surely one of us would have noticed if he were missing two, right?"

"Something to keep an eye on," Julianne said.

We found the saloon empty and unlit. I led the way through the batwing doors and across the dusty floor. Before we stepped behind the bar, I went to the back door, unfastened the bolt, and eased it open.

"Master adventurers should always know their exits," I said in a hushed voice.

We jumped over the bar and found a cellar door made of two thick wooden slabs. A sliver of dim light leaked through the crack where the two pieces met. We opened them and climbed down a bamboo ladder, into the dank-smelling basement.

In the middle of a wide, half-lit room, the strange bartender sat at a wooden table. Next to him was the biggest man I'd ever seen. He was bald and his fingers were splayed out in front of him, each one the size of a cucumber. His jaws looked like they could chew through metal, and a long, reddish scar stretched across his face—from his left ear to the right side of his chin.

An oil lantern hung on a nail from one of the rafters above the two men. It cast shadows across the walls of the room, which were lined with a bizarre collection of items: more lanterns, a rack that held six cutlasses, mildewing clothes, clay jugs, barrels, a stack of stained glass windows, and a giant pile of rocks.

The bartender motioned us to the table. "G'day, mates, take a seat. I'm afraid I never did give my name. Call me Pemburu."

We crossed the dirt floor and sat down on slatted chairs under the sputtering lantern light. I noticed that Pemburu had all ten of his fingers. The colossus next to him had ten fingers too.

"Hello, friend," I said, smiling and reaching out a hand toward the giant. "What's your name?"

The man lifted a meaty paw toward mine, but Pemburu swatted it away and glared at me. "He doesn't talk."

I studied the bartender's massive comrade. His back was rigid and he'd balled his hands into two enormous fists, like two hams resting on the table.

Julianne scowled. "Why won't you introduce us?"

"Seems only polite," Jeeves said. "But I suppose an Australian wouldn't understand that."

Pemburu glowered at them, then turned back toward me.

"His name is Gunting," he said, biting off every word. "It's a nickname, from a story you don't want to hear. It means *scissors*."

"His name is Scissors?" I asked.

Pemburu did a cutting motion with his fingers, and I looked at the jagged scar that crossed Gunting's face.

"Now," the barkeep went on, "why don't you three tell me why you're in Borneo?"

"It's like I told you earlier," I said. "We're hunting for the nefarious Zeetan Z."

Gunting's shoulders twitched.

"And why do you reckon you want to find him?" Pemburu asked.

"In a minute," Julianne said. "First, why do you have those swords? And the old-fashioned lanterns in the corner? And those barrels and clothes?"

Pemburu's eyes narrowed, and he scratched his cheek with one fingernail. "You're a nosy one, aren't you?" He turned back to me. "No one in these parts will talk to you about Zeetan Z. Don't you know how deadly he is?"

I pressed my hands to the table and leaned forward. "As deadly as a deathstalker scorpion riding on the back of a funnel-web spider?"

"Bingo."

"Well, we aren't afraid of him," I said.

Pemburu let out a low whistle; the light from the lantern made his face look sunken and ghostly. I glanced at Jeeves, who was also looking at the cutlasses. His forehead was beaded with sweat.

"Don't you see the danger, gang?" Pemburu asked quietly. "Zeetan Z would cut you to shreds. He'd cut *me* to shreds, and I reckon I'm tougher than you. Why don't you pack up your swags and go back to where you came from?"

The lantern choked greasy smoke, and for a split second the room went black. When the wick flared up again, I turned toward Pemburu, blood rushing to my face.

"Because," I said, "we think that Zeetan Z kidnapped my parents."

As soon as the words spilled out, I knew I'd said too much. My eyes darted over to Julianne. She pushed her chair farther out and stood up.

"I think perhaps we should look elsewhere," Jeeves said, voice trembling. "You gentlemen have a nice—"

Gunting slammed one meaty fist on the table, and the room fell silent. He drew a scrap of paper and a pencil from his pocket and scratched out a note, which he showed to Pemburu. The barman read it, nodded, then turned back to us with a sticky-sweet smile.

"Have you three ever heard the phrase 'The lion lies in the light'?" he asked.

The room seemed to tilt. Clearly, these two knew more about Zeetan Z than they were letting on.

"No," I lied. "Not once. Never."

Gunting flipped the paper over and scratched out another note. He showed it to Pemburu, who read it and shook his head. Gunting wrote something else and underlined it three times. Pemburu barely glanced at the words.

"That's always your way," he muttered. "This time we do things my way, understand?"

Gunting looked at the table and nodded slowly.

"Good," Pemburu said.

The word had hardly left his mouth when the giant's massive arm shot out to grab my shirt collar. Before I could do anything heroic, he lifted me up and flung me across the basement. I landed right on the giant pile of rocks. Luckily, **Ronald Zupan** is incredibly resistant to pain.

I was on my feet in a flash, only to see Pemburu lunge for Julianne as Gunting went after Jeeves with his arms stretched wide. I picked up one of the rocks and heaved it at the towering rogue. He turned around just in time to see it coming, but it only bounced off his massive chest.

"Strange," I said, "rock is supposed to beat scissors!"

The distraction gave Jeeves just enough time to pick up a stained glass window and smash it over Gunting's head. The glass shattered everywhere, but Gunting hardly noticed that either. He grabbed the window frame from around his neck and tore it in two. All the commotion was enough for Julianne to dodge away from Pemburu and slip, swift as a shadow, over to the rack of swords. She picked up one

for herself and sent another spiraling through the air, into my outstretched hand.

"En garde!" we said at once.

I went after Gunting while Julianne attacked Pemburu. Two expert fencers against two unarmed men should have been no problem, but when I thrust my cutlass at Gunting's shoulder, the sword only skidded away. The giant picked up a chair and threw it at me.

FACT: It hurt a lot worse than the rocks did.

"Is your blade dull?" Julianne yelled across the room.

"It could hardly saw through a stick of butter!" I called as Gunting charged again.

Before the colossus could get his meaty hands on me, Jeeves broke another stained glass window across his pumpkin-sized skull. Gunting grasped wildly at the air and tumbled backward onto the rock pile.

"I think the swords are props," Julianne yelled across the room, "from Josh Brigand's pirate movie!"

In seconds, Gunting was on his feet again, breathing like an enraged bull. My short, extraordinary life flashed before my eyes.

"Dull swords call for a new plan!" I yelled to my friends.

"What's that?" Jeeves asked, voice quavering.

"Run!"

Julianne spun twice, slapped Pemburu across the face

with the flat of her cutlass blade, and dashed straight to the bamboo ladder. I ducked under Gunting's outstretched arms and followed her, looking over my shoulder the whole time. Jeeves picked up a desk lamp in each hand and began backpedaling after us. Just before he started to climb, he reared back and threw one lamp at Gunting and the other at Pemburu.

They were both direct hits! Pemburu collapsed and Gunting staggered backward. His mouth fell open, and I saw that instead of a tongue, he had a pink stump. I shuddered.

"Nice work, Jeeves!" Julianne yelled.

"That's what comes from years of playing cricket," Jeeves panted as we scrambled out of the basement and slammed the cellar doors behind us.

"Oh, here we go with the cricket," I huffed.

We quickly wedged the doors shut with a table and piled chairs on top.

"It's a wonderful game," Jeeves said, pressing his back up to our stronghold and digging his heels into the dirt floor.

"There's a tea break," I said. "How can that be a sport?"

The entire room shook as Gunting threw his massive body against the cellar door. The three of us held it shut with all our might.

"Just because it has a tea—"

"*Enough!*" Julianne yelled.

Gunting hit the cellar again, and it sent us skidding into the back side of the bar. We leaped over the countertop and bolted through the back door of the saloon. Seconds later, Gunting burst out after us. He gained steadily, yelling garbled words with each step. Once we got to the jungle path, we could hear his heavy footfalls thudding behind us.

Finally, the motorbike came into view, bathed in a silver pool of moonlight. I quickly slid my sword through my belt and jumped onto the driver's seat. Julianne dove aboard behind me, and Jeeves swung his long legs into the sidecar.

"*Ghaaaaaahh!*" he screamed.

> **FACT:** I could tell that he'd just sat on his dear friend Carter for the second time in one day.

I kick-started the engine but it didn't fire. I tried again. Nothing. The sound of Gunting's snorts and snarls drew closer. I jammed my foot on the kick-start harder than ever. This time, the engine burped once and sputtered to life.

Without a moment to spare, I opened the throttle and we rumbled along the jungle path. The road angled downhill, but even with gravity on our side, Gunting closed in. Julianne climbed to her feet—one foot on the edge of the sidecar, the other on the seat of the motorbike. She steadied herself by holding my shoulder with one hand and gripped the sword she'd stolen from the saloon with the other.

The giant was so close behind that we could feel his hot breath. I watched him in the side-view mirror, waving his arms wildly as Julianne used her cutlass to swat him back.

I glanced into the sidecar and saw Carter turn his attention away from Jeeves and toward our attacker. He flared his hood. A mask of horror came across Gunting's face, and his legs seemed to give way beneath him.

Before I could deduce what was happening, the handlebars wobbled, and I had to turn back to the rocky track. The jungle echoed with the crash of boulders and Gunting's screams.

"WHAHAHAHAHAHAHAHA!
AYEYETAHHHHHHHHHH!
GHWWWHWEEEEEEEE!
RRRRRUUUUUUUU . . ."

It was like the death wail of a ringed bandicoot. And after that, nothing.

FROM THE DESK OF
Thomas Halladay

Errors in the Chapter "Shadowy Meetings!"

1. Ronald is not "incredibly resistant
to pain" as he likes to claim. Landing on
rocks didn't hurt because, just like the
swords, the rocks were movie props. They were
probably made of papier-mâché, which would
explain why Gunting deflected them so easily.
As everyone knows, scissors beats paper.

2. The stained glass windows were
probably movie props too, but after seeing
the way Pemburu collapsed when I wound up and
threw the lamp at him, I'd wager those were
real.

3. I keep catching the absurd implication
that I'd somehow become "dear friends" with
Carter the cobra. There's not a grain of truth
in it. And if you're thinking to yourself,

"This butler sure does go on and on about a defanged snake," let me just say: even the bite of a defanged snake can leave quite a bruise.

15
Deductions in the Dark!

The giant had disappeared into thin air. All we could hear of him were his groans echoing somewhere behind us. We drove on in silence.

"I think we lost him," Julianne panted. "Do you think we lost him?"

Carter slithered onto Jeeves's lap and coiled up there. The butler frowned. "It looked almost as if he . . . fell right through the ground."

I didn't stop to investigate. In the words of Helen Zupan, "When a villain tries to break you, make a break for it and don't hit the brake until you're sure they're gone . . . or broken."

Finally, I saw a gray split in the inky undergrowth and drove straight into it. Creepers and vines tore across our faces.

Thirty feet into the bush I flicked off the headlamp and soon after that I killed the motor.

"What now?" Jeeves asked.

"We wait for morning," I said.

There was no way to mark the hours—the thick jungle canopy blocked the stars out completely. I volunteered to take the first watch, and Julianne made good use of her violin by propping the case under her head like a pillow. Soon, she and Jeeves both slid silently into the land of dreams. I sat with my new cutlass in my left hand and Carter coiled around my right arm, alone with my thoughts and the swirling snake-head moths.

I was starting to drift off when I heard rustling by my side. My body tensed up. "Who's there?"

"It's me," came Julianne's voice.

I couldn't see her, but I spoke in her direction—eager to share my latest dazzling theory. "Gunting and Pemburu knew my parents' clue. They must be in cahoots with Zeetan Z himself. That also explains why they have all those props from the movie starring Johnny—"

"*Josh*," Julianne said.

"Blinkhard."

"*Brigand*. Are you jealous?"

I picked up a pebble and threw it into the blackness. "Me? Of Jim Brickhead? Why would I possibly be jealous of . . . ?" I hesitated. "Do you think he's impressive?"

"I've only seen him in movies," Julianne said. "But you act a little weird every time his name comes up."

I scoffed. "Not at all. Your hero sounds like a bit of a dolt, no offense. **Ronald Zupan** is a *real* master adventurer."

"But you said yesterday that you'd never been on any of your parents' expedit—"

"After this dazzling rescue, my parents will never risk leaving me behind again. What would Jolly Biffman say to that?"

Julianne didn't answer. The only sound was the jungle orchestra swelling and tightening around us.

"*Any*way," she said after a long pause, "I agree that Pemburu and Gunting are in cahoots with Zeetan Z . . . sort of. I don't think Pemburu is a pirate. He wasn't the one who asked about 'the lion lies in the light'—he didn't say that until Gunting wrote him a note."

"Interesting theory, Sato," I said. "So let's suppose that Pemburu is just a comrade of the nefarious gang."

"What about Gunting?" she asked. "Do you think *he's* one of Zeetan Z's crew?"

"Probably."

I heard rustling as Julianne shifted closer to me. "It seemed like they were disagreeing about something . . . I wish we could see those notes Gunting wrote."

"We could try to find him," I said. "Jeeves said it was like he fell through the ground. What if he's still there?"

"Good luck trying to convince Jeeves to go back to where

a giant tried to crush us all to death," Julianne said. "No, I think we'll have to come up with something else."

We dropped into a long silence, punctuated by the buzz of insects and the croaks of far-off tree frogs.

I thought Julianne had fallen back to sleep when she spoke again. "Question, Ronald. Once we rescue them, do you think your parents would do me a favor? Like, to say 'thanks'?"

I didn't have to think twice. "Of course."

"What if it's complicated?"

"The Zupan Family Crest reads, 'The More Complicated the Better.'"

Julianne let a soft little laugh flee into the darkness.

"I'm serious," I said. "Unless, of course, the favor is to help you meet Judd Broad-face and sail off in his ship."

Julianne sighed. "It isn't about Josh Brigand. It *is* about a ship though."

Somewhere in the jungle, an owl gave a single, lonesome hoot.

"Many astounding adventures take place on the high seas," I said. "Tell me more."

I couldn't see Julianne, but I could feel her hesitate.

"When I was three, my parents decided to go sailing

around the world," she said. "They'd planned it for years and packed everything into a tiny ship called the *Alma*. But off the coast of Chile, we were caught in a storm."

There was another long pause.

"Two weeks later, a band of rumrunners found me playing with a fiddler crab on Alejandro Selkirk Island, but my parents were never seen again."

Some sort of bug scampered across my ankle, and I brushed it away. "So that's the favor? You want Francisco and Helen to find your parents? Sato, you've come to the right family. The Zupans have located treasure in the depths of pyramids, they've uncovered artifacts in long-abandoned mine shafts, they've—"

"My parents weren't kidnapped," Julianne interrupted. "They weren't international adventurers like yours. They just liked to sail, and one day they got caught in a storm. That's all."

A strange sensation washed over me—I felt sad for her sadness. My parents may have been in the clutches of a dastardly pirate, but they had **Ronald Zupan** to save them. Julianne's parents wouldn't get a heroic rescue. Three different times I opened my mouth to say something, and three different times I stopped myself.

"What's the favor then?" I finally asked.

When Julianne spoke, the words came slowly. Even the bugs seemed to hush at the tone of her voice. "I thought maybe, when this is all over, Francisco and Helen could help me find the wreck and recover some keepsakes."

"Treasure hunting," I murmured.

"You could call it that. Everything my parents owned was on the ship. I thought if I could just find it, I'd have something to hang on to. My grandfather told me about a music box . . ."

She trailed off. I let my sword fall to the ground and set my hand delicately on her shoulder.

"I swear that my parents will help you," I said, "and me too, of course. And Jeeves is dead asleep, but I bet anything he'd help."

We sat in silence for a long time, both thinking about our parents. We heard a distant roar somewhere in the jungle and scooted back-to-back, watching for yellow eyes lurking in the bushes.

I tried to stay awake. As Helen Zupan says, "A master adventurer has to lessen the need for shut-eye. It's a lesson you'll learn quickly when traveling in dangerous territory."

Over and over, my eyelids drooped, but I forced them open again. Finally, the rise and fall of Julianne's breathing, coupled with the hum of the moths and Jeeves's soft snores, overpowered me, and I disappeared into dreamland.

FROM THE DESK OF
Thomas Halladay

An Error in the Chapter "Deductions in the Dark!"

1. Ronald told Julianne that I was dead asleep during their conversation, but I'd actually woken up when I heard them rustling. As nerve-racking as our whole ordeal had been, I was glad to see the two of them getting along. This might sound surprising, but Ronald doesn't have many friends his age, and I liked the fact that Julianne wasn't afraid to stand up to him. Quite the backbone, that girl.

It might have been a very nice little moment . . . if only there wasn't an angry giant on the loose, a deadly pirate hiding nearby, and a pet king cobra that wouldn't stop biting me.

16

Monsoon Storms!

I awoke to tiny pinpricks rippling across my neck and face. I leaned my head up to look for the culprit and saw a twig that had fallen on me in the night. I tried to shake it off but it held firm. I grabbed for it and it came alive in my fingers—limbs pedaling through the air.

Tiny bubbles of spit frothed from its mouth.

"I know just how you feel, my long-thoraxed friend," I said to the colossal stick bug. "Last night **Ronald Zupan** was also roughly handled by a giant."

I set the insect on a branch and looked down at my shoulder, where Gunting had smashed me with the chair. My entire side throbbed. An ugly purple bruise spread halfway down my arm. I crawled out of our jungle cocoon to find my friends sitting in a clearing between two towering trees.

Julianne was busy scrawling notes in her adventure journal. "Good morning," she said without looking up.

She finished writing and rolled a pale-green fruit as big as a watermelon in my direction. I cradled it in my lap and tore away the tough shell to reveal yellow pods of flesh.

"Thank you," I said, sucking a piece of sweet fruit away from a smooth black seed.

"Did you sleep okay?" Jeeves asked. He was tinkering with the engine of the motorbike.

I massaged my shoulder. "Like a three-toed—"

"You were thrashing quite a bit, is why I ask."

Before I could say anything else, Carter slithered out of the jungle with a rat in his mouth. He began to slowly swallow it in front of me. The rat's fur was matted and slick and its legs twitched. My stomach did a spiraling backflip.

Julianne stood up and stretched her arms as high as they'd go. "So, does anyone have a plan?"

I sucked down another section of fruit. "We passed a hill that looked like a skull yesterday—it was higher than all the others. If we climb to the top of that and look around, we might be able to see something . . . like a river. I mean, if they have Joff Biffhead's ship, the pirates must be close to water, right?"

"If the only alternative is going to look for a tongueless giant," Jeeves said, "I'll take the hill any day."

Julianne stood up and tied her scarf around her waist. Then she slipped her sword between the scarf and her hip.

"But if we climb the hill and don't find anything," I added, "then we'll have no choice but to go Gunting hunting. He and Pemburu are the only leads we've got, and we *need* a clue."

"Let's hope it doesn't come to that," Jeeves said.

I rose to my feet and a terrible pain shot down my side. I stumbled and had to brace myself against a tree.

"You sure you're feeling all right?" Julianne asked.

"Sato, you seem to be suggesting that I have a massive bruise across my shoulder and that my ribs ache every time I stand." I hunched over until I could catch my breath. "To which I say"—I squeezed my eyes shut in pain—"*I'm perfectly fine.*"

Jeeves ran his tongue across his upper teeth, making his lip bulge. "Indeed."

When we were ready to depart, I eased myself into the sidecar. Carter basked on my lap. I could see where the tiny claws of the rat strained against the inside of his stomach.

Jeeves drove back the way we'd come—heading toward the main road. At first, finding the way was easy; our tire tracks were pressed deep into the soft ground. But after a few miles we arrived at a rocky section where two paths crossed, and we had to slow to a crawl to see the prints.

With my body leaning out of the sidecar and my head angled toward the path, I couldn't hear anything over the death cough of the motorbike. I didn't notice the clouds gathering overhead until the first raindrop splashed down on my outstretched neck.

I had just enough time to glance skyward before the crash of thunder split the air and the rain began to hammer down in full force. The tracks blurred in seconds, washing away in long, muddy streaks. Our wheels spun and spat. Julianne and I had our adventure hats to protect our heads. Jeeves, on the other hand, looked like a drowning llama.

"Here!" Julianne called over the rain.

She passed him the flight goggles, transforming him into a drowning llama with goggles on. We came to another fork in the road.

"Which way?" Jeeves asked, his voice half-swallowed by the storm.

We stalled at the crossroads. Then started to slide backward. The wheels skidded. The front of the bike swung around completely, and the ground crumbled beneath us. We began hurtling toward a deep ravine that ran alongside the path.

There was no way to stop; we were caught in a mudslide.

"Abandon motorbike!" I yelled.

"I've got Carter," Julianne cried, gathering up the snake in her arms.

I grabbed the atlas and dove from the sidecar. A raging river of mud flowed toward the bottom of the gully, and I skidded down it as fast as I could go. A wave of debris rushed behind me, ready to swallow me whole. When the hill bottomed out, I hit the ground running. My sword slapped against my leg as I stumbled through the undergrowth, hardly able to see over the atlas.

My toe caught on a root and suddenly I was airborne— my ankle came into view next to my ear, then a flash of ROCK, the sky, a bush, my elbow, ROCK, sky again, and finally a big, speckled ROCK waiting right in my landing space.

I had just enough time to think, "This is bad" before I lost my grip on the atlas and everything went flying.

FACT: Correct as usual!

"*Ronald . . . Roooonald.*" The voice swam into my ears from across an ocean.

I opened my eyes. Julianne Sato stood over me, blocking the rain from thrumming down on my face. "Are you okay?"

My head throbbed.

"Naturally," I groaned. "**Ronald Zupan** is highly resistant to—"

"I know, I know," she said, leaning down to brush some mud from my forehead. She smiled and it made my brain feel foggy—probably just the impact from landing.

I reached out to pet Carter, who was draped across Julianne's shoulders. The rain continued to pound away.

"Where's Jeeves?" I wondered, fishing a plug of mud out of my ear.

Julianne's eyes widened. Seconds later, I hobbled beside her as we rushed back to the bottom of the hill. We found the brave butler lying facedown in a quagmire of twisted branches and muck. It took both of us, plus Carter latched on to the tail of Jeeves's coat, to hoist him to his feet.

Once he could stand without swaying, Jeeves yanked off the flight goggles. This left him with a bandit mask of pale skin surrounded by thickly caked mud.

The three of us slowly turned to look at the motorbike. It was upside down, buried to its tires in debris. Jeeves brushed his fingertips against the spinning rear wheel. His face and body continued to shed chunks of mud.

"You feel all right?" Julianne asked. "About your motor-bike, I mean."

Jeeves looked down dismally.

I cleared my throat. "It's times like these I'm reminded of the wise words of Francisco Zupan, who says—"

Julianne reached behind Jeeves and poked me in the ribs. I leaned back to look at her, and she slowly shook her head.

"It's . . . an unfortunate loss," I stammered. "I know you treasured it."

The rain surged again—the drops splatted and pinged

against the underbelly of the motorbike. Finally, Jeeves turned around and straightened his jacket.

Julianne used her free hand to pick up her violin from the mud before it washed away, as I collected the spilled contents of the atlas. The note from my parents with

The lion lies in the light.

written at the bottom was still inside the false book, wet but not blurred.

"Over here," Julianne called out, waving from under an acacia tree.

We huddled together under the spreading branches, just as another slab of mud crumbled and slid into the gully, piling on top of the motorbike. Only the muffler could be seen now.

Jeeves turned away from the wreckage. "Believe it or not, Ronald, I think I'd actually like to hear Francisco's saying."

"'He who endures will conquer,'" I said. "'So will he who never gets stung by a blister beetle.'"

"He who endures will conquer." Jeeves gathered himself up. "Very well then . . . to use your phrase: *onward*."

A Note on the Sayings of Helen and Francisco Zupan

As you may have noticed, my employers are full of sayings. Helen speaks in homonyms—words that sound the same but mean different things. Francisco's phrases usually have something to do with bugs and are little help to a butler. Naturally, Ronald quotes them both as if their words are pure genius.

I've gotten in the habit of blocking out these lines when Ronald repeats them. He might get halfway through a pearl of wisdom from Francisco about the dangers of "kissing bugs and overpacking" before I even notice.

And yet, somehow, these words landed: "He who endures will conquer." Forget the next bit, about the blister beetle; it's the first part that matters. True words, indeed. Some days—when your motorbike is submerged in mud, you're soaking wet, and a warm cup of tea seems lifetimes away—you just have to put one foot in front of the next.

17

Alone!

We were worried the road might collapse again, so we tried tracing a path through the jungle instead. The plan was still to find the skull-shaped hill I'd seen the day before. If that didn't help, we'd have no choice but to go back and look for Gunting.

Twisted banyans shot up through the clouds and sent tangled roots plunging down into the earth. Smaller trees filled in the gaps between them. Thanks to the thick jungle, the rain didn't hit us directly. Instead, the water ran down the leaves in tiny streams, which all seemed to trickle right down the back of my neck.

Progress was slow. Jeeves carried the atlas, and Julianne and I used our dull cutlasses to swat at the tangled vines that crossed our path. Before long we were trudging forward in complete silence.

After about half an hour, Julianne stopped. "Where's the road?"

I looked up. "It's right over . . ."

I ran a few steps toward where I thought the road was, but there was just more jungle. I dodged around a giant tree and went a little farther. Nothing.

"It must have turned," Jeeves said.

"Or we turned away from it," Julianne tried.

"No fear," I said. "Master adventurers are blessed with an extraordinary sense of direction."

We adjusted our course and hiked on, certain that we'd hit the road again soon. As we walked, we nibbled squares of chocolate from inside the atlas and ate sunset-colored papayas collected off the jungle floor. The papaya trees were everywhere, tucked between taller trees, and the sweet scent of their fruit perfumed the whole rainforest.

At some point, the rain stopped and the sun came out, filtering down weakly through the jungle. The haze vanished and our wet clothes gripped us like the paws of spider monkeys. Each step was a battle. It was like Helen Zupan always says, "Sometimes, it's an amazing feat just to move your feet."

Julianne stopped a second time. "We're walking in circles. That's the same tree we saw twenty minutes ago."

I inspected the tree in question. "Hmmm, you're no doubt saying that because the blotchy fungus on the trunk is shaped like a flamingo—which does seem *vaguely* familiar to other trees we've encountered. I dare say it's a distant cousin, a far-flung relative, a genetic—"

"Definitively the same one," Jeeves interrupted.

Julianne nodded. "One hundred percent."

FACT: There are times in any master adventurer's life when all eyes are watching him and he has to do something bold and brilliant.

"Friends," I said, rolling up my sleeves, "we have no way to know where the road is, or why so many trees in this jungle have fungus that looks like flamingos. Also, the jungle is too thick to see the hill we're looking for."

"Where are you going with this?" Jeeves asked.

I patted the trunk of the flamingo tree. "We might not be able to find the hill, but we can do the next best thing. I'll ascend this mighty giant and take in the terrain. Then I'll make a highly accurate map."

It was a rousing speech—slightly disrupted by a yelp of pain when Carter bit Jeeves's ear.

Julianne peered up into the branches. "Make sure you keep an eye out for clouded leopards up there."

"Perhaps the leopards should keep an eye out for *me*," I said, throwing her a bold grin.

"No, I mean it. There's a page about Borneo's clouded leopards in this guide to mammals that I have back home.

They hide in trees during the day and get very aggressive if you disturb them. I think that was what roared late last night."

I tipped my adventure hat to thank her for the advice, grabbed hold of the flamingo tree, and swooped quickly upward, swinging from one branch to the next, scrambling as fast as I could. With the cicadas buzzing encouragingly, I thought of my parents and how every branch got me closer to rescuing them. I imagined how proud they'd be of their son. They'd surely bring me on their next adventure as a reward for my blazing bravery.

Before I knew it, I was a hundred feet off the ground and gaining speed. In the tree next to mine, I saw a family of red-haired orangutans. They bared their teeth and tugged on their beards, as if to say, "Well done, brave sir! Bravo!" I didn't have my own dazzling facial hair to pull on at the moment, so I offered a toothy smile instead.

"Can your movie star Jeb Broofus climb like this?" I called down to Julianne.

She answered with a loud scream.

"I thought not!" I yelled back.

Jeeves added to the uproar. The jungle was too thick for me to see their admiring faces, and I couldn't make out a single word they said, but they both sounded frighteningly impressed by my climbing.

Soon the branches thinned out. I settled myself into a spot where the last thick branch met the trunk of the tree and looked out over the rainforest canopy. All around me the sun blazed.

"I'm at the top!" I announced.

Far below, my friends were still frantically celebrating my spectacular climb. Their words were muffled, but I managed to make out a single, drawn-out syllable: "*Aaaaaaaaap.*"

"What was that?" I yelled back. "Map? Of course I'll make a map!"

It was a stunning view. In the distance, fog-shrouded hills dotted the horizon on three sides. To the north of my tree,

I saw a few different streams cutting through the jungle. I looked farther and spotted the road, the skull hill, and the village with two lazy rivers snaking wide paths around it. Beyond that, the horizon got murky where the rivers met the ocean.

The top of the tree swayed gently. Jeeves and Julianne were still yelling, but all I could decipher was that final syllable, "*Aáaaappp!*"

"Yes, yes! Map! I've got it!"

Just as I reached for a pencil, a breeze came up and the treetop swayed. I wrapped both arms around the trunk to steady myself, but the pencil slipped from my fingers. Before I could even lunge for it, it had vanished below me.

"Uh . . . friends," I yelled down, "did either of you happen to see a pencil falling from the sky?"

When I couldn't hear an answer, I had no choice but to climb back down. Halfway to the bottom, I met the orangutans again. This time the group's mood had taken a foul turn. They screeched and pelted me with figs. When the figs ran out, they threw—

FACT: A gentleman explorer doesn't always tell what a bunch of primates threw at him.

The point is, I wanted to get down in a hurry. The orangutans woke up every bird in the area, and the jungle chorus was so loud that the racket drowned out Jeeves and Julianne altogether. I glanced below me, but I still couldn't see them.

"It was an incredible view up there," I announced, "but my pencil fell and . . ."

I prepared to swing to the ground dramatically on an emerald-colored vine—until I discovered that the emerald-colored vine was actually an emerald-colored tree snake.

I fell like a flailing wildebeest. "*Oof!*"

After a minute, I dusted off, sat up, and settled my adventure hat back on my head.

"Carter, did you see your green cousin?" I asked. "The mysteries of the jungle are uncoiling all around us."

No one answered. I clambered to my feet and still didn't see a soul.

"Jeeves! Julianne! *Carter!*"

For one terrifying moment, even the menacing monkeys were silent. My friends were gone.

Errors in the Chapter "Alone!"

1. It wasn't "MAP" that Julianne and I yelled; it was "TRAP!" We'd stumbled into a spring-loaded net and were dangling twenty feet above the ground for at least ten minutes. Carter had been captured too, but after he bit me twice on the nose, I pushed him through a hole in the net and he slipped to the ground. As Julianne and I struggled, I took great relief in thinking that I might never see that snake again.

2. Ronald doesn't mention exactly what it was that the orangutans threw at him after they ran out of figs. Very respectable. I'll show the same restraint and withhold comment.

3. Of course . . . it *is* my duty to report the facts as they happened.

4. He wouldn't mind, would he?

5. Oh, what's the harm? It was dung!

6. That's poop, you know. They were throwing poop. Got him pretty good too.

18
Odd Villains!

My head swiveled left and right. Had Jeeves, Julianne, and Carter gone to chase down a lead? Or was something more sinister afoot? What if they were now captives of the dastardly Zeetan Z, just like my parents? One thing was clear: my friends of both the human and serpentine variety had vanished into thin air.

Suddenly the air *did* seem thin indeed—each breath came quick and shallow. I doubled over to calm myself and felt the spine of my adventure journal pressing against my hip. I reached for it, hoping to uncover a morsel of advice.

The leather was swollen with water and the paper clung together in chunks, but the India ink was unblurred. Inside, there were notes on wrestling a rabid warthog but nothing about finding lost compatriots.

NOTES ON WRESTLING A RABID WARTHOG

FRANCISCO
1. Sneak up on the beast. Warthogs are almost impossible to catch running across the open savanna.
2. Grab the back legs first and hoist the animal off the ground.
3. Flip your foe on its back and wrap it up in a bear hug.

HELEN
1. Keep clear of the tusks, being gored by a warthog means weeks of pain.
2. Be sure not to get kicked. Those short legs are incredibly powerful.
3. Avoid the warthog's teeth at all costs. The beast can bite a chunk out of your leg without the least bit of trouble and remember . . . rabies!

JEEVES
1. There's absolutely no reason to wrestle a rabid warthog. Meanwhile, there are plenty of good reasons for picking up your socks from the living room floor.

Near the back of the notebook, I came to a piece of creased newspaper, yellowed by time. As I gently unfolded the page and saw the smeared headline, I realized that I had the article practically memorized.

MASTER ADVENTURER DISCOVERED ALIVE (AND LIVING LIKE A KING) IN THE AMAZON!

Rio de Janeiro, Brazil—World-renowned adventurer Francisco Zupan walked out of the Amazon Rainforest this week after being given up for dead more than a month ago.

When reporters asked Zupan about his ordeal, he said, "I had a wonderful time with the Matis Indians, the Jaguar People. They taught me to track tapir by getting low, where the greatest clues are sure to hide. When it was time for me to say good-bye, they gave me gifts of pottery and woven baskets."

International media expecting a haggard, half-dead Zupan were in for a "wowser"—even the adventurer's trademark beard seemed to be in fine shape. Zupan's first move was to send word to his wife, Helen, who was at home with the couple's young son.

"I had guessed that my husband was the guest of the Matis," Mrs. Zupan told reporters who showed up at her Bay City home. "I thank them for sending him home in good health and fine spirits."

I folded the article back up and returned the adventure journal to my pocket. Jeeves had given the page to me one stormy night, when I woke up missing my parents. He said it was proof that the two of them had a way of landing on their feet.

This time around, I didn't have Jeeves to convince me that things would turn out all right. He was gone too, and I was alone, with only a dull sword and my wits to protect me. My skin prickled.

"I have to come up with a plan," I said aloud.

I decided to follow Francisco's advice, handed down by the Jaguar People. I crouched close to the jungle floor to look for clues. Sure enough, there was a wide dent in the fallen leaves and soft soil. Next, I found a few fibers from a rope. Had Zeetan Z caught my friends in a trap? I shuddered at the thought.

"*Eeeeeech!*" An orangutan screeched overhead, and I leaped to my feet.

"Not now, exotic beast," I yelled, shielding my face. "I'm looking for clues."

The ape didn't throw anything, so I peeked at him through the spaces between my fingers.

FACT: The greatest clues may hide close to the ground, but the clue I found was dangling overhead.

Fifteen feet up, there was a long piece of rope twisted around a tree branch. One end of the rope had been cut, but I quickly traced the other end down the trunk of the tree and into the undergrowth. Behind a tangle of vines, I uncovered a system of pulleys, connected to a lever.

It was a devilish trap. My comrades must have stumbled across a trip wire and gone rocketing into the branches. I looked behind the tree and saw a pile of stones—the counterweight for this crude device. I stepped delicately back to the clearing. On second glance, I could make out expertly disguised contraptions everywhere. To my left, there were carved spikes hidden in the husk of a fallen log. To my right, I saw a wire strung between two strangler fig roots.

"Someone is hunting in this jungle," I said to myself. "But for what?" A terrible thought crossed my mind. "Or *whom*."

The orangutan screeched again, then raced up into the canopy. I heard a rustle of leaves behind me and spun around, sword at the ready, only to find myself face-to-face with a seven-foot-long king cobra. His olive-colored scales shone in the midday sun.

"Carter!" I boomed. "Am I ever happy to see you. Things have been looking grim for **Ronald Zupan**."

My trustworthy pet rocketed toward me and clamped his jaws onto my cheek.

"You're right," I said, stroking his head gently, "we should stick together. The jungle is thick with danger."

After freeing myself, I knelt back down to look for more

evidence. It wasn't long before I found a set of strange boot prints—different from what Jeeves, Julianne, and I wore. Their owner had walked into the clearing alone and walked out with two captives.

I took up the trail with Carter at my side. We tracked the prints closely, stopping every few feet to listen for cries of help. All we heard was the loud caw of a rhinoceros hornbill perched overhead.

I looked up at the bird as it lifted into the air in a dramatic swirl of color. After that, the jungle went eerily silent for a moment, and then the spell was broken.

Ra-TACHET-click. A small man skipped out from behind the trunk of a tree. He was holding a bright orange flare gun, aimed right at me.

"*Nog odd itch,*" he cried in a shrill voice.

A blue handkerchief covered the man's mouth. His head was hooded in a thinning clump of snowy curls and his skin was dry and weathered. I couldn't see his features, except for two nervously twitching eyes. Clearly, this was the same man who'd captured my friends.

"NOG. ODD. *ITCH!*"

I raised my arms high and forced myself to breathe. "Sorry, friend, I don't know the Malaysian tongue."

My eyes caught on the stranger's cowboy boots, which were the same bright blue as his bandana and bedazzled with gemstones. He was nothing like I'd imagined Zeetan Z, but I had to consider the possibility that this was also the villain who had my parents.

"I ib speekig anglist!" he yelled.

"A melee of Malay," I said, hoping to calm him down. "Lovely language, but it's Greek to me."

The stranger tore off the bandana and stuffed it into his pocket.

"I said, I *am* speaking English." His voice skittered and trembled, just like his hands. "I don't want you or the snake to move another inch, understand?"

The man's small eyes scanned another wide circle through the jungle. He scratched his beard feverishly. "If you're looking for your friends, they're all tied up!"

He waved the flare gun at me again, and I noticed that he was wearing lambskin gloves even though it was sweltering.

"Tied up!" The man cackled. "It's a joke!"

I plastered on a smile. "Good one."

The stranger tottered a few steps closer, motioning with his flare gun. "Enough of that; you're coming with me."

A Note on What I Was Thinking at This Very Moment

While the odd man with the flare gun was busy with Ronald, Julianne and I were a few hundred yards away, in some sort of tree house. Our captor had tied our hands and feet to our chairs and cinched bandanas over our mouths.

As I sat, fighting against the knots that held me tight, I said to myself, "Either Ronald will do something uncannily brilliant and set us free . . . or we're going to die here, in a tree house in Borneo."

I could not think of any other way for our ordeal to finish.

19

Ship in the Clouds!

I walked in front of the madman, with Carter slithering beside me. The scoundrel didn't need to tell me the path; the ground was still soft from the rain and it was easy to follow the prints that Julianne and Jeeves had left behind. They wove between trees and under giant spiderwebs and ended at the base of a massive strangler fig.

The wild, exposed roots of the tree shot down from above, overlapping and twisting together. There was only one gap, and past it I could see an empty space. The fig had grown around some other tree a long time ago. Now, there was nothing left inside but darkness.

My captor jammed his flare gun into my back. "In there!"

I looked up. Overhead, disguised by a thicket of branches and roots, I could make out the vague shape of a

boat. I stepped between the twisted roots into a tight crevice and Carter slid in after me. A rope ladder hung down from above.

"I'll climb first," the stranger said, stepping past me. "If you try any funny business, your friends are goners. *Capisce? Claro?*"

I opened my mouth to say something back but he cut me off.

"And no snakes allowed!"

I watched as the man scampered up the rope ladder. In another second, I heard the click of a latch and a slanting ray of light brightened the center of the tree trunk.

"Be brave and stand watch," I said to Carter. "You'll be biting Jeeves again in no time."

I grabbed hold of the ladder and started to climb. The strange villain tapped his feet and waved me forward with his flare gun. At the top of the ladder, I found myself in some sort of tree *ship*.

For a second, I wondered if it was the same vessel that had been stolen from the movie set, but I didn't have any time to puzzle over it. The stranger was waving his gun again.

"Here are your friends," he said. "All tied up! Get the joke now?"

My eyes adjusted to the dim room and I saw Jeeves and Julianne, sitting in crude chairs made from knotty fig branches. They were bound hand and foot and had bandanas cinched tightly across their mouths. The atlas and Julianne's violin case both rested open on the floor between them.

"Lose the sword," my captor snarled. "Tie your feet."

He waved his flare gun toward a third chair. I sat down across from my friends and the man kicked a long length of rope toward me. I pushed my sword away and pretended to fumble with the rope, tying a loose bow.

"No, no, no! You're not even trying," he said, blinking rapidly. His voice skipped and hiccupped. "Tie it tighter. Tighter!"

I tied my legs with a double clove hitch and the stranger stepped closer to me. "You smell putrid."

"I had a run-in with a troop of orangutans," I said.

The man's mood changed for a second. "Threw figs at you, did they? Smells like a little dung too, eh? Were they accurate marksmen?"

"You could say that."

He stepped behind me and tied my hands together. I forced my wrists as far apart as I could manage, so that there would be a little space to wiggle when he was done. The stranger's flare gun bumped my spine as he wove the rope in serpentine coils.

"A constrictor knot," I said.

The villain leaned close to my ear and put one gloved hand on my shoulder. "And no one *ever* unties constrictor knots."

Little did the rogue know that **Ronald Zupan** had spent years preparing for this very moment. Over and over, I'd had Jeeves tie me up and leave me in my room until I could escape. It was his favorite among all our different training exercises.

The strange villain pulled up another crate and sat facing me with his back to Julianne and Jeeves. My eyes roamed around the tree ship. The branches and giant roots acted as ribs, with boards nailed across them. There were room dividers made from sailcloth. This couldn't be Jax Brixton's old ship—it would have taken months to make.

Every few feet, there was a porthole with a brass spyglass pointing out of it. A ship's bell was bolted to a branch, and around a canvas corner I could see a second room.

"Now," the stranger said, lifting the flare gun, "tell me why you came to Borneo. Who hired you?"

I glanced at Jeeves and Julianne. I had never seen my dear butler look so scared.

"Out with it!" the scalawag snapped.

"No one hired us," I said. "I came for my parents."

"What are you talking about, *parents*?"

I did my best to unscramble what was going on. Was this man a pirate himself? He couldn't be Zeetan Z, *could he*?

The stranger shook the flare gun barrel just a few feet from me. "*Talk!*"

All the pestering had worn down my steel nerves. "**Ronald Zupan** does not cower to rogues!" I snapped.

The stranger's gloved trigger finger twitched, and the barrel of the flare gun flashed.

FSSSSSST!

A glowing white flare rocketed across the room, bounced off the wall of strangler roots, and spun across the floor, spitting sparks everywhere, burning so brightly that I had to squeeze my eyes shut.

FACT: Perhaps occasionally cowering to rogues isn't such a terrible idea.

FROM THE DESK OF
Thomas Halladay

A Note on What I Was Thinking at THIS Very Moment

We're going to die here, in a tree house in Borneo!

We're going to die here, in a tree house in Borneo!

We're going to die here, in a tree house in Borneo!

We're going to die here, in a tree house in Borneo!

We're going to die here, in a tree house in Borneo!

We're going to die here, in a tree house in Borneo!

We're going to die here, in a tree house in Borneo!

We're going to die here, in a tree house in Borneo!

We're going to die here, in a tree house in Borneo!

20

Secrets Uncovered!

The gun-waving madman stomped out the flare. The smell of sulfur stung my nostrils, and the smoke made me cough until I felt light-headed. Jeeves screamed through the cloth tied across his mouth, and Julianne fought wildly against her knots.

"That will teach you," the villain said. "Never argue with a man with a flare gun. Especially when that flare gun has a loose trigger."

"A sword is the only weapon of a master adventurer," I said as the stranger loaded another cartridge.

I shifted in my seat and the rope that held my hands snagged on part of the chair. Making sure not to struggle, I used the leverage to my advantage and my pinkie found a crease where it could start to dig into the constrictor knot's coils.

"Enough blabbing," the scalawag spat, leaning in close. "Let's get back to why you're here."

My eyes stared straight ahead while my fingers worked on the knot. "We're looking for something."

"Of course you are," my foe snorted with a bitter laugh. He edged nervously around to my other side. "You three are bounty hunters come to find my hiding spot."

Hiding spot? The man didn't sound like a bloodthirsty sea devil—I decided he couldn't be Zeetan Z. Maybe he was the dreaded pirate's scout?

"We *are* on a mission," I admitted. "You're right about that."

"To capture me!" The man twitched and shivered at once. "Admit it!"

I gritted my teeth. "Setting Francisco and Helen Zupan free is more important than apprehending a two-bit rascal like you."

My enemy frowned. "Francisco and Helen? Are those names a cipher? Are they anagrams for my own name? Like Deterring Chef Jake or Kerchief Garden Jet?"

"Francisco and Helen aren't a cipher," I said. "They're my parents. They've been kidnapped . . . probably by one of your fellow pirates."

The little man shuddered again. "Don't say 'pirates' in here. Never say the word 'pirates.'"

I tried to buy time. "You'd rather I say 'buccaneer'? 'Sea rover'? 'Gentleman of Fortune'? *'Parent-stealer'*?"

The stranger stood up and walked to the closest port-hole. He aimed the spyglass and peered out at the jungle. I'd managed to loosen the top coil of the constrictor knot and separate my wrists a few inches. Slowly, I began unwinding the complex twists and turns of the knot's second layer.

I stared at Jeeves, and in my head I heard him calling out instructions, just like he used to do back home. *Over, under, pass through, side twist, pass through, reverse the whole thing now.*

I tried to think of ways to stall and decided to follow the advice of Helen Zupan, who says, "When captured by villains, tell them your tale. It might just save your tail."

I swallowed once. "My parents always promised they'd never miss my birthday. That's how I knew something was wrong."

The man wheeled to face me. "What are you gibbering about?"

"I came to Borneo to find them. Along with my trusty team of . . . well, I'm the leader, of course, but right after me are my savvy sidekicks—"

Julianne glared at me across the room.

"Nevertheless, we will not fail," I said. "So, you have a choice: let us go now or suffer the consequences."

A loud peal of laughter burst from the stranger, and a sharp-toothed smile spread across his face. "Oh my, my," he said. "I think I understand what's going on here. I think I do, but do you? No, I don't think you do!"

I hesitated, both pinkies wedged deep inside the constrictor knot.

"You thought *I* was in cahoots with Zeetan Z!" the man gasped. "Is that right?"

"Well," I said, feeling a little defensive, "maybe you're a lookout or some other sort of spy."

"Me?" the stranger scoffed. "Only a fool would think that. Why don't you try to work out my name, boy? I just gave you an anagram—all you have to do is scramble the letters."

Turning the letters of Kerchief Garden Jet into some other name would buy me vital seconds while I tried to untie the knot. *Over, around, double-twist, pass through . . .*

"Your name," I said, drawing a breath, "is Hendrick Age-Feet Jr."

The man twirled the flare gun lazily on his finger. "If you can't even figure out who I am, you have no business trying to find Zeetan Z."

Even though my heart was racing, Jeeves's voice in my head was calm and steady. *Around, double-pass, twist, under . . .*

"That was my first guess," I said. "How about . . . Dr. He Reject Fake Gin?"

The stranger jerked the flare gun toward me. "Wrong again!"

"Frighten Creek Jade?"

"That's not it either!"

As my brain searched for another anagram, I noticed the muscles of Julianne's right arm twitching. The rope that once bound her hands was puddled on the floor behind her.

"What about . . . Arched Feet Jerking?" I asked.

The madman shook his head. I stared right into his eyes—I didn't want him to look away. If he turned and saw what Julianne was doing, it was all over for us.

"Knifed Recharge Jet."

He danced and skipped in front of me. "You'll never guess it! You've got no mind for wordplay! No head for clues!"

It was an insult that **Ronald Zupan** wouldn't take sitting down—except I was still tied to my chair. I risked another glance at Julianne. She was stealthily untying the ropes at her feet. Jeeves looked ready to faint as his eyes flashed between the two of us and our crazed captor.

"Chafed Egret Jerkin," I tried.

The strange man threw back his head and cackled. Julianne stood and picked up her violin from its case without a sound. She crept forward, ready to put it to good use.

"No one could guess it," I said. "There must be a thousand possibilities."

Over, pass through, wind around, twist, good, Ronald, you're almost there. I could definitely feel the knot getting looser.

"To think I was scared of you!" The man looked crazed now, beads of sweat slid down his forehead into his eyes and he blinked them away.

I dug my nails into the constrictor knot and the last coils came undone. My hands were free.

Julianne was close enough to make a lunge, but instead of attacking, she peeled the bandana away from her mouth.

"Oh . . . ," she said, "the anagram—"

At the sound of a voice right behind him, the stranger spun, leading with the flare gun. Before he got all the way around, I lunged for him, grabbing his elbow.

"*Sato!*" I yelled.

FSSSSSSST POP!

The shot shattered one of the porthole windows, and the flare went rocketing out into the jungle. With my legs still tied to the chair, I dragged the stranger to the floor. The villain wrestled free, and I struggled to pin him again.

"Don't move," Julianne said. She held her violin high, ready to strike.

The madman squirmed under my weight, trying to face me. "Y-you untied a constrictor knot."

I ground an elbow into his ribs and looked up at Julianne. "I bet Jasper Broomhill has never saved your life like that!"

"Ronald," Julianne said, dropping her violin to her side, "I think you can let him go. He's not a threat."

"What do you mean?" I asked.

"I just figured out the anagram."

"You did?" the stranger asked, wriggling beneath me.

"Mhuh Dwib?" Jeeves's voice came muffled through his gag.

"Jacked Feet Herring?" I tried.

"Close," Julianne said. "It's Three-Fingered Jack."

FROM THE DESK OF
Thomas Halladay

An Error of My Own from the Chapter "Secrets Uncovered!"

1. I'd been sure that I was going to die in a tree house in Borneo. Certain of it. I was passing the time by writing my obituary in my head: "Good butler, except for when he took two children to Borneo and they were killed by a madman. Other than that, bang-up job."

And yet . . . somehow, miraculously, we didn't die.

I suppose I have Ronald to thank for that.

There, I said it.

21
New Allies!

I untied my ankles from the chair and stood up. Here was the man my parents' files had talked about, the only man to ever escape Zeetan Z.

He took off his tan gloves and dropped them to the floor with a wooden *clack*. His right hand was missing the pinkie and ring finger, and I quickly deduced that the glove had been stuffed with fakes.

"That's me." He offered a slight wave. "Three-Fingered Jack."

"Why didn't you tell us?" I asked.

"How could I risk it? Strange things have been happening around here." He leaned close.

"Just yesterday there was an explosion in the jungle. An explosion! Surely it was Zeetan Z burning me out."

"That was our plane," Julianne said as she untied Jeeves. "We had a rough landing."

Three-Fingered Jack frowned. "Still, Zeetan Z doesn't like the idea that he left a survivor. I figured you three were bounty hunters, come to track me down."

Julianne finished with Jeeves's last knot.

"Jeeves," I said, "come meet another man who loathes Zeetan Z. An ally."

Jeeves tore away the bandana that covered his mouth. "*Ally?*" he scoffed. "We aren't allies!"

Three-Fingered Jack looked hurt. "Is this about me catching you in a trap, holding you hostage, and shooting at the children with a flare gun?"

"Yes," Jeeves said, "precisely."

"That's water under the bridge, though. It's in the past."

"It was two minutes ago!" Jeeves snapped.

The strange hermit's shoulders slumped, and he stared at the floor. Luckily, **Ronald Zupan** is an expert at navigating sticky social situations.

"You can make it up to us by inviting my pet cobra into your tree house," I said. "The snake is very attached to Jeeves."

"*Literally* attached most of the time," Julianne added.

Three-Fingered Jack twitched. "The snake? Well . . . bring him up then. The more the merrier, I suppose. Eh?"

As I climbed down the rope ladder to collect Carter, I could hear Three-Fingered Jack ask the others, "It's well trained, this snake?"

"Not at all," Jeeves grumbled.

I hoisted Carter into the tree house, and Julianne helped me pry his mouth off the bridge of my nose.

Jeeves wheeled toward Three-Fingered Jack. "If you *really* want to make things right, you could tell us everything you know about Zeetan Z."

Three-Fingered Jack took two cautious steps away from Carter. "Patience, patience! We'll discuss it over dinner. I haven't had guests in ages!"

He dodged behind a wall of canvas into another room. A second later, we could hear him clattering around in the kitchen. Jeeves, Julianne, and I crowded together for a parley.

"Friends," I whispered, "we have an odd bird on our hands."

Julianne looked at the burned-out flare on the floor. "I think he's been alone in this jungle too long."

"Which is why," Jeeves said, "the sooner we leave the better."

Three-Fingered Jack started whistling while he cooked.

"By the way," Jeeves said to me, "that was very brave . . . how you handled everything."

Julianne nodded her agreement. "I've never heard of anyone untying a constrictor knot."

"What do you mean?" I asked. "You untied one too. Plus you figured out the anagram."

"That anagram almost got me shot with a flare," Julianne said. She glanced down at Carter, who was curled between our feet. "Also, mine wasn't a constrictor knot . . . it was a double clove."

"Sato," I said, puffing my chest like a frigate bird, "are you saying you're *impressed*?"

She rolled her eyes. "I'm saying that I should go see what information I can get out of Three-Fingered Jack."

Julianne walked around the canvas wall, into the next room. "You have to admit," I called after her, "I *was* pretty spectacular!"

Jeeves and I followed her into the dining room of the tree ship with Carter hanging on Jeeves's leg. A wall of scrap wood separated Three-Fingered Jack's kitchen from the rest of the room. The wall wasn't quite as tall as him, so we could see his white curls bobbing back and forth as he worked on dinner.

"This recipe is something that I've perfected over all my many days in this jungle," our host called. "Just you wait!"

A thick oak table hung on ropes from the ceiling in the center of the dining room. We dragged the four chairs in from the main room and sat down.

I cut straight to the point. "Do you have any leads on Zeetan Z?"

Three-Fingered Jack peeked out from behind the wall with a mortar and pestle in his hands and wagged his head back and forth. "When Zeetan Z and his crew attacked the movie set *Buccaneers of the South Seas*, it caused an uproar. The pirates had stolen a replica ship owned by a very famous actor."

"We know," I said, "old Josie Blightface."

Julianne shot me a look. "That joke is wearing thin."

"Ronald's parents came to Borneo to search for that pirate ship," Jeeves explained. "Apparently, they've been enemies of Zeetan Z and the Liars' Club for years." His mouth tightened. "Though their longest-serving employee hardly knew a thing about it."

Three-Fingered Jack ducked behind the wall again, but we could hear him easily enough.

"I searched for the pirate ship too," he said. "I figured I would finally discover Zeetan Z's lair. But the trail went cold." We could hear a wooden spoon clanking inside a pot. "That is, until just two nights ago, when I saw a fire burning in the jungle. I snuck closer and there sat a pack of the filthiest souls you could ever imagine."

He described a gang of haunted-looking rogues with machetes at their waists, wearing gaudy earrings and bright silks, feasting on roasted pig.

"That sounds more like the old-fashioned type of pirates," Julianne said. "Maybe it was the movie crew getting back to work, filming a scene for *Buccaneers of the South Seas*?"

"I wondered the same thing," Three-Fingered Jack said, his voice quavering. "But as I crept closer, I saw that there were no cameras, no crew. It could have been a rehearsal, but then why the costumes? But the true nub of the matter is that these pirates looked too real to be fake."

"So they *were* Zeetan Z's men?" I asked.

Three-Fingered Jack poked his head out of the kitchen again. "Bingo! But dressed up as old-fashioned pirates, in costumes. Zeetan Z is already a bit of a showman, if you think about it. He pretended to be a lost fisherman when he took my ship. He probably disguised himself to kidnap your parents too."

"Naturally," I said. "My parents are master adventurers; they could never have been captured without great trickery."

Three-Fingered Jack was back in the kitchen now. "I believe that Zeetan Z and his crew really like the items they stole from the movie set. In fact, not only were they dressed in the old-fashioned pirate costumes, but they also had bound booklets in front of them. They were practically screaming the ridiculous lines back and forth."

"Scripts from the movie?" Julianne asked.

"Bingo again! Pirates *acting* like pirates! And you should

have heard them, calling one another 'dear old messmate' and talking about 'scurvy dogs' and 'bilge-sucking ruffians.'"

"Bilge-sucking ruffian is a pretty good insult," I admitted.

"Did you manage to get any solid information?" Jeeves asked. "Any clue you remember hearing?"

Three-Fingered Jack paused. "It was hard to make out . . . mostly jibber from the movie script. I remember one of them asking '*What will we do with all these bees?*' and then another kept repeating, '*The lion lies in the light.*'"

The phrase stopped us cold and we traded silent looks.

After a minute, Three-Fingered Jack poked his head out from the kitchen. "What did I say?"

"That's a clue from my parents about where the Lion of Lyros is hidden," I said.

"The Lion of Lyros? The old statue?"

"You've heard of it?" I asked.

"Everyone has," Three-Fingered Jack said. "But I always thought it was in a museum. I didn't know that collectors had it."

"It's my parents' most prized possession. When Zeetan Z captured them he must have figured out that it was his chance to get the lion too. He even sent a gang of thieves called the FIB to our house to search for it."

"That conniving devil!" our host said.

Julianne frowned as she tried to puzzle out some thought. "Let me see if I have this straight . . . Your parents came to

Borneo to try to get back Josh Brigand's ship, right? But instead of capturing Zeetan Z, he captures them?"

"Through some mysterious malfeasance," I said. "Yes."

"But how does Zeetan Z know the clue, 'The lion lies in the light'?"

She was right; that part *was* confusing. It made sense that Zeetan Z would know that my parents had the Lion of Lyros . . . but how did he find the same clue we discovered in the atlas?

Jeeves wore a pained look. "I believe," he said, "Francisco and Helen must have given Zeetan Z that riddle to protect themselves. If the pirate can't solve it, he can't hurt them. But *after* he finds the lion, then . . ."

His point was as clear as Icelandic crystal.

> FACT: If I ever wanted to see my parents again, we'd have to rescue them before the pirates figured out the meaning of "The lion lies in the light."

A Confession by Thomas Halladay

As it finally became clear how much danger the Zupans were in, I began to feel a sense of guilt creeping over me. As I mentioned earlier, right in my jacket pocket I had an acceptance letter for a new job with none other than the movie star Josh Brigand himself. Even though I knew better, I felt like I'd betrayed my employers. As if this was somehow all my fault.

I tried to force it out of my thoughts by reminding myself of all the secrets the Zupans had hidden from me. Surely, I deserved a secret too, and no one ever had to know. I'd get rid of the letter the first chance I got.

22

A Strange Meal!

As Three-Fingered Jack's stew bubbled in the kitchen, Julianne sprang to her feet and paced circles around the table. I could tell that she was working on some kind of theory.

"So Pemburu met us at the saloon and got word to Zeetan Z," she said. "Then Zeetan Z sent Gunting to find out what we knew."

"And rip our arms off," Jeeves added. He was pacing too, but it was harder for him because Carter was still wrapped around his leg.

"Which means," I said, hopping up and walking in circles along with them, "that Zeetan Z is hidden somewhere close. Close enough that Pemburu could send word to the pirates after we came to the saloon, and they could send Gunting back so quickly."

My friends nodded thoughtfully. Our enemy was nearby, but where? Hidden right under our noses somehow?

Julianne spun toward the kitchen. "What did you do after you saw the pirates?"

"Oh, for the best-laid plans!" Three-Fingered Jack chirped. "My idea was to wait until they fell asleep, then attack. But as I readied myself to spring on them, the flare gun accidentally fired." He stepped out from behind the wall and wiggled the stumps of his missing fingers. "As you've seen, I'm not too handy with the thing."

"Then what?" I asked.

Three-Fingered Jack eyed me, like he was deciding whether to tell me a secret. After a second, he fluttered his hands toward the ceiling. "Disappeared into thin air. Like ghosts. The next day I got my nerve back and went to their fire. All that was left behind were smoldering coals."

"Nothing else?" Julianne pressed.

Our strange host looked through one of the porthole windows out into the jungle. He didn't say anything for a long time, and then finally his face broke into a forced smile. "Smells like dinner!"

Julianne scowled as we set the table. It was plain as day that the hermit was hiding something.

After we sat down, Three-Fingered Jack ladled us each a big bowl of soup. "To new friends! I'm sure this tasty meal will make everything right between us!"

Without another word, the hermit dove into his stew like

a starving ferret. As he shoveled spoonful after spoonful into his mouth, I looked down into my bowl, then back at my compatriots. Jeeves's lips were drawn into two thin lines. Julianne's skin had a greenish tint.

Three-Fingered Jack realized that he was the only one eating and pointed his spoon at us. "Go on, have some!" He tapped his bowl. "I'll bet you'd never guess my secret ingredient."

FACT: Yes, we would. It was easy.

"Worms," we said in unison.

Three-Fingered Jack was taken aback for just a second, then wagged his spoon at us. "But not *just* worms. There are millipedes in there too, plus a few grubs. So much protein can be found in insects! It's a very healthful diet. Is it healthful? Health-ish?"

I thought about pushing away my bowl, but I remembered another one of my mother's sayings: "There's no quicker way to show strangers you come in peace, than to eat a piece of any food they offer."

I dug up a spoonful, hesitated, then took a bite.

"So," Three-Fingered Jack asked, his eyebrows jumping, "how does it taste?"

"Exactly like I imagined," I said, forcing a smile.

"Indeed," Jeeves said with a grimace. "The flavor is *quite* wormy."

"The texture is wormy too," Julianne added after her own bite. "The millipedes crunch a little."

Three-Fingered Jack sat up straighter in his chair and beamed at us. "Oh, I'm *so* glad you like it. It feels nice to have houseguests who enjoy my cooking!"

He merrily ladled out his next serving of worm stew, while Jeeves, Julianne, and I all stared at one another with our mouths half-open. The first chance we got, we pushed our bowls aside and launched into the story of Gunting and Pemburu attacking us in the saloon basement. When we arrived at the bit about Jeeves throwing the lamps, Three-Fingered Jack turned to me.

"I have to admit," he said, "I've never really understood cricket either. Which ones are the wickets?"

"Who knows?" I said. "And what kind of game has tea breaks?"

Jeeves slapped his spoon down on the table. "That does it. Here and now, I'm going to explain the rules to all of you. It's a marvelous game, I promise. First . . ."

At the mention of cricket, my eyelids started to droop, but Jeeves couldn't be swayed.

"So," he droned on a few minutes later, "we count the wickets of the third test, then eat a plate of cucumber sandwiches. Ronald, don't you see? It's like baseball without the diamond—"

The second the word "diamond" left Jeeves's mouth, Three-Fingered Jack looked like something had snapped inside of him. He kicked out his chair and swiveled his head feverishly.

"*Diamonds! Diamonds!*" he screamed, gripping the edge of the table with his hands. "Zeetan Z! He wants diamonds! He's tearing my ship apart. *Diamond Jack! That must mean real diamonds! Where are they hidden?*" His tone dropped. "But I'm telling the truth! There are no diamonds!"

Julianne reached over and laid her hand on Three-Fingered Jack's trembling arm. He jerked away and looked down at her as if he'd never seen her face before. His breathing was ragged, and his head swiveled left and right, as if the pirates might spring on him at any moment.

"His blade flashes in the moonlight. I swear over and over, 'There are no diamonds, the Duchess of York called me that because she thought my mind sparkled.' Zeetan Z doesn't believe me. *Sheenk!* My fingers! My fingers! I have to get away. For a moment, the giant loses his grasp on me! I leap into the blackness—swimming, bleeding, waiting for the sharks."

For a long second, Three-Fingered Jack stared across the table at us, rabid, wild, terrified. Then his body went slack and he fainted—right into the last bowl of worm stew.

By the time our host awoke, the dishes were done and Jeeves had found three hammocks for us to string up in the dining room.

"I'm sorry," the hermit mumbled as he stood up on wobbly legs. "Sometimes I get so . . . so . . ."

"It's been a long day," Julianne said with a soft smile.

"Quite," Jeeves agreed. "I think we should all get some sleep."

I noticed him eyeing me, and I was sure we were thinking the same thing: What about my parents? Did they still have all their fingers?

Jeeves and I both went to wash up at the same time, then crawled into our hammocks. We could hear Julianne brushing her teeth in the kitchen. On the way to his room, Three-Fingered Jack tugged on a rope and a huge section of the palm-frond roof eased open.

"This way you can see the stars," he said. "Close it right away if it starts to rain, though. I imagine we'll have some real monsoon storms soon. I don't want a flood in here."

The hermit left us alone and Jeeves fell asleep almost instantly. Julianne and I stayed awake though. We gazed up at the stars and moon, shining through the tree branches. Carter was coiled on the floor right next to me, and I reached down to brush my fingers across his smooth scales.

After a few peaceful minutes, the view was blocked by thousands of bats swooping overhead. They twisted and spun like inky ribbons caught in the wind.

"I wonder where they're going," Julianne whispered.

I knew she was just trying to help me get my mind off my parents, but I couldn't come up with a good answer— so I stayed quiet. We watched the bats until they thinned out and the dappled moonlight fell like a silver blanket across our hammocks again.

"Help is on the way," I whispered, hoping that somehow my parents might hear me.

An Omission from the Chapter
"A Strange Meal!"

Ronald left out a conversation we had while washing
up for bed, but I think it's worth sharing:

Ronald: How are you holding up, Jeeves?
Me: Well, Three-Fingered Jack's story was
troubling, the details were quite—
Ronald: (splashing his face with water from
a tub) The Lost Ruins of Tikal, the False
Prince of Greenland, the Case of the Czar's
Hat.
Me: Those are different adventures your
parents went on, right?
Ronald: (splashing more water) The Vanishing
Shroud of Cairo, the Shanghai Switch, the
Turkish Tango.
Me: Wasn't that the time they had to escape
from—

All at once, Ronald plunged his entire head
and shoulders into the washbasin. No sooner had he
popped back up than he reached into his pocket and
slapped his mustache on. It had lost most of its stick
and flopped quite a bit, but I decided not to say
anything.

> **Ronald:** I know you're worried, Jeeves, but my
> parents have gotten out of plenty of tight
> scrapes, and they're sure to get out of this
> one too.
> **Me:** Oh, I wasn't trying to say—
> **Ronald:** My point is, we've got three dashing
> adventurers and one deadly reptile, and all
> Zeetan Z has is an army of bloodthirsty
> pirates. There's no need to panic, I promise.

With that, he said good night and I wandered
toward my hammock in a bit of a daze.

23
Orangutan Standoff!

I awoke to the sound of Three-Fingered Jack's chirpy voice drifting out of the kitchen. It was hard to follow everything he said—something about how he'd found the wreckage of his old ship a few days after the pirate attack, then dragged it piece-by-piece into the jungle to build his tree house.

My eyes eased open and the room swam into focus. I looked down at my shoulder. The bruise had gone deep purple at the middle and sickly green around the edges. My mustache had come off in the night and I could feel it stuck to my forehead. I peeled it off, pocketed it, and yawned like a Bengal tiger.

"Is that you, Ronald?" Jeeves asked. "I assume you slept like a—"

"Three-toed sloth," I said. "Of course."

I sat up in my hammock, my bare feet brushing against

the floorboards. Beside me, a nylon cord stretched across the room with our mud-stained socks hung out to dry. I went to peek in the main room, where I found Julianne hard at work, with Carter coiled beside her. She'd borrowed a whetstone from Three-Fingered Jack and was putting an edge on our cutlasses.

"Sharp as ever, Sato," I said, giving her the best smile I could muster up.

Julianne inspected the blade of her sword before scraping it across the length of the stone again. I padded back into the dining room and saw Three-Fingered Jack standing beside my hammock, holding the atlas.

"This is far too big to lug around," he said, dropping it with a thud. "Load what you need into this."

He handed me a canvas sailor's bag, and I knelt down to open my father's treasured book. Everything was still there—the squares of melted chocolate, the playing cards, the waterproof fire-starting kit, the grapefruit-sized candle, and the sealed envelope that read, *To **Ronald** Only to be read in a case of IMPENDING MUTINY!*

Underneath everything else, I found the small strip of paper.

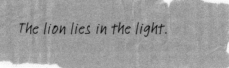

The lion lies in the light.

I held the clue up for Three-Fingered Jack to see. "This is what the pirates were saying?"

"Yes, quite! They got that line from your parents?"

"I think so. Gunting wrote the same thing on a piece of paper in the basement of Pemburu's saloon."

Three-Fingered Jack's eyes sparked with an idea. "Say, how big is the Lion of Lyros?"

"Small," I said. "Three and a half inches tall."

"Three and a half inches," Three-Fingered Jack said. "That's small enough to fit inside of that candle. *In* the light . . . But surely you already checked—"

In the other room, Julianne's sword clanked to the ground. Jeeves dodged out of the kitchen, his mouth wide and his cup of tea sloshing everywhere.

In the light! How had we missed it? Had I forgotten the time Francisco and Helen threw a cheese wheel off their sinking ship, only to discover that an incredibly valuable collection of Dutch coins had been hidden inside the sixty-two pounds of Gouda.

"Next time I see something made of wax," my mother told me, "I'll give it a few whacks before I toss it out."

I grabbed the crimson candle. It was heavy and easily big enough to hide the statue inside.

"My brilliant parents have done it again!" I said. I opened my hand for Julianne to flip a freshly sharpened blade across the room. "I'll slice it open like a puma falling upon a wild boar."

"No!" Jeeves yelled. He sprinted toward me, spilling the rest of his tea.

FACT: Over the years, the good butler has become very sensitive about sword throwing indoors.

Jeeves snatched the candle and weighed it in his hand. "The Lion of Lyros is thousands of years old. If it bangs against a rock, it could chip and be ruined. This wax protects it perfectly—surely that's what your parents were thinking when they covered it like this."

He had a point. The lion was worthless if it was chipped. Three Fingered Jack gave me a sewing needle, which I heated up and pressed into the red wax. After about an inch, I hit something solid. The lion was *in* the light, just like the clue said.

"We'll leave it the way it is," I announced. "Besides, Francisco Zupan always says that a candle is the second-best thing to have on an adventure, after bug spray."

I held the candle up and stared at it. We had the lion now. We could use it to get my parents back, *if* we could just find Zeetan Z. I stuffed the candle into the sailor's sack, then loaded in the rest of the items. Three-Fingered Jack wanted the cards to play solitaire, so we traded for one of his spyglasses and some dried papaya pieces.

The atlas was muddy and wet, but after what had happened with Shakespeare, I wanted to make sure my parents could get it back. I pushed it into a corner of the room and made Three-Fingered Jack promise to hang on to it.

"Agreed," Three-Fingered Jack said.

We tried to settle on a plan while we ate sliced papayas with honey for breakfast.

"Maybe it's still worth trying to go to the top of the skull hill," I said. "The only other thing I can think of is to try to find Gunting, capture him, and ransom him to Pemburu for directions to Zeetan Z's lair. My parents did that once, on a gambling boat heading down the Mekong River."

"I hardly need to mention that it sounds dangerous," Jeeves said, "but I suppose every idea will sound dangerous."

Julianne took another bite of papaya. "First, I want to go to the campfire—where Jack saw the pirates." She turned to our strange host. "Could you draw us a map, showing that spot and the road back toward town?"

Three-Fingered Jack tapped his chin with a spoon, then smiled strangely. "I'll do it just as you say! A map that shows the road *and* the spot that I saw the pirates."

He raced over to a cabinet and took out a fountain pen and a pot of black ink. Then he tore the cover off a warped notebook and hunched in the corner, excitedly drawing and muttering to himself.

We were just finishing breakfast when we heard a loud screech overhead and saw a family of familiar-looking orangutans perched on the edge of the open roof. Three-Fingered Jack put aside his pen and ink and sprang to his feet.

"Meet my orangutan army!" he said as the apes slapped their thighs. "They will help me defeat Zeetan Z."

Jeeves arched an eyebrow.

"Don't look so skeptical! I've trained them to follow my commands and throw things at my enemies!"

"You haven't trained them very well," I grumbled. "All I did was smile at them."

"Of course," Three-Fingered Jack said. "If you bared your teeth at them, even if you were just smiling, it would seem very aggressive. And did you yell? That sends them into a panic."

The orangutans slipped one by one to the floor of the tree house, which didn't seem to sit well with Carter. He flared his hood and hissed at them until the beasts scampered off into the kitchen.

"I've already taught them to throw figs," Three-Fingered Jack bragged, "and papayas. Soon, they'll be ready for homemade coconut explosives, and then we'll confront Zeetan Z."

"Once you find him, you mean," Julianne said. She watched the hermit closely.

"What?" he asked, still dreaming about his revenge.

"You'll confront Zeetan Z *once* you find him," Julianne said. "You told us that . . ."

She narrowed her eyes. Three-Fingered Jack looked as guilty as a Guatemalan civet with chicken feathers plastered to its face.

"You know where he is," Julianne said in a calm, steady voice. "You know and you aren't telling us."

The hermit stared at the floor. "I . . . I think I worked out an *idea* of where he is. I'm not certain of—"

"*He's got my parents!*" I yelled, charging toward him.

I'd barely taken two steps before the whole pack of orangutans leaped out of the kitchen, holding whisks and spoons and handfuls of wriggling worms that hadn't made it into the stew. Even Carter couldn't scare them away this time.

They drew back their arms, ready to throw, and I skidded to a halt.

"Now let's all calm down," Three-Fingered Jack said. He motioned to the orangutans to lower their weapons. "It's true . . . I haven't been fully honest. You seemed like bumblers when you got caught in my trap, but you untied my knots and solved the anagram, so I thought maybe I misjudged you." He wet his lips and went on. "I was all ready to tell you everything over breakfast, but you hadn't even thought about the lion hiding in the candle, so then again, you seemed like bumblers."

Julianne's eyes blazed. "But this isn't a game!"

"Of course not," Three-Fingered Jack agreed. "It's much more serious. And let's not forget that I *have* helped you, in bits and pieces. I agreed to make you a map of the saloon and the spot where I saw the pirates, right? I told you where the lion is, didn't I? I just want to see Zeetan Z punished for his evil deeds."

"But if you tell us where he is——" Jeeves said.

"If I tell you where he is and you fail," Three-Fingered Jack broke in, "he's sure to change hideouts, and all my planning will be for nothing."

"So you won't tell us what you know?" I asked from between gritted teeth.

"If you could wait until my orangutans are fully trained, just a few days more, maybe a week . . ."

"*We don't have a week,*" I snapped.

"I'll make you a deal then," the strange hermit said,

bouncing from foot to foot. "If you're the best people to defeat Zeetan Z, you'll have to prove it. I'll give you a clue. With the clue and the map, you should be able to solve the mystery."

Jeeves snorted in disgust.

"Spill it," Julianne said.

Three-Fingered Jack pondered for a second. Julianne and I both pulled out our adventure journals to scratch down the words.

"Chase the glistening sword that carves through stone," the hermit said. "It will lead to the *belly of the beast*." He bit his lip in concentration, then gave up with a shrug. "I wanted to make it rhyme at the end there, but oh well. And here . . ." He dodged back to where he'd been sitting and picked up the old notebook cover. "Your map."

"What is this?" I demanded. "There are no landmarks, it's just three *X*s and all this ink. Did you spill it?"

"That's for me to know and you to figure out," Three-Fingered Jack said, giving us a strange grin. "Now I think you should be going—I have orangutans to train."

The hermit nod-ded at the biggest orangutan and the beast drew back his arm menacingly. There was nothing to do but pick up our things, open the hatch, and climb down the rope ladder. Julianne carried her violin case, I carried the sailor's sack, and Jeeves wore Carter slung around his neck like a scale-covered scarf.

When we set foot on the soft soil in the little cavern at the center of the strangler fig, we looked back up into the tree house. Three-Fingered Jack was silhouetted in the light, backed by his crew of primates.

"What does Zeetan Z look like?" I called up when I reached the ground. "Tell us that at least."

The strange hermit was quiet for a moment, then spoke in a low, trembling voice. "His eyes. That's all I remember. They haunt me, those eyes. Who cares the color—if they had any color at all. And yet, when I dream, when I dream . . . they're all I see."

He shuddered and fell back, out of sight, and the biggest orangutan stepped forward and slammed the hatch of the tree ship.

Errors in the Chapter "Orangutan Standoff!"

1. When Ronald says that I dashed from the kitchen with tea "sloshing everywhere," I have to admit that bit of clumsiness was done on purpose. No butler worth his bow tie would spill tea on accident. The truth is, judging by the taste, Three-Fingered Jack uses the same key ingredients for his tea as he does for his stew.

2. Not so much an error as something Ronald left out: the tree house seemed to make Carter particularly edgy, which led to the snake's biting more than usual, which led to *me* feeling grumpy. Add to that the fact that I'd spent the morning drinking worm tea and been kept up all night by Ronald's nightmares and . . . just keep in mind during the chapters to come that I wasn't feeling top-notch.

24

Bloodsuckers!

"**D**id you see that?" Julianne said excitedly as we stepped out of the strangler fig.

I turned to face her, shielding my eyes against the bright sunlight. "See what?"

"There was no ink on Three-Fingered Jack's hands." She was peering closely at the black blotches on the map. "I don't think these are spills. I think he made them on purpose, as part of the clue."

I glanced over her shoulder. "So we just have to solve the riddle, or figure out the meaning of the blotches, and we'll know where Zeetan Z is?"

"Well," Jeeves said with a sigh. "As much as I dread Zeetan Z, I'm glad we don't have to see that giant, Gunting, again."

We walked toward where Three-Fingered Jack saw the

pirates. There weren't any trails marked on the map, so we slashed a path through the jungle—rolling the riddle over and over in our heads.

"The glistening sword that carves through stone . . . will lead to the belly of the beast."

I led the way, using my freshly sharpened cutlass to hack at the creepers and vines. After about an hour of hiking, we were dripping sweat and decided to take a break.

Julianne collapsed on a mat of fallen banana leaves and I sat beside her. "Glistening sword . . . *glistening* sword . . . glistening *sword*?"

She slapped at a mosquito buzzing around her ankle. "It kind of made me think of Excalibur. You know, the sword in the stone?"

"Right," I said. "But the sword Three-Fingered Jack talked about carves *through* the rock—it doesn't get stuck in it."

"Perhaps it's not a real sword or a real stone, but a metaphor," Jeeves tried. "Like Occam's razor."

I frowned and swatted another mosquito. "What's Occam's razor? Was he some sort of master adventurer?"

"He was a scholar," Jeeves said, "and it wasn't a real razor. It was an *idea*, about cutting right to the point and how sometimes the simplest solutions are right in front of your face."

I pondered it. "Sounds very un-Zupanian to me. If a master adventurer wants to make a name for himself, he can't always do things the easy way. He's got to be blazingly creative—like when I booby-trapped my room using a thousand silver ball bearings."

The memory didn't sit well with Jeeves, and he stormed into the bushes, grumbling to himself and rubbing his temples so hard I thought he'd give himself a rash.

I snuck a look at Julianne, who was still mouthing the words "glistening sword." There was something I'd been meaning to ask her, and I wanted to do it while we were alone.

"A question, Sato."

"Yes?" she said.

"Have you ever felt . . . I mean about Zeetan Z or . . ."

"Yes?"

"Like, maybe your courage isn't quite screwed to the sticking place?"

"Do you mean *scared*?" she asked.

I turned to watch a bird hopping along a tree branch and ran my tongue over the tops of my molars.

"I don't know if you've noticed," Julianne went on, "but I kind of have a thing about drowning. I even turned my violin into a life preserver."

I shifted slightly. "My parent's adventure applications say that master adventurers fear nothing."

"That's crazy." Julianne flicked another mosquito away from her arm. "Look at all the things your dad says about bugs. He sounds terrified of them."

I'd never thought of that.

Julianne kept going. "I'm scared of open water, your dad fears bugs, Jeeves fears . . . most of the things that have happened on this trip. What about your mom?"

"Helen fears having her favorite books eaten," I said.

Julianne chuckled. "See? Everyone's afraid of something. What about you?"

My back stiffened. "**Ronald Zupan** was born fearless."

Julianne gently flicked a mosquito off my shirt. "*Right*. But what if you *did* fear something?"

"I—"

"You don't, I get that." Julianne waved me off. "But what

if it wasn't the real you, just . . . someone like you. An *almost* Ronald."

I shrugged.

"I bet he might be scared of something bad happening to his parents," Julianne said, watching me on the sly.

A few lazy wisps of fog drifted uphill toward us. I felt pressure behind my eyes and squeezed them shut for a few seconds.

"Maybe," I admitted. "Perhaps I could imagine this almost-Ronald worrying about that."

"It's only natural," Julianne went on, waving away more mosquitoes. "And maybe he'd feel like he had to impress everyone and be spectacular all the time."

"Yeah," I said, shrugging one shoulder. "I guess."

A giant leaf twirled down to the jungle floor.

"Or," Julianne said, "he'd always feel like he had to be daring and bold and to—"

I set my hand on her arm. "Let's not pile it on. Almost-Ronald probably has plenty to think about."

Julianne flashed me a private smile and I swatted at yet another mosquito.

"Jeeves," she said, wrinkling her brow.

"You're wrong on that one," I countered. "What would almost-Ronald possibly have to fear from Jeeves, he's—"

"*Look!*" Her eyes were wide, and she pointed over my shoulder.

I turned to see Jeeves barreling toward me at full tilt, with Carter around his neck and a giant gray cloud hovering behind him.

"*Mosquitoes!*" he screamed. "*I'm being eaten alive!*"

In seconds, the buzzing haze of mosquitoes surrounded us, swallowing us up. They swarmed so thick that when you swatted one you squashed sixty. We cut a path toward the river, but the winged devils only got hungrier, their droning hum ringing through the forest.

Jeeves broke into the lead and flailed downhill, ripping and kicking through the undergrowth like a madman. Julianne and I raced behind him, tearing through bright green vines and oar-shaped leaves. Fifty feet ahead, we watched him dive, face-first, into a foggy abyss.

I caught my leg on a vine and landed in a bed of muck.

"Unhand me, rapscallion," I yelled, using my sword to hack at the coiled creeper.

Julianne sprinted past me as I wobbled to my feet, flattened ten mosquitoes on my forearm, and charged forward. When I arrived at the lip of the ravine, my eyes caught on a half-buried envelope. Perhaps it was a clue! I quickly bent to pluck it from the mud, then leaped into the thickening mist, sliding downhill.

Where the ravine met the river bottom, spirals of mist rose up out of the ground and melted together into low-hanging clouds. I stood up, caked in mud. There were fewer mosquitoes now, but red bumps were already starting to swell on every inch of my exposed skin.

Up ahead, I could hear Jeeves and Julianne panting and squelching across the swampy ground. I started to walk after them. It was too foggy to see anything; all I could make out were the trees closest to me. They sprouted from the soil like legs of ancient monsters, with gnarled roots and spiny bark.

I carefully unfolded the damp letter I'd plucked from the mud.

FROM THE DESK OF
Thomas Halladay

Dear Mr. Brigand,

   It was my pleasure to meet you at the going-away party for Wiggins. He's a fine man and a longtime friend. I was flattered that you offered me the chance to replace him, and, as promised, I've given it a lot of thought.

   After careful consideration, I have decided I'd like to take the job. The Zupans are adventurous people, to be sure, but I think they'd be happier with someone a bit more daring. I am quite certain that their son, Ronald, would prefer that. As for me, the quiet existence you described sounds ideal. Life with the Zupans is rather chaotic, and I think the time is ripe for a change.

   Sincerely,

   Tom Halladay

I felt like an Arabian camel had kicked me in the chest. My throat tightened.

FACT: Jeeves was planning on leaving the Zupans to go work for Julianne's favorite movie star.

I dropped the letter into a copper-colored puddle, then stomped on it. My boot sank deep into the muck and I lost my balance. I jerked upright again and wrenched my leg from the oily mud. My foot came free with a loud *burp*. Bootless.

"Dazzling," I said, flopping down.

I rolled onto my side and plunged my arm deep into the pit to fish for my boot. No luck. I used my sword to poke around, without success. I had a brief vision of Jeeves serving pancakes to some actor—then tore off my second boot and hurtled it deep into the forest.

I stomped forward in my socks, trying to figure out exactly what I wanted to say to Jeeves. I found him with Julianne, standing in the fog at the edge of a gurgling stream.

"Where'd your boots go?" Julianne asked me.

"I'd rather not talk about it."

"Leech," she said, pointing down at my calf. "They were in those puddles."

I looked down to see a swollen, sluglike menace fattening itself on my blood. Without a word, I bent over to peel the

207

sucking mouth of the leech off my skin. It released me with a slight *pop*, leaving behind a speckled ring of red. I coldly threw it into the stream.

"Bloodsuckers everywhere," Jeeves said with a smirk, scratching his mosquito bites.

I glowered at him as I pulled another leech off the back of my knee. "My thoughts *exactly*."

Errors in the Chapter "Bloodsuckers!"

1. Occam's idea about "the easiest solution being the best" was a good one, no matter what Ronald says. I was quite tired of people who lived by the slogan, "The more complicated the better."

2. Ronald booby-trapping his room with ball bearings wasn't "blazingly creative," it was dotty. I'M THE ONLY PERSON BESIDES RONALD AND HIS PARENTS WHO EVER GOES IN HIS ROOM!

3. Oh, let's not make such a big thing about the letter to Josh Brigand. I'd suffered enough cobra bites, slept in enough three-legged beds, and slipped on enough ball bearings to last me a lifetime. No, it wasn't ideal for Ronald to find the letter when his parents were missing, but nothing could be

done about that now. Besides, I *did* want to
quit. As the *Ganymede Guide to Butlering*
says, "A butler who doesn't feel important
should find someone else to serve. There is
nothing less satisfying than trying to help
someone who insists they don't need it."

25
Mutinies!

When we finished peeling all the leeches off, Julianne took out Three-Fingered Jack's map. I turned away from Jeeves to look at the water. It tumbled over mossy rocks and filled deep pools, guarded by ancient boulders.

"The pirates had their campfire somewhere over . . . there," Julianne said, peering down at the *X*, then pointing across the river.

She bounded across the tops of rocks, toward the opposite bank. I followed and Jeeves trailed behind us. Once we got to the other side, Julianne held the map toward me. Without anything but a few black blotches, it was hard to tell exactly where the campfire had been. I started walking upstream, and Jeeves, Julianne, and Carter went in the other direction.

It was only a matter of minutes before I found a small fire

pit, ringed with stones. Inside were burned pieces of wood and a half-melted glass bottle.

"Sato," I called. "I found it!"

Julianne ran along the riverbank in my direction. Jeeves trotted behind her, carrying Carter. We all stood together, looking down at the ashes.

"Not much help, is it?" Jeeves asked. "I thought there might be a clue or . . ."

Julianne had already spun away from the fire pit and was scanning the ground, pausing every few seconds to study the map. After a few more steps, she stopped, looked down at something, then spun around.

"I think you two will want to see this."

I raced over to her. She was kneeling now, staring at a spot on the riverbank. When I got closer, I could see the swirling mist disappearing through a curtain of emerald vines.

"A cave!" I said.

Julianne glanced back at me, beaming with excitement. "And look at the map. One of Three-Fingered Jack's blotches is just downstream from the campfire. Exactly where we are now."

"But there are so many blotches," Jeeves said. "It's probably just a coincidence, right?"

I ignored the boy-betraying butler and crouched behind Julianne. She peeled back the neon-stemmed plants and leafy mosses and leaned inside the cave. There was a narrow tunnel, just big enough to crawl through, running right beside the river. A thin rivulet of water flowed along its length.

I drew a deep breath of the dank, moist cave air. "The shimmering sword that cuts though stone will lead to the belly of the beast," I said. "Three-Fingered Jack must have meant water! Water is the sword!"

Jeeves leaned in behind us. "Are you two saying what I think you're saying?"

Julianne turned her head. "Remember how Three-Fingered Jack said that after his flare gun went off, the pirates seemed to disappear into thin air? I think he came back and found out that they hid in this cave."

"So you think this little tunnel leads to Zeetan Z?" Jeeves asked. "Is that the idea?"

Julianne started to answer, but I spoke for her.

"Sato," I said, "I apologize for Jeeves's thickheadedness. He doesn't really care about finding my parents."

"What are you—"

"He only cares about actors like Jiffer Bridgehead," I finished.

Jeeves's mouth opened, and his hand shot to his jacket pocket.

"I found your letter in the mud," I said, glaring at him.

Julianne backed out of the cave and looked up at us. "What are you two talking about?"

I stared straight at Jeeves while I answered. "My butler is going to work for your favorite movie star."

"You *are?*" Julianne asked.

"I hadn't officially sent the letter yet," Jeeves said, glaring right back at me. "But I was certainly leaning in that direction. Why don't *you* try having a cobra bite you every time you dare settle down for a cup of tea."

I kicked a loose piece of moss with my bare foot.

"Josh Brigand," Julianne said. "What are the chances?"

"Quite high," Jeeves said icily. "There aren't many butlers left these days."

A mosquito perched right on the tip of my nose and I batted it away.

FACT: Mosquitoes and leeches are hardly impressive enough to make **Ronald Zupan** miserable, but there I was, miserable nonetheless.

Jeeves drew a deep breath. "Can we talk about my job prospects later? You two might be on to something with this tunnel idea. But where does the tunnel lead? Are you saying it might open up in a—"

"You never wanted to come on this trip!" I said to him. "You only started helping when you realized you could get your new boss his ship back!"

Jeeves rolled his eyes. "Don't be ridiculous. I've known your parents longer than you've been alive!"

"But you—"

"You're wrong," Jeeves said flatly. "You *are* wrong

sometimes, Ronald. And you aren't immune to poison either. And you don't sleep like a three-toed sloth—you've been moaning in your sleep this entire trip."

I felt my whole body start to shake.

"Ronald," Julianne said, "can you pass me the candle?"

I looked down and saw her crawling back inside the cave.

"Just one second," I said. "We're not finished here."

"I'm going to investigate," Julianne said. "I don't want to listen to you two argue. There might be clues and—"

"*I'm* the leader of this expedition!" I snapped.

Julianne's lower legs were the only part of her body not inside the tunnel, and I watched them tense up. Then, after a pause, she started crawling forward again, until the thin curtain of green fell back into place and she was completely out of sight.

"Ronald," Jeeves said, "since you don't value my help, I think I'll go investigate on my own."

He unwound Carter from his neck and set the cobra on the ground.

"Go then!" I yelled. "A mutiny!"

He started to trudge upstream, slapping at mosquitoes as he walked. "Call it what you like."

"Farewell, Jeeves," I called after him. "Have fun butlering for Judas Brutus."

"*My name isn't Jeeves!*" he yelled back, without turning around.

I watched him until the river curved and he was out of

sight, then stooped down to look inside the tunnel. The entrance was smooth gray clay. Thin trails of water slid along the floor, down into the blackness. Every few feet, a cream-colored cone jutted from the ceiling.

Up ahead I could see Julianne sitting in a tiny pool of light that streamed in from a small hole in the cave ceiling.

"So," I called ahead, hurrying after her, "maybe the pirates have some sort of hideout down here?"

"Great deduction," Julianne said coldly.

The tone of her voice froze me. I could feel Carter winding around my ankles. I took off my adventure hat and wiped my face with my shoulder. The silence dangled between us, like we were separated by a wall of spiderwebs.

"Sato," I said, chewing my lip.

There was a long pause.

"I . . . I should have given you the candle . . . when you asked before."

"Yep," she said flatly.

"I was mad. The mosquitoes . . . and Jeeves's leaving . . . I didn't want to miss out on a discovery."

"So you're saying you were wrong?" Julianne asked.

She shifted her body slightly toward me. I looked down at Carter, who had decided it was the perfect time to bite my elbow.

"Wrong is such a relative term," I said.

Julianne started crawling forward again. I called after her: "I—I'm saying . . . possibly."

She kept going.

"Probably!"

She went forward some more.

"Fine! I was wrong not to give you the candle and wrong to say I was the leader."

She stopped.

"The truth is, you've done just as much for this expedition as I have," I said. "You got us swords in the basement of the bar, and you figured out that Gherkin Reject-Fade was Three-Fingered Jack."

"And?" she asked, wriggling around to face me.

"And you found this tunnel."

"And?"

I fiddled with the leather strap on my adventure hat.

"And I'm sorry," I said.

I didn't move. My knees pressed into the floor. A droplet of water landed on the crown of my head and made my whole body shiver.

"Sato, I'm sure you already deduced this, but I think the shimmering sword is the water and these caves might lead to the belly of the beast—"

"A giant cave full of bats," Julianne interrupted, a hint of excitement returning to her voice. "Remember all those bats last night? Any cave big enough for all of them would also be big enough to stash Josh Brigand's ship."

"You figured all that out?" I asked. A wave of jealousy washed over me, but I pushed it away. "Well, it's time to put the idea to the test. I'm going forward. Jeeves is probably halfway to the village already. I won't blame you if you mutiny too."

"No," Julianne said. "I'm coming with you."

"Because it was your discovery?"

She shook her head. "Because that's what partners in dazzling schemes and grand adventures do. They stick together."

An Error in the Chapter "Mutinies!"

1. I wasn't halfway to the village, as Ronald supposed. I wasn't going to leave him. I just needed a few minutes to cool off. I walked upstream, then doubled back downstream, then kicked a rock with my boot—which was a bad idea. Finally, I sat down on the bank of the river to think the whole thing through. I couldn't exactly abandon two children in Borneo. But after all my time with Ronald, he hardly seemed to listen to a word I said.

I was still deciding what to do when I heard the sound of leaves crunching behind me. I had only a split second to think *It might have been a bad idea to yell in this pirate-infested jungle* before the thought was interrupted by the click of a revolver.

"Hands up, Pommy!"

26

A Momentous Decision!

I crawled to meet Julianne below the small hole in the cave roof. Carter slithered close behind. Plants had taken root in the sandy soil around the hole, and delicate green stems stretched up toward the sky. At that moment, I remembered my father's letter.

"Wait just one second," I said.

I opened the sailor's bag and pulled out the envelope marked:

To Ronald Only to be read in a case of
IMPENDING MUTINY!

I broke the wax seal and read the letter silently.

Hello Son,

  I'm sure you look in the atlas often, but I hope you'll never have to read this letter. If you do, it means your companions have lost faith in you and decided to mutiny.

  My advice: you have to continue on. Wasting time in the darkest jungles arguing with a mutineer will put the whole expedition at risk. If they don't trust your leadership, you are better off without them. It's for the safety of your entire team.

  Remember: doubting friends are worse than enemies, and fire ants are the worst of all.

  Stay brave,
  Francisco Zupan

"What did it say?" Julianne asked as I folded the letter and tucked it away.

I drew a breath. My skin prickled and itched. "Jeeves has abandoned the expedition. Francisco says we should go on without him."

Julianne's face was partly veiled in shadow, so I couldn't

tell if she thought it was a dazzling idea or not. I reread the letter. Julianne drummed her fingers against her violin case.

"What do *you* think?" she asked.

I itched the swelling mosquito bite on my nose and thought through our options. Then, I drew the candle from inside the sailor's sack, lit it with one of the fireproof matches, and passed it up to Julianne. "My father is right. Lead the way."

Julianne took the candle and crawled forward slowly. The path inside the cave began to wind downhill, the ceiling opened up a foot or two—but only enough for us to shuffle forward, squatting over our feet, arms tight around our knees. Droplets of water fell from the roof, and somewhere far below we could hear a distant surging river.

I knew I should follow my father's advice, but for some reason I felt like a musk ox was sitting on my rib cage. I could hardly breathe as our tunnel took us deeper into the center of the earth.

"He *did* push on when he lost his motorbike," I said, shuffling forward a little slower. "That was brave."

The slope grew steeper. I pressed my fingers against the walls to slow down; my bare feet slid over the smooth floor of the tunnel.

"And he held his own when we fought Gunting and Pemburu," Julianne added.

I smiled, remembering how proud Jeeves looked after he knocked the villains out with two desk lamps. But the feeling quickly faded. "To think that all that time he already had the letter to Jock Bragman in his pocket."

Julianne didn't say a thing. We were steadily gaining momentum. Soon, there would be no chance to climb back the way we came. It would be too steep.

I felt Carter bite my ankle. "I know you'll miss him," I muttered to the snake, "but remember, *he* left us."

As we slipped deeper into the abyss, the tunnel curved. We tried to slow ourselves down by dragging our hands against the cave wall. In the words of Helen Zupan, "When exploring a treacherous, unlit hole, proceed with caution and you'll come home whole."

The flickering candle revealed a stalactite up ahead. It was long and narrow—reminding me of a face I'd seen almost every day since I was born.

"*Stop!*" I boomed.

Julianne had already ducked under the stalactite, but her right hand shot out behind her and she managed to grab it. Carter and I slammed into her back. For a split second the candle was airborne. It did a slow flip, wick still burning, before Julianne snatched it out of the air with her left hand. The flame hissed against her palm—leaving us in darkness.

I held the back of Julianne's shirt with one hand and the stalactite with the other. Carter cinched himself around my thigh.

"What are you doing?" Julianne asked, panting.

"Hand me the candle, then spin yourself around," I said in as calm a voice as I could manage.

I found good footholds and Julianne passed me the candle. Then she released the stalactite so that she could grab the walls with both hands.

"Sato, I'm making a bold decision," I said. "I'm going back for Jeeves."

I moved forward, searching for places to grip along the sloping cave floor.

"After all," I added, "he never finished explaining how cricket works."

Julianne didn't speak. I knew I was going against Francisco's advice, but at least the Norwegian musk ox sitting on my ribs was finally gone.

When we arrived back at the hole in the tunnel ceiling, I stopped so we could both catch our breath.

"I was hoping you'd decide to go back for him," Julianne said. "And I have to admit, I'm impressed."

"Well, Sato . . . ," I said, turning to face her.

I trailed off. Her bowler hat was tipped back on her head, and her hair was flecked with dried mud. The weak light trickling into the cave revealed those golden speckles in her eyes.

"Yes?"

Whatever I'd been about to say had vanished completely. "Onward," I finally managed.

I turned back to face the mouth of the cave, but before I could start crawling again, a loud voice rang out above us.

"Listen, Pommy! If you don't tell me where Gunting is, there's gonna be trouble!"

Julianne's eyes flashed. "*That's Pemburu*," she mouthed.

The next voice was Jeeves's—he sounded terrified. "Th-the giant? How would I know where the giant is? The last time I saw him, he was trying to murder us."

I snuffed out the candle. A few pieces of sandy gravel fell inside the cave. Jeeves and Pemburu were standing practically on top of the hole in the tunnel's roof.

FACT: My butler was in grave danger.

"Then tell me where the two little grommets are hiding," Pemburu went on. "I bet I can make *them* talk!"

Silence.

"*Where. Are. They?*" Pemburu yelled, louder this time.

Suddenly, we were cast into darkness. Someone had stepped right over the opening in the ceiling of the tunnel. Pebbles and loose dirt sprinkled our hair.

"M-miles away." Jeeves's voice was muffled now. "We argued and they left me. Hours ago. I'll probably never see them again."

"Mutiny, eh?" Pemburu growled. "And Gunting? What happened to him?"

"He . . . he seemed to fall into a hole."

"Take me there," Pemburu said.

"I . . ." Jeeves's voice seemed to catch in his throat. "Please put the pistol away."

"You shut—*ughha! Agg! Gmich!* A blinking mozzie just went right down my throat! I'll continue this little chat when we're away from the river."

We heard Jeeves and Pemburu march off. When we were sure they were gone, we crawled out of the tunnel on hands and knees. Even through the haze, the sunlight was so bright that we had to shield our eyes.

"Sato," I said, my fingers tightening around the grip of my sword, "change of plans. We've got a butler to rescue."

FROM THE DESK OF
Thomas Halladay

Errors in the Chapter "A Momentous Decision!"

1. I take issue with the idea that Ronald was reminded of my face by looking at a stalactite. I've asked a number of people about this, and they promise me that I don't look anything like a stalactite, a stalagmite, or any other part of a cave.

2. I was the one who stepped on the hole of the tunnel roof, and I did it on purpose. It was a sly move, if I do say so myself.

3. I told Pemburu that I'd never see Ronald and Julianne again, but I wasn't so sure. In fact, I had a glimmer of hope that I would see them very soon. I'm not short on complaints about young Ronald Zupan, but with Pemburu leading me into the jungle, I moved forward thinking, "The Ronald I know would circle back for a friend."

27

Dazzling Rescue!

Julianne and I crouched low to track the footprints leading away from the river while Carter slithered behind. The jungle grew thicker with each step. It wasn't more than a few minutes before we spotted Pemburu and Jeeves—three hundred feet ahead, standing in a ring of spiny ferns, veiled by mist.

Pemburu kicked Jeeves, and he stumbled forward. Julianne, Carter, and I darted between trees, closing in, peeking out to watch, never making a sound. Every few minutes we could hear Pemburu curse at the mosquitoes, Jeeves, or both at once.

"We have to attack before he gets close to town," Julianne said in a hushed tone. "We don't want to meet any more of Pemburu's friends."

Jeeves and Pemburu had stopped walking. They stood in a clearing between two mighty fig trees, while Pemburu used his belt to cinch Jeeves's hands behind his back.

"I don't want you throwing anything, do I, mate?" Pemburu said. Even from far away it was easy to spot a giant purple knot bulging on the villain's forehead, where Jeeves had hit him with the lamp a few nights earlier.

Julianne tapped my elbow. "Do you have a plan?"

I pulled out my adventure notebook and riffled through the pages. There were entries on riding a yak, fighting off a bull shark, identifying fake Persian cutlery—but nothing that seemed to fit our situation.

"Sato, I'm stumped. Any ideas?"

She set down her violin case and rolled up her sleeves. "Well, I was thinking we could *pretend* to surrender, as a diversion. Then, when Pemburu is distracted, we attack." She paused and tucked a few loose strands of hair behind her ears. "That's where it gets sticky."

"No," I broke in, "*that's* the moment where I leap from a tree and knock the villain unconscious!"

Julianne's eyebrows shot up. "You're going to jump out of a tree? That sounds crazy. It sounds difficult. It sounds—"

"Perfect?"

Julianne couldn't help but smile. "Yeah . . . if we can pull it off."

In the distance, Pemburu finished tying Jeeves's hands,

which made me realize our plan's fatal flaw. "But they'll be long gone before we can cut down a few vines and weave them into a rope."

"Already done."

Julianne clicked open her violin case and removed the violin. Lying underneath was a perfectly woven coil of rope made from thin green vines.

"I made it when you were napping that first afternoon," she said. "I thought we might anchor it to a tree branch if we ever had to rescue someone from a raging river."

"Sato," I said, "you're astounding."

She shrugged. "Everyone's afraid of something, right? For me it's drowning. The real question is, is it strong enough?"

I fingered the braided vines. "The last rope I trusted my life to was made of dresses. This'll do just fine."

The jungle canopy above us was so dense it would be simple to climb from one tree to the next all the way to where Pemburu and Jeeves stood. Julianne untied her purple scarf from around her waist and retied it onto the tip of her sword.

I threw the rope over my shoulder. "Keep him talking until I can drop down on his head."

As I started off, Carter bit my knee.

"Good luck to you too, my friend," I said, petting the serpent.

Julianne and Carter started toward the clearing as I scampered up into the tree. Once I had climbed high enough,

the branches were wrapped up in patches of moss and flowering vines—I jumped easily from one to the next.

When I'd cut the distance in half, I looked down through a space between branches and saw Julianne waving her sword with the purple scarf tied to it.

"Pemburu!" she called through the fog. "You win."

The villain jerked his body all the way around in one swift movement. "Well, if it isn't that little sheila who was traveling with this butler."

Jeeves's face looked just like it had the night before when he was served worm stew. "Julianne, what are you doing here?"

"Surrendering, I reckon," the bartender said.

Julianne dipped her chin.

Pemburu took a cautious step forward. He popped his knuckles one by one. "But I see you've got the flag tied onto your sword there . . . And as I remember, you're pretty handy with that thing. Is this a trap?"

Overhead, I started softly running along the branches. The next time I looked down, Pemburu was eyeing Julianne coldly.

"And is that a snake in the grass?" he asked. "He sort of puts a damper on our situation."

They were only ten feet away from each other now. Pemburu held up his hand for her to stop. "Where's the boy?"

I found the spot to stage my gambit and tied off one end of Julianne's rope.

"We mutinied from Ronald," Julianne said.

I heard Jeeves let out a groan.

"So he's not with you?" asked Pemburu, still scanning the surrounding jungle.

Julianne shook her head. "Nope."

I wrapped the rope of vines around my right wrist and drew my sword in my left hand. My toes wriggled out to the very edge of a mighty, moss-covered branch.

"Well, put your sword down and come over," Pemburu said. "I'd better tie you up too."

The moment of truth was upon me. I took a deep breath, counted to three, and dove into the air. When the rope went taut, my feet swung out ahead of my body, but I held my sword steady.

"Dastardly dog!" I screamed.

Pemburu's eyes flooded with terror.

> **FACT:** I missed him by about a foot.

> **DOUBLE FACT:** At the end of my arc, I went spinning back in the other direction and smashed squarely into the rogue before he had time to turn around.

Pemburu hit the jungle floor with a thud. I gathered myself as he rolled into a gap between two trees. Julianne rushed at him, sword drawn.

"No!" Jeeves screamed. "He's got a— "

But it was too late. Pemburu was up on his knees. He was dazed, shocked, and panicked, but he'd also managed to draw a pistol from his waistband.

"— gun," Jeeves finished weakly.

No one moved. I'd knocked the wind out of the scoundrel, and he sucked in short gulps of air.

"Like . . . I said . . . before," he finally choked out, "you're in danger, gang. You should have gone home when you had the chance. Now drop your swords and put your hands high."

Carter reared back and flared his hood; the sun made his scales shine. Julianne and I stepped into fencing stance.

"I'm serious," Pemburu said.

"We are too," I replied.

I glanced over at Jeeves; his face was tight. "Y-you came back for me."

"Of course I did, Jeeves. You're family."

The moment was shattered by the

CRACK!

    CRACK!

      CRACK!

of gunshots.

Pemburu was standing now—pistol pointed skyward—staggering toward us. "I said, *Drop. Your. Swords!*" He started to draw the revolver level. "Or it'll be the last mistake you ever make."

FROM THE DESK OF
Thomas Halladay

An Error in the Chapter "Dazzling Rescue!"

1. Ronald left it out, but when he called
me family, he also called me by my real
name . . . Tom.

   Of course, there wasn't much time to smile
about it, what with yet another armed madman
closing in.

28

Cornered!

Carter wound through the grass toward Pemburu—hissing like he'd just met his one true enemy. Pemburu slowly cocked the hammer of his pistol.

"Carter!" I yelled, starting after him.

"Grrrrrrrrrrrrr." A throaty growl rumbled through the jungle, sending a cold shiver down my spine.

Pemburu glanced into the trees and his voice faltered. "What was *that*?"

"Grrrrrrrrrrrrrrrr." The noise was somewhere overhead, getting louder and closer.

"Ronald." Julianne's voice quavered. "Do you remember what I told you about clouded leopards?"

"Sato, this is hardly the time—"

"How they live in trees? And hate to be disturbed?"

"Grrraaaawww!"

"Like by people climbing near their homes. Or firing guns in the air."

"Oh dear," Jeeves said.

The terrible roar shot up in pitch.

"RAAAAYYYYWWWWWWR!"

There was a flash of fur and claws as a clouded leopard darted down the trunk of the same tree I'd just leaped out of. His coat was covered with islands of black speckles swimming in a sea of tan. His lips were drawn tight, revealing his teeth.

They were big teeth. Big and sharp.

"Crikey!" Pemburu started to run, tripped, fell flat, then popped frantically to his feet and tore into the undergrowth.

The leopard darted after him, bounding with long, graceful strides. They disappeared from sight—then reappeared to the right of us, in a clearing. Pemburu was facing the leopard now. He aimed the gun and fired two shots. Both missed. One bullet buried itself in the dirt; the other sank into a mighty tree, sending up a spray of bark. Pemburu set his feet and squeezed off a third shot—this time exploding a rock just a few inches away from the leopard's left forepaw.

The leopard hesitated. Pemburu squinted down the sight of the gun. He held the pistol as steadily as his quaking arms would allow.

"Don't shoot!" I screamed.

The leopard spun to face me. Pemburu pulled the trigger. The gun clicked empty—but the leopard was curious about the master adventurer with the loud mouth. He began slinking in our direction, swiping his tongue across his cheeks in wide circles.

"Th-that's no way to treat the brave soul who just tried to save you," I said, taking a step backward.

The beast zigzagged slowly toward me. Carter poised to strike, but even the deadliest snake known to man would have been no match. I hefted the serpent up and draped his body across my shoulders. Julianne's sword sung through the air, slicing cleanly through the belt that bound Jeeves's wrists.

We started to run, Jeeves and Julianne out in front. The leopard came bounding after us, roaring as he went. We tore through the bushes, dodged trees, and hurdled over petrified

logs. I could hear the leopard's footfalls not far behind us. A quick glance over my shoulder showed the beast only twenty feet back, gliding across the jungle floor.

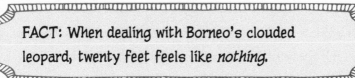

FACT: When dealing with Borneo's clouded leopard, twenty feet feels like *nothing*.

Carter and I were first in line to be devoured. There was no way to outrun the mighty jungle cat, so I spun to face him, sword shifting with each step backward. Carter lifted off my shoulder and flared his hood. The leopard was close enough to pounce.

"I was trying to help," I explained.

He clawed the air.

"Also, Jeeves would taste terrible. Too bony."

The leopard let out a long, low, rumbling growl. His eyes gleamed. So did his teeth. I kept backing up until I bumped into my friends. For some reason they'd stopped running.

"Ronald, we have a problem," Jeeves said in a faint voice.

"I noticed."

"Another one." The words seemed to stick in Julianne's throat. "Bigger."

The leopard breathed through his nose. Every muscle on his body stood out, pulsing with energy.

"Bigger than an angry leopard?" I asked.

"There's a hole in the ground," she replied, "and it's too wide to run around."

I risked looking over my shoulder. We'd come to a gaping split in the jungle floor.

My mouth suddenly felt bone dry. "This is bad."

"Horrible," Julianne said.

"Catastrophic," Jeeves added.

The leopard angled his head, glowered at me, and slowly paced toward us—pushing me back against my friends and pushing them closer to the edge of the giant, inky sinkhole. He had us cornered and he knew it.

Then the Most Curious Thing Happened

We were right up against a massive hole in the ground, with a leopard breathing down our necks. And there was Julianne Sato, calm as could be, taking Three-Fingered Jack's map out of her pocket.

"WHAT ARE YOU DOING?" I screamed inside my head. But no actual words came out. Julianne just kept on studying the map, peering closely at it and looking back at the sinkhole.

Then it hit me. I peered over the ledge to see a deep blue pool, and I was struck with a hunch of my own about what was coming next.

29

The Belly of the Beast!

The leopard took a few more steady steps forward, then lifted a heavy paw and swatted at the tip of my sword.

"Go away, you varlet," I said. "*Please.*"

Julianne was the first to speak. "Do you two remember the map—those inky blots?"

"What about them?" I asked, my eyes still locked on the prowling leopard.

"Well, the ink spot near where Three-Fingered Jack saw the pirates turned out to be where the tunnel was, right? The shimmering sword that cuts through stone . . ."

The clouded leopard rocked on his hind legs, pulsing forward and back. His mouth was open and his breath had the coppery smell of raw flesh.

"And I'm not sure exactly where we are now," Julianne

went on, "but there's a really big ink spot in the corner of the map. It *might* be this."

"I worried you might say that," Jeeves muttered.

"I don't like it any more than you do," Julianne said, "but what if Three-Fingered Jack marked all the holes in the ground because he thinks they all lead to some sort of . . . underground world?"

"The belly of the beast," I muttered, trying to keep the leopard back.

"Three-Fingered Jack might be wrong though," Jeeves said. "Let's remember that he's batty."

The leopard growled again. His hot breath seemed to coat my skin. There was no telling when he would spring.

"All the evidence points in the same direction," I said. *"Down."*

I swiveled my head long enough to see that we'd backed up to the farthest edge of the cliff. Dirt and rock crumbled from under our feet and disappeared into blackness. From this angle I could see into the middle of the cavern. The water was dark blue.

"I think it's deep enough."

Jeeves's voice sounded weak. "Never in my life have I wanted so badly for one of your hunches to be right."

The leopard licked a wide arc across his nose, and his muscles tightened. I braced myself, holding my sword steady. "On the count of—"

Without warning the leopard sprang—but we were already airborne. Julianne had grabbed my wrist and yanked me from behind. My adventure hat fell off as we soared into the abyss.

"*Ooooooooohhhhhhhhhh nooooooooooooo!*" Jeeves yelled as we somersaulted down, down, down into the sinkhole.

I drew a breath. *Splash! Splash! Ker-splash!*

When my lungs tightened I started to kick, bursting to the surface with a whoop. "Right out of the jaws of death!"

We were in a massive, domed cavern. The split in the ground above lit the room, and the water sparkled brilliant blue where the sun hit it. The reflection shimmered along the walls.

"Everyone feel all right?" I asked.

Jeeves shook out his hair and flashed a smile that took over his whole face. "To tell you the truth . . . yes."

"What about you, Sato? Lost the adventure hat but didn't drown, I see?"

She gulped, her eyes panicky, her head swiveling left and right.

"I know I said there wouldn't be open water, but this is in a cave . . . so it's not *technically* open."

Julianne was treading water with her violin–life preserver under one arm. "It's not that," she said. "Where's Carter?"

I felt every ounce of joy drain out of my body. I scanned the water for my trusted cobra. Jeeves kicked out for the far corners of the cave, while I dove under to search the bottom. I reached the riverbed in four strokes and clawed blindly at the gravel and sand, ignoring the pressure in my lungs.

Finally, I had to go back up for air. I dove again and came up empty-handed a second time.

"We've got to find him!" I yelled, between heaving breaths.

"*Ahgripr-snagish-blostle!*" Jeeves cried from deep in the shadows.

"Please, Jeeves! Help!"

"Graffle-bladnish-pripple!"

"Stop complaining," I yelled. "Your dear friend Carter needs you!"

"Mickle-brimple!"

I hesitated. The muffled yell was accompanied by wild splashing. Julianne and I kicked toward the sound. Jeeves swam into the light.

"Carter! You're alive!"

"Miff wu pweeze," came Jeeves's muffled voice.

Julianne's laughter pinged off the walls of the giant grotto as she unraveled the serpent from my beloved butler's head.

"If you had told me three days ago that I'd gladly have a cobra coiled around my head, I'd have called you crazy," Jeeves said.

"That's the thing about thrilling adventures," I replied with a smile. "They change you, whether you know it or not."

On the downstream side of the cave a pile of boulders jutted out of the water. We swam to it and pulled ourselves up onto the rocks, drawing heaving breaths. The sun streamed in from the sinkhole and danced across the surface of the underground lake. The water glowed as blue as the feathers of a Malaccan bird of paradise.

I angled my head to see if the leopard was still at the edge of the cliff, but the stalactites and the pitch of the cave blocked my sight line. I hoped the beast would be satisfied eating the two adventure hats we'd left behind.

"So it's an underground river," Jeeves said, "which hopefully leads us to Zeetan Z's lair."

"Hopefully," Julianne said. "And we can only find out by swimming downriver in the darkness."

There was a long moment of silence as the three of us peered downstream and thought about the peril we would soon face. From where we stood, the river curved around a corner and disappeared. The cave walls were steep and slick-looking, without banks.

We rolled our pants above the knees, and Julianne and Jeeves took off their boots. The sailor's sack was full of water, but our items were mostly intact. I fished Francisco's soggy letter out of the bag.

"So you read the mutiny letter?" Jeeves asked.

"Indeed," I replied.

"And?"

"And I came back for you."

Jeeves eyed the wet paper. "But what did the letter say? May I read it?"

I shook my head. "I'd rather you not."

"Really, I insist."

He reached for the soggy page, but I didn't want his feelings hurt by Francisco's harsh words for mutineers. So I did something that I hadn't done since devouring Shakespeare.

FACT: I ate the letter whole.

As Helen Zupan says, "The most adventurous people are carnivorous readers."

Jeeves watched with a furrowed brow as I chewed. "Well, I'm glad we're all back to being sensible."

"Right you are," I boomed, swallowing the paper down.

It was time to set off. Carter slid into the water first, sending tiny waves rippling out toward the edges of the cave. Jeeves and I kicked off the rocks after him.

Julianne pulled out a bootlace and used it to tie her hair up, then gripped her violin case tight with one arm and eased herself into the river. "Can we . . ."

"Speak and it's done," I said.

"Stay close?"

"Your best plan yet, Sato."

We crowded shoulder to shoulder and let the river pull us along. At the end of the grotto, the cave grew tighter and darker. The only sound was the echoing *plop* of droplets falling off the long strands of moss hanging overhead. After a few hundred feet, the current sped up. The sailor's bag was coated in a thin layer of tar—so as long as I kept it upright, it floated easily beside me. Julianne used her violin case like a kickboard, and we swam in a small knot, with Carter circling us.

"Onward into the belly of the beast," I said. "If that's still the right word when traveling underground. Maybe it's downward? Or *sideward*?"

Whatever the word was, if our deductions were right, we were headed for a meeting with the dastardly Zeetan Z.

One Thing I Wasn't Thinking About as We Entered the River

1. Mutiny.

The time for arguing, splitting up, or rushing off in a state of anger was over. Talk of new jobs could wait. Ronald, Julianne, and, yes, even Carter needed me and—if my plan was to leave Borneo in one piece—they'd just proved that I needed them too.

We were in it together now. All for one and one for all, as the saying goes.

30

Sea Devils Around the Bend!

As we rounded the first bend in the river, we saw the outlines of stalactites hanging from the cave ceiling, looking just like the teeth of the leopard we'd evaded. If we were really headed into the belly of the beast, this was like passing through its jaws.

The darkness grew heavier, pressing in on us. The only noise was water lapping against the walls of the cave or burping in small pockets that had been carved from the rock. Soon, the light dimmed completely.

After what felt like a month, I spoke. "Jeeves?"

"Yes."

"Julianne?"

"I'm here."

"Carter?"

"He latched on to me a few minutes ago," Jeeves said. "Got the nape of my neck this time."

"I'll get him off," I offered.

"Or I could," Julianne said.

"No, I'd like to hold him actually," Jeeves insisted. "I mean . . . just for the snake's sake, of course."

"I'm glad you two made friends," I said. "No true master adventurer is afraid of snakes."

Jeeves sighed, but he didn't argue. After another minute in the darkness, I fished the waterproof matches out of my pocket. We could still use the candle, even if it *did* have a priceless artifact inside. I lit the wick. The flickering light felt warming, like my mother's Thai coconut soup on a rainy day.

We passed into another wide room and gasped in unison.

"Look at that!"

"Dazzling."

"Lovely."

The roof of the cave was covered in tiny glowworms. Not a few here and there, but thousands, millions of them. As our eyes adjusted, we could see their brilliant tendrils trailing down below them.

I blew out the candle, and the glowworms shone even brighter.

"How many matches left?" Julianne asked.

I cringed and counted the matches with my fingers— there were only seven. Hopefully they would all light.

We drifted silently downstream, below the whorls of glowworms. They lined the ceiling like endless stars—crowded together in florescent green constellations. It was a welcome distraction, but it didn't last long.

Just a few hundred feet ahead, a low moan echoed through the cavern. *"Graghaaaaa. Grumaaaaaash."*

"What. Is. That?" Jeeves asked. "Not the leopard?"

Up ahead, the path made by glowworms on the ceiling wound around another corner.

"Whatever it is, it's close," Julianne said. "And we're closing in on it."

We floated into the next room in complete silence. About sixty feet downstream there was a hole in the cave roof—this one much smaller than the one we'd dove into. It let in slanting rays of afternoon sun and cast a dim, dusty light through our lost world. Below the collapsed roof, we saw a massive figure writhing in agony.

I drew the spyglass from the sailor's sack and pressed it to my eye. "The giant!" I said. "Gunting!"

I thought back to when he chased us and it all made sense. Gunting must have fallen into a sinkhole and landed on a pile of rubble. He was still there, sprawled on a patch of sand, surrounded by jagged stones.

"I *knew* it," I said. "Rocks beat scissors after all."

We floated closer. Gunting's leg looked

twisted in all the wrong ways. His head lolled back and forth; his massive, scarred face was streaked with grime and tear tracks. I counted back the hours he'd been in the cave. It was even longer than Francisco spent at the bottom of the Well of Souls the year before I was born.

I stopped swimming and tried to think of what my parents would do, but there weren't any tongueless giants in their stories.

"We have to help him," I announced.

"Are you *mad*?" Jeeves asked. "We'll do nothing of the sort."

"And leave him to die?"

"Swimming down a pitch-black river is bad enough," Julianne said. "And Gunting wasn't exactly friendly to us before."

They had a point, but just then Gunting forced his head up and let out a miserable wail. It was so loud that a family of bats started bickering somewhere in the far reaches of the room.

"The truest way to prove you've grown is to help a villain as he groans in pain," I said.

"Did Helen say that?" Jeeves asked. "I don't remember that one."

"Then consider it a **Ronald Zupan** original."

I could deduce by their silence that my friends weren't convinced about helping the brute, so I shouldered the sailor's sack and swam toward him alone.

"Ronald!" Jeeves called after me. "When this turns into a catastrophe, I'm going to say 'I told you so!'"

I waded up onto the sand and stood just a few feet from Gunting. The giant forced his head up and opened his eyes.

"Hello," I said, "I'm the master adventurer you tried to squash a few nights ago."

Gunting let out another low, garbled cry. I'd thought he was seven feet tall back in the saloon, but now, stretched out, it looked more like seven and a half.

"I'm going to take that to mean you apologize," I said, "or you surrender. Either way, I graciously accept."

I took another cautious step forward, dripping water. Gunting stayed still. I looked at his leg and saw that not only was it broken, it was pinned down under a rock.

"We know Zeetan Z is down here," I went on. "We know he has my parents, and we know he wants the Lion of Lyros. You practically gave that part away with your note in the saloon."

I took the last few squares of chocolate out of the sailor's sack and tossed them onto Gunting's lap. Then I drew one match out of the box and flicked that to him too.

"Now listen, you villainous oaf," I said. "Your leg is broken and you're sure to die if you stay down here. Up above, your friend Pemburu is wandering the jungle, searching for us. Eat the chocolate to get a little strength, then use the match to start a fire with twigs and whatever else you can find. He'll see the smoke and come rescue you."

The giant let out another miserable groan.

"I'm glad you see it that way," I said, looking into his glassy eyes.

He pointed overhead, toward the surface.

"Yes," I said. "Go above."

He shook his head, pointed at me, and gestured to the sinkhole again. He laced his fingers together and mimed giving me a boost up.

"Me?" I asked.

He nodded forcefully.

"No chance," I said. "I have two master adventurers to rescue from a dastardly pirate."

Backing toward the river, I saw Gunting's eyes squeeze shut in agony. I hesitated, watching him, then took two careful steps toward his twisted leg. I wrapped my arms around the boulder that pinned it down and rocked it back and forth. He screamed and wailed each time, snot bubbling out of his nostrils, but I got enough momentum to roll the massive stone off him.

"There," I said, "now you can crawl up to the surface, even without Pemburu's help."

With that, I dove into the water and swam away as fast as I could. Once I got into the center of the river, I turned to face Gunting one more time and saw him gulping down the squares of chocolate. His eyes steadied and there was a look on his face I couldn't explain. He pointed above ground again and again, but when I shook my head, his features tightened and his jaw muscles pulsed.

FACT: The expression wasn't quite as grateful as I'd hoped.

Jeeves and Julianne met me a few hundred yards downstream.

"What did you say to him?" Julianne asked.

"I gave him one match to start a signal fire," I said. "And told him that we were going to find Zeetan Z."

"I wish you hadn't mentioned that last bit," Jeeves said through gritted teeth. "It would be far better if he didn't know our plans."

We kicked forward, drifting downriver into the farther reaches of the cave.

"Fear not," I assured my friends, "he's too weak to chase after us."

They didn't say anything, but I noticed that Julianne started swimming a little quicker.

"He'll never try it," I promised. "He likes me. It's my best hunch yet. Call it a Zupanian instinc—"

My brave words were drowned out by a roar coming from upstream, followed by the sound of something massive splashing in the water. Jeeves said a few words that shouldn't be repeated. Julianne repeated them.

There was no denying it; Gunting was chasing us.

FROM THE DESK OF
Thomas Halladay

What We Were Up Against

1. An injured giant with a desire to crush us following from behind.

2. The deadliest pirate to live in more than two hundred years hidden somewhere in the dark maze of caverns up ahead.

What We Had in Our Favor

1. My cricket arm.

2. Ronald and Julianne's fencing skill.

3. One nonvenomous venomous snake, which was starting to behave a tad sluggishly.

If I were a betting man, I'd have put every shilling I had on the villains—that is, if I could find someone to bet on us.

31
Chilling Ruses!

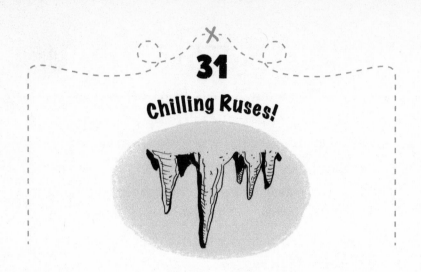

Now *we* were fortune's fools! Caught in a cave with an over-sized rogue, haunted by the sound of his arms as they slapped the water like wind-ravaged palm trees. The current carried us downstream until the cave was midnight black again.

"Jeeves, you've always wanted me to admit when I was wrong," I said, kicking forward, hoping not to run into a wall. "This seems like a good place to start."

"Let's just focus on getting away," Jeeves huffed.

We raced toward the middle of the river, where the current was the strongest.

"But I *did* tell you so," he added.

"We both did," Julianne said between heaving breaths. "But maybe there's something good to come out of it."

I started kicking double time. "Way to see the bright side, Sato . . . What is it?"

"He's hurt and hungry. Would he really bother to follow us if we were headed the wrong way?"

"He must be trying to catch us before we can get to Zeetan Z," Jeeves said. He was panting heavily, and I remembered that he had to do the swimming for Carter too.

Up ahead, there was another hole in the cave ceiling. The light was weak and pinkish. It would be night soon and even the sinkholes would be as dark as the pupils of a pygmy marmoset.

In the faint light, we could spy Gunting's hulking form swimming behind us. He was gaining. My feet scraped the river bottom.

"Stand up and run!" Julianne yelled.

We charged forward, churning up the stones and sand, pulling farther away from the giant until the cave narrowed and the water got deeper again. Then we were back to swimming, racing for the next curve.

"He made it to the shallow bit," Jeeves called, looking over his shoulder.

We all spun around. Gunting couldn't stand on his leg— he was crawling and clawing across the gravelly riverbed.

"His energy won't last," I declared. "The fiend hasn't eaten more than a few bites of chocolate in days."

A rock the size of a hedgehog smashed into the cave ceiling just above my head and sprayed shards everywhere.

"How about we don't make any more guesses about Gunting?" Jeeves panted.

We raced around two tight bends in the river, bumping off the slick cave walls as we went.

"I have an idea," Julianne said.

"Good, because we need it." My heart was hammering so fast I thought it might jump out of my chest.

"Let's let him get ahead of us," she said. "That way it's *us* following him instead of the other way around. I bet he'll lead us right to Zeetan Z."

Gunting let out a monstrous roar and another rock shattered against the cave wall.

"*And*," Jeeves added, "it's harder to throw rocks upstream when you're fighting the current."

The next time the river curved, we raced straight to the darkest edges of the cavern, where the water lapped against the limestone. We tried to find someplace to hide, but the walls had been polished smooth by the river. We drifted forward, feeling blindly for a rock to grab.

"I can touch over here," Jeeves whispered. "Just barely."

Julianne and I swam toward his voice and gripped his jacket. Carter was looped around Jeeves's neck; I pressed my face against the snake's body.

We could hear Gunting splashing his way toward us. We didn't move or speak, just held each other tight and hoped he'd swim right by. The water was deep and Jeeves swayed back and forth under our weight.

Now that we were still, the giant had no way to tell where

we were, and he slipped right past us. For a few long minutes, we stayed put. Even the scattered patches of glowworms on the cave ceiling seemed sinister now. Their eerie green light looked haunted.

"We can't let him get too far ahead," I said, after we'd each had time to catch our breath. "If he's going to Zeetan Z, he's also leading us right to my parents. We've got to keep swimming."

Things I Was Looking Forward to If We Made It Out of Our Predicament Alive

1. A meal of roast beef and potatoes, with sticky toffee pudding for dessert.

2. A warm bath.

3. A few hours curled up with a good book.

4. A long sleep. Perhaps a week straight. Maybe more.

As we swam, I repeated those four things over and over to myself—*meal, bath, book, sleep; meal, bath, book, sleep; meal, bath, book, sleep.* I wish I could say that it helped.

32

Endless Night!

We swam after Gunting as fast as we could, but a new problem bubbled to the surface. What if he tried hiding in a corner of the cave, just like we had, to catch us by surprise? We flinched at every far-off flutter of sound, and every *plop* of water made us cringe.

After what felt like a year of unlit horror, we spotted him up ahead. He'd just entered a section of cave that was brighter than any room we'd been in since the first grotto. For a second, I thought the light came from more glowworms, but as we continued on, I felt a breeze and realized that we were entering a narrow canyon. The limestone walls still towered overhead, but there was only sky above us.

To our right, two sandbars ran along the side of the canyon, separated from each other by twenty feet of swirling water, where the river lapped against the rock wall. At the upstream end of the first beach, there was a grove of giant bamboo stretching toward the cliff tops.

"Grrrrrruuuuuuu!"

"We've been spotted," Jeeves said.

Sure enough, Gunting was staring straight at us. He let out another scream before rolling onto his stomach and swimming toward the first sandbar, but the current was too strong and he shot past it. He clawed up onto the second beach instead.

"What do we do now?" Julianne asked, voice trembling.

Gunting was waiting for us to pass with his enormous body half in the water. If we tried to slip by him, he'd have a good shot at catching us.

"To shore!" I called.

We kicked sideways and made it to the first sandbar, just below the bamboo grove. The section of river that separated our patch of sand from Gunting's was a frothy whirlpool. There was no way an injured giant could swim upstream to reach us . . . or so we hoped.

Jeeves drew the spyglass from his pocket and opened it with a few swift clicks. A half-moon shone down on the canyon; its light made the surface of the river look like rippling silver.

"We'll rest and make a plan," I said to my friends. "We can take turns keeping a lookout."

The night air was sticky. Carter slithered off Jeeves's

shoulders and coiled into a tight knot, half-wedged under a river rock that was still warm from the sun. Jeeves handed me the spyglass and I studied Gunting's treacherous glare for a few minutes.

"I tried to help you," I whispered to myself, clicking the spyglass shut. "You could be up on the surface, getting your leg fixed."

I emptied the contents of the sailor's sack on the sand and we ate the last pieces of papaya. When it got colder, Julianne and I went to the bamboo grove and chopped down a few colossal shoots, dragging them back to make a fire inside a ring of smooth rocks.

We sat in silence for a long time before Jeeves cleared his throat and spoke to me from across the fire.

"Tomorrow, or whenever it comes, we'll face Zeetan Z." The smoke and shadows made him look grizzled.

"The sooner the better," I said.

"Our lives will hang in the balance: yours, mine, Julianne's, Carter's, and your parents'."

I nodded.

"Whatever comes," he went on, "remember, you don't have to try to impress anyone."

I scratched a mosquito bite on my elbow. "Jeeves, I never *try* to be impressive. It comes naturally."

He paused again, rolling another piece of bamboo toward the coals. "I know how badly you want to be chosen for one of your parents' expeditions, is all." His voice was calm and level. "But you can't convince people of how brave or smart or skilled you are. You've got to trust that they'll see it."

I found a wood chip in the sand beside me and flicked it into the flames. "I'm not really sure what you're getting at."

Julianne set down her violin and hugged her knees. "Ronald," she said, "do you know why I beat you in the city fencing championship?"

I didn't like where this was going. I stood, faced the river, and used the sole of my foot to shove a stubby green piece of bamboo into the current.

"During our match, you were winning," she said. "I was on my heels . . . until you tried to use Bonetti's Spiral Attack."

I wheeled around. "Bonetti was a genius and you know it."

"Bonetti was a showman," Julianne said without missing a beat. "Do you remember DiMazo's technique? The one we learned the first week of class? That's how I beat you. It's like Jeeves said about Occam's razor—sometimes the easiest solution is the best."

We stared at one another across the fire. I set my hand on the hilt of my sword and thought back to my match against Julianne for what was surely the ten millionth time.

"I recall all of that," Jeeves said. "The turn in the match came just as Francisco and Helen walked into the stadium. You tried to get fancy."

A piece of bamboo hissed and whistled in the flames. I felt my jaw muscles tighten.

"You can wave your sword in circles all you want," Julianne finished, "but you should know that if you hadn't, you would have beaten me." The corners of her mouth curled upward. "Or at least you would have had a chance."

With that, she lay down on the sand and turned to face the canyon wall. She had her purple scarf wrapped across her back and it shimmered in the firelight.

"I'll take the watch," Jeeves said. "You two get some sleep."

Carter was coiled in a tight ball, with his head tucked beneath his middle. I stooped over to pet him, and his body trembled under my touch.

"Snakes aren't meant to spend a long time without heat or sun," Jeeves said, his brow furrowed. "I'm worried about him."

I brought the deadly serpent inside my shirt, over my chest, to try to warm him up. Next, I made myself a bed in the sand and stared up into the night sky. The words of my friends rolled over and over in my head like a three-banded armadillo . . .

The pirate Zeetan Z was charging out of the water toward me, a sword in his hand. I *felt* him, even though I couldn't see his face. I tried to force my head up but my body was bound tight. How had he found us?

I strained and tried to scream. Nothing. My enemy stood right above me now, and I looked up at him. His eyeholes were empty. Just black.

He was grabbing at me. I had to fight. I had get up. I lashed out. My balled fist cracked against something solid.

"Owww!"

My eyelids snapped open. Jeeves was on his knees by my side. His nose dripped blood. I sat up and looked at the water. It was calm and Gunting was still on his beach, slumped over. Carter slipped out of my shirt and into my lap. I panted, trying to catch my breath.

"Another nightmare," Jeeves said, pinching the bridge of his nose.

"They're getting worse," I gasped.

Jeeves fished into his pocket for a kerchief. "I noticed."

It took me a few minutes to calm down. "I'm sorry."

"You know," Jeeves said, dabbing his nose, "your father had a bout of terrible nightmares, right around the time you were born." He pulled the handkerchief away from his face. It was blotted with blood. "The more people you care about, the more there is to scare you in the world. And yet, if you didn't care about people, there would be nothing worth protecting."

I thought about what he said for a long time. "That's very wise, Jeeves. Is it okay if I write that in my adventure journal?"

Jeeves smiled. "I'd be honored."

"I mean, I might spice up the words a little, but still . . ."

The two of us sat in silence until Jeeves's head started to droop forward between his knees. I gently rolled him onto his side, noticing a crust of dried blood around his left nostril. Next, I stood up and stoked the fire so that it lit the whole canyon with a dancing red glow.

I wandered along the waterline, upstream, until I reached the bamboo grove. Jeeves's words about protecting the things you care about played over and over in my head. Then, gazing up at the bamboo, I had one of my most Zupanian ideas yet.

I drew my sword and chopped at the biggest of the closely crowded shoots.

SHEENK. CLACK! CLACK! CLACK!

The bamboo gave a groan and toppled. I picked another one.

CLACK! CLACK! CLACK!

"What are you doing over there?" Jeeves groaned from the fireside.

"Thrilling plan," I called downstream. "Brilliant scheme! Not to worry."

"That's *exactly* the sort of thing that worries me," he mumbled groggily.

Working by moonlight, I made a raft for us to sail down-river on. When bamboo sap coated my sword, I collected it and rolled it into a ball. It would be the perfect fuel for a torch as we navigated the dark cave.

As soon as I was done, I guided the raft upstream along the shoreline until it was hidden from sight by what was left of the bamboo grove.

I stepped back to admire my work, then crossed the sandbank to take one more look at Gunting before lying down next to Carter. By the time I fell asleep, the sky had already begun dissolving from black to purplish-gray.

FROM THE DESK OF
Thomas Halladay

A Conversation between Julianne Sato and
Tom Halladay (Part II)

In the morning, while Ronald slept, Julianne and I
both went to the water's edge to wash up.

Me: Your grandfather probably won't be too
happy with me when this is all over.
Julianne: Bring him that piñata full of candy
he was hoping for, and you'll be surprised how
understanding he can be.

There was a long pause as she brushed her teeth
with river water, then stashed her toothbrush in a
cargo-pant pocket.

Me: I do wish you and Ronald had a more bold
and daring butler to help you right now.
Julianne: You keep saying things like that,
but as far as I can tell, you're as bold and

daring as they come. I bet you'd be bored to
death butlering for Josh Brigand. I read in a
magazine that he gets four Swedish massages
every week and only goes out when he
absolutely has to.

Me: Excitement is overrated.

Julianne: I don't think you really believe
that. Not for a second.

33

Help from Above!

I woke up flat on my back. The sun hadn't crossed the side of the canyon yet, but the sky was already bright. My eyes slowly climbed the crags and edges jutting out of the rock wall.

I heard talking and sat up to find Julianne and Jeeves walking toward the fire pit from the river. Something was different about my good butler—more than just his swollen nose.

"Did you shave?" I asked.

His face flushed. "Just passed the edge of Julianne's sword across my cheeks."

"But you left the beginnings of a mustache?"

He lifted a single shoulder.

Julianne shot me a look. "Dashing, don't you think?"

"There's no denying it," I said with a smile.

Carter slid across the sand and tucked into a nook in the

canyon wall. I stood up and walked to the bottom of our sandbar with the spyglass. Gunting was awake now; his brow was knitted and his massive shoulders shone with sweat. Each hand held a smooth, mango-shaped rock. Beside the river's edge, he'd made a pyramid with ten or twelve of them.

"Friends," I called over my shoulder, "we have trouble."

They rushed over and we stood in a row. Gunting jabbed a meaty finger at us, then traced a path upward along the rock wall. He kept pointing, more and more urgently with one hand.

"He wants us to climb out," Julianne said.

I cupped my hands around my mouth. "We're here to rescue Francisco and Helen Zupan. We're not leaving without them!"

Gunting's face bunched in anger, and he pointed to the top of the cliffs again. "*Greeeeegh!*"

"I hope your cricket arm is rested," I said to Jeeves. "He's going to throw those rocks at us; we need to be ready to return fire."

Jeeves sucked his teeth, measuring the distance in his head. "Cricket bowlers don't often have to throw at an eight-foot colossus."

"It would make the game more interesting," I said. I noticed a piece of bamboo floating along the shoreline and remembered the raft. "Come this way. I want to show you two something."

I led them to the upstream end of the sandbank, where the raft waited at the water's edge.

"This way we won't have to swim for the rest of the trip," I told them, "*plus* we'll have light!"

Julianne looked ready to smile, but the moment was shattered by a **CRACK!** overhead. A stone exploded against the rock wall. Fragments scattered everywhere. Another rock came soaring overhead and splashed into the water beyond the sandbar.

"*Get down!*" Jeeves screamed.

My deduction was spot on: Gunting was hurling the rocks he'd gathered. One of them hit a thick bamboo shoot and split it in half. The broken end came down like a guillotine between Julianne and me.

"Carter!" I yelled.

I started for the fire pit, but Jeeves grabbed my arm and wrenched me back. "You'll be killed! I'll go."

I shook free. "Impossible. I need the skills of a cricketeer to cover me."

"I'll handle the supplies," Julianne said.

The three of us bolted out of the bamboo grove, toward the campfire. Gunting's stones tore through the air—missing us by just a few feet every time. Jeeves snatched up a rock and hurled it toward the giant, but the throw was short and it thudded to the sand. Gunting reared back again, launching a shot in my direction.

"*Ronald!*" Jeeves screamed.

I dove to the ground and the rock exploded against the canyon wall. Carter slithered out from his hiding place. I scrabbled toward him on hands and knees and flung him across my shoulders.

"I've got him!"

I sprang to my feet and began to run. Julianne snatched her violin case and the sailor's sack from beside the fire just as a stone slammed into the coals, sending a wave of embers spraying up into the air. We ran into the bamboo grove, rolling over a sand dune and down the other side. Jeeves came panting after us, and we took cover behind a clump of five sturdy shoots.

One more rock splashed into the river—then the attack stopped just as suddenly as it had begun.

"He's waiting for us to make a move," I said between heaving breaths.

Julianne took the spyglass and crawled to the edge of the sandbar to investigate. I followed her.

"You're right," she whispered. "He's on his knees in the water. Two rocks left."

I stood up to get a clearer look. "He's going to wait until—"

THLOOOOOOSH!

I sat up out of the water, dazed. Black seeds and gobs of orange fruit coated my body. Loud screeches echoed through the canyon, and I looked up at the cliffs.

> FACT: I'd been hit square in the chest by a papaya, thrown by one of Three-Fingered Jack's orangutans.

I scrambled for cover just as another papaya hit a bamboo shoot and rained gooey pulp down on me. The orangutan army hooted and cheered, hurling piece after piece of rotten fruit.

I jumped up and pointed over at Gunting. "*Him,* you apes! Not us!"

Julianne grabbed me and dragged me down to the ground just as another papaya whistled overhead. "That's why they came," she said. "The yelling."

The orangutans kept up their bombardment, and soon we were covered with mushy fruit. I glanced toward the water and saw half of a papaya bobbing right at the shoreline. I dodged out of the bamboo grove to grab it and ran it back to Jeeves.

"Hit Gunting and I bet he'll scream," I said. "Then maybe the orangutans will start attacking him instead of us."

Jeeves rubbed his shoulder. "My last throw was off. I'm a touch rusty."

"You can do it," Julianne said.

I grabbed Jeeves's arm. "Look at your mustache! You were born to be an adventurer."

Without a word, he ducked out of the bamboo grove, reared back, and hurled the piece of fruit at Gunting. The giant was distracted by the orangutans and didn't see it coming until it was too late. As the overripe fruit traveled a perfect arc toward him, the rogue turned his head, and the papaya exploded against his massive chin.

Screams of rage rebounded off the canyon walls and Three-Fingered Jack's orangutans scrambled downstream along the high rock ledge to investigate. A few of the bigger orangutans threw papayas at him. One direct shot filled Gunting's ear with black seeds. Julianne, Jeeves, Carter, and I all crawled out onto the sand to watch.

Another perfectly aimed papaya spiraled right for Gunting's giant head, but at the very last second he caught it. Then the giant's muscles rippled and he threw the papaya right back at the biggest orangutan. It was a direct hit, and the ape somersaulted backward, groaning in pain. The other orangutans backed off, looking ready to scurry away.

I was sure the plan had failed, but at that moment, Three-Fingered Jack himself stepped to the edge of the cliff.

"Well, hello down there!" he called to us. "Looks like

you're not such bumblers after all! Headed for the belly of the beast?"

"Indeed!" I yelled back. "But we could use a little help to get there!"

Gunting saw the hermit and roared—waving wildly at us and pointing to the top of the cliffs again. It was as if he thought Three-Fingered Jack could convince us to abandon our mission.

As the yells bounced through the canyon, Thee-Fingered Jack stared down at Gunting, his head tilted curiously. Then he slowly raised his arms and a loud hoot went up in the jungle. More than fifty orangutans rushed to the cliff's edge, and a hail of papayas soared into the canyon. Gunting was an easy target—papaya after papaya pummeled him, until he was covered in fruit mush.

The giant toppled backward into the water, arms flailing. The orangutans slapped their thighs in celebration. Gunting flopped and screamed, trying to fight his way back to land. It was hopeless. Over and over the rain of papayas knocked him back.

Finally, he had no choice but to turn downstream. The current swept him along and he swam ahead, into the next section of the cave.

FROM THE DESK OF
Thomas Halladay

An Addition to the Chapter "Help from Above!"

Have I mentioned I'm a cricketer? I have, right? I thought I might have lost some fire on the old bowl, but you should have *seen* the look on Gunting's face when I hit him with that papaya!

I mean, I hit him like he was the last remaining wicket before third tea break in a five-day test match. It was marvelous!

34
Life-and-Death Decisions!

"**W**e have to follow him!" Julianne yelled as the current carried Gunting down river.

"What?" Jeeves cried. "He almost killed us!"

"If he gets to Zeetan Z, then the whole pirate gang will be ready and waiting when we get there!"

Jeeves opened his mouth to argue.

"It's the only way," I said, grabbing his arm. "To the raft!"

We ran upstream, shoved the raft off the sandbar, and crawled aboard. I got to my feet and used a piece of bamboo to pole us into the current. Julianne secured the torch so that it could stand up without someone holding it.

A small, fire-red orangutan was still caught up in the excitement and hurled one last papaya at us. It was right on target, but Julianne turned at the last second and sliced it in half, midflight. One of the halves spun on the deck like a top. I picked it up, took a hearty bite, and gave Three-Fingered Jack a wave.

"Breakfast and a rescue in one!" I yelled. "Farewell strange hermit!"

He waved back with his mangled hand as we curved around the first bend in the river. "Good luck in the belly of the beast!"

We entered another tunnel. After a sunlit morning the cave suddenly felt darker than ever. Somewhere overhead, bats bickered and squeaked.

I dropped my papaya, steering us into the middle of the river while Jeeves lit the torch. Julianne held her cutlass high and kept her violin case poised like a shield. If Gunting was waiting, we'd be ready.

"There he is," Julianne said, pointing with the tip of her blade.

The giant drifted on his back, watching for us. When he saw the raft, he flopped over and started to swim farther ahead. The sputtering torchlight danced across the smooth stone arch of the cave roof. Just below it, we saw a split in the river.

Gunting arrived at this crossroads, hesitated for just a second, and swam left.

"What do we do?" Jeeves asked. "He might be tricking us!"

"I'll steer to the middle," I said. "You two brace the raft against the rock. We'll make a plan there."

I held a steady line and we crashed into the rock wall. The current swept past us to the left and right.

"Look," Jeeves said.

Right above our heads, the torch cast its flickering glow on a symbol carved into the stone and filled in with green lichen.

Julianne's eyes widened. "The dot must be some sort of code."

"It's simple," Jeeves said. "A dot on the left means we go left, just like Gunting . . . right?"

The tail of the raft got caught up in the current. I jammed the pole into the riverbed and leaned on it with my bruised shoulder. A jolt of pain shot all the way down to my hip.

Julianne's eyes frantically scanned the symbol for some extra clue. "Pirates used to use black dots to mean death."

One corner of the raft dipped below the surface and cool water washed over our legs.

Jeeves looked at me. "Any hunches?"

"Here's a hunch," I said, fighting against the pole. "Choosing wrong could get us all killed."

"We're losing him!" Julianne warned.

Already, the sound of Gunting's swimming had been drowned out. Beneath us, the river sucked at the nose of the raft and it swung hard to the left. The pole skidded across the river bottom. Jeeves lost his balance and landed on his back. The raft spun once, bounced against a wall, and sucked us down the left side of the split.

"Was that on purpose?" Julianne asked, her voice filled with panic.

"That *is* the question, isn't it?" I said, after a moment of petrified silence. "I'll have an answer just as soon as we know if it was the right choice."

Julianne stepped as close as she could to the torch, which was already weakening. Working quickly, she tore her scarf down the middle, tied one piece of the fabric around her waist and used the other to cinch her violin case to the small of her back.

We bounced off an exposed rock and bumped down a series of small rapids.

"There he is!" Jeeves called.

Up ahead, Gunting was lit by sunlight seeping into a jagged crack along the cave ceiling. The light cast shadows through the cave—making the giant's scarred face look more ghastly than ever.

"Another fork in the river!" I announced.

My words were muffled by the sound of surging water. The two rivers had joined again and the current sped up. The river sloshed up over the sides of the raft and we thudded against a submerged rock. All three of us fell to our knees.

When we got to our feet again, we saw that Gunting had his back up against the wall where the river split. His arms were spread wide.

"Why isn't he going?" Jeeves cried. "*Go, you devil!*"

I dragged the bamboo pole, but it was little use.

"He's going to wait," I yelled. "He wants to catch us as we pass."

Julianne stepped to the front edge of the raft with her sword at the ready. Jeeves stood at the middle of the raft with Carter. He yanked on the torch pole so that it wasn't connected to the raft anymore and held it out over Julianne's head like an angler fish.

Gunting started waving us toward the right side of the fork.

"Look!" Julianne pointed with the tip of her sword. Just above Gunting's head, lit by the torch, we saw a second symbol:

"Two dots left!" Julianne called out. "This is the second split. So we go left again?"

"Gunting is trying to force us right!" Jeeves yelled. "That definitely means we should go left!"

I didn't say anything. Both ideas made sense, so I steered the raft to the far left side of the tunnel. But there was something strange going on. I couldn't quite puzzle out the look on Gunting's face, and a constrictor knot had started tightening in the pit of my stomach.

As we boomed past him, Gunting gripped the wall with one hand and leaned out toward us. He wasn't about to tangle with Julianne's sword, but he still made a grab for the back corner of the raft. We slipped past him by just a few inches.

When he saw that he'd missed us, Gunting's eyes squeezed shut in agony. The expression felt like the last piece of a puzzle. Over and over, the giant had tried to get us to leave the cave. He'd missed us with every boulder he threw, but he'd hit the leader of the orangutans with a papaya on the first try. And what was the note he'd written to Pemburu back in the saloon? They were arguing over something, and they didn't attack until Pemburu said, "We do things my way this time."

I jerked the bamboo steering pole out of the water and stretched it toward the giant. Gunting lunged into the middle of the river to try to grab it, but my deductions had come too late. He had to swim back to the wall to keep from getting carried downstream. As he gripped the wall with one hand, Gunting let out a miserable wail that echoed through the cave.

"*What in the world are you doing?*" Jeeves demanded.

"We're going the wrong way!" I yelled. "Gunting doesn't want to hurt us, he's just been trying to scare us away."

Jeeves scoffed. "Need I remind you that he spent the morning throwing boulders at us?"

"He could have hit us if he wanted to," I grunted, trying desperately to slow down the raft.

Julianne turned her head to face me. "So if he doesn't want to hurt us, and he tried to stop us from going down this way, then . . ."

FACT: We were headed for trouble.

FROM THE DESK OF
Thomas Halladay

Errors in the Chapter "Life-and-Death Decisions!"

None. Sadly, dangerously, Ronald is telling it
exactly like it happened.

35

Treacherous Traps!

The current dragged our raft deeper into the tunnel, and the river narrowed until we could touch the walls on either side. The ceiling was just a few feet over Jeeves's head.

"Friends," I announced, "I believe we're caught in—"

"Spiderwebs," Julianne said from the bow.

"I was going to say 'a trap,'" I said as the first sticky threads clung to my arms and face, "but—*agk*—yes, spiderwebs!"

These weren't ordinary spiderwebs, either. In the last of the dying torchlight, we saw the shadowy outlines of entombed bats tangled in the crisscrossing lines. I passed the steering pole to Jeeves and went to stand at the front of the raft with Julianne. We swung our swords back and forth to clear a path.

The tightness of the tunnel magnified the sound of the churning water as the current rushed along. Jeeves did his best to slow our progress, but we only gained speed. I felt the hairy legs of a spider the size of an orange scurry across my wrist and shook my arm to get it off, nearly flinging my sword into the darkness.

TWANG!

I jerked my arm back. I'd struck something tauter and tougher to break than a spiderweb. *A trip wire!*

"Get upstream!" I yelled.

In an instant, the tunnel filled with the echo of boulders cracking against one another. Pinpricks of sunlight sliced through the tunnel.

AND
    THE
        CAVE
            BEGAN
                TO
                    COLLAPSE.

We leaped off the back of the raft just as a colossal boulder landed on the bow. It catapulted us and we flew into the air—splashing into the river, kicking to the surface, and swimming away from the falling rocks as if our lives depended on it.

The sound of the cave collapsing was deafening. Then, just as quickly as it had started, the noise stopped and the tunnel fell silent. We let the current suck us back downstream.

"Trip wire," I panted. "I hit it with my sword."

In the gray half-light I could see huge rocks piled out of the water. I found footing and stood up. I could make out Julianne and Jeeves on either side of me. Neither of them said a word.

The rocks had dammed the river, and it quickly began to rise. We looked overhead. It was impossible to tell just what sort of mechanism had held the boulders in place. They'd left behind a gaping cavity in the cave ceiling. A few thin shafts of light filtered down from above.

I slung the sailor's sack over my shoulder and began to scramble up the rocks. Julianne followed silently. Jeeves brought up the rear, with Carter looped around his shoulder.

The boulders had bounced and stacked unevenly. Before we could get over the barrier, we had to wriggle between the jagged edges of the stones and the clammy cave ceiling.

On the back side of the rock pile, a few bamboo shoots from our ruined raft jutted out from between boulders at odd angles. The water on our side of the dam was just a few inches deep. Julianne silently peeled a spiderweb out of her hair. Jeeves pressed his hands against Carter's body to try to warm our cold-blooded compatriot.

Another monstrous crack echoed overhead, and we flinched in unison. It wasn't rocks this time; it was thunder. Up above, we could hear a monsoon storm begin lashing the jungle. The little bit of light coming in dimmed, and I imagined the clouds filling in to block out the sun.

Streams of muddy water dripped through the tiny holes in the cave ceiling and splashed against the mound of boulders. It made a sound like clockwork: **CLICK-CLICK-CLICK-CLICK-CLICK.** Or maybe the clockwork sound came from the clicking jaws of Goliath tarantulas, I couldn't be sure.

We dragged ourselves forward, listening to the steady clicking, too tired to speak. After we took a few cautious steps, the slivers of light faded away.

I drew the candle from the sailor's sack and lit the wick. It sputtered and fizzled out. I tried a second match. The flame caught—burning blue at first, then pale yellow. Only two matches left.

The bottom of the river was smooth but not slick. I walked in the lead, with the candle in one hand and my sword in the other, looking up at the spiderwebs that crisscrossed overhead. We listened with our ears pricked to the continuous **CLICK-CLICK-CLICK.**

"What *is* that sound?" Jeeves asked.

Up ahead, the two rivers joined up again. It couldn't have been far, maybe fifty feet. Beyond that there was more light, probably another sinkhole.

"*Freeze!*" Julianne's voice rebounded through the tunnel. She slowly came up beside me. "There, look."

An inch away from my neck was another trip wire. I lifted the candle high, then swung it out wide to study the cave walls.

*CLICK-CLICK-CLICK-
CLICK-CLICK-
CLICK.*

Jeeves craned his neck to look above us. "Oh no," he said. "See that?"

He pointed to an arrow tucked inside a divot in the limestone on the left side of the tunnel. I went on tiptoes to inspect it. The arrow was made of bamboo, and its sharpened point was aimed right at us.

Behind us, the water breached the rock pile and started gushing over. In seconds, it had risen to my knees.

*CLICK-CLICK-CLICK-
CLICK-CLICK-
CLICK.*

"The course of an adventure never did run smoothly," I said with a low whistle. "The arrows must be catapulted somehow. Mind those wires, Sato."

There was a second arrow just past the trip wire and a third pointing down from the cave roof. They were hidden in every small crevasse or split in the rock. I passed Julianne the candle and she leaned close to study the trip wire.

"It's just tied off to a bolt," she reported. "It doesn't lead to anything."

We stepped under it.

"And there's another," said Jeeves.

A second wire crossed the tunnel. This one would have been underwater if the boulders hadn't dammed the river. It was tied to the wall, just like the first one.

We moved on, one inch at a time. We came to a third trip wire, then a fourth.

"Why would Zeetan Z set up all these fake trip wires?" Jeeves asked.

"Oh no." Julianne's voice was flooded with fear. "He's trying to slow us down."

CLICK!
CLICK!
CLICK!
CLICK!
CLICK!
CLICK!
CLICK!

The sound ticked faster now, like it was racing toward a finish line. I realized that it wasn't rain. Or spiders. It was another trap—some sort of mechanical gear system, ticking down to our doom.

"*Run!*" I yelled.

We sprinted for the end of the tunnel, tearing through false trip wires, trying to get away from whatever new danger was coming. In front of us, the tunnel opened up. It wasn't far off at all now.

There was a loud twang up ahead of us, and an arrow clacked against the limestone.

"Back!" I yelled.

The current was already up to our waists—we did our best to charge against it. The river pulled at us like the fingers of death itself, trying to drag us toward a grisly fate. The next arrow that whizzed through the tunnel came from the upstream side. Then more arrows. The sound built as a barrage of arrows swept toward us from both directions. One whistled past me and the left side of my face went hot.

"*Down!*" Jeeves screamed.

We plunged into the shallow water. Jeeves must've found something along the wall to grab on to. He reached out with one long arm and hooked us toward him. I searched blindly until I found Julianne's hand. Her fingernails dug into my palm; her hair washed across my face. My heart pounded in my ears.

Jeeves was the first one to rise to the surface. A second

later, he pulled Julianne and me up, both gasping. The arrows had stopped. Julianne fought to catch her breath. Jeeves and I steadied her against a wave-shaped curve where the tunnel wall jutted into the river.

"I'm okay," she panted. "I'm okay, I'm okay, I'm okay, I'm okay, I'm okay, I'm okay, I'm okay, I'm okay, I'm okay, I'm okay."

The more she said it, the less convincing it sounded. She shuddered and drew an uneven breath. I relit the candle and rested one hand lightly on her shoulder.

Her eyes focused on me; I could see them glisten with tears. Her pupils were the size of dimes.

"We have to get out of here," Julianne said. "We have to get out of this cave."

I wanted to promise her that we would. I wanted to swear on the Zupan name that we would evade each treacherous trap laid by Zeetan Z. But I wasn't so sure anymore.

"Carter isn't moving," Jeeves said after a minute.

I felt a lump leap into my throat. "Is he . . . ?"

Jeeves shook his head. "He isn't dead. I think he's gone into a torpor."

I reached up toward Jeeves's shoulder and brushed my fingertips across the cobra's head. "What's a . . . a . . ." I trailed off and blinked once, twice. My dazzlingly sharp thoughts had gone adrift. Jeeves looked at me, then back to the snake.

"Torpor is when the snake can't keep his body heat

up," he explained. "He grows sluggish and falls into a deep sleep."

"Deeeeeeeeep sleeeeeeeeeeeeeeeep," I slurred. My tongue felt like it was swollen. Something strange was happening to my body—I slumped against the cave wall.

"Ronald, you're bleeding," said Julianne. She grabbed my arm and tried to hold me up.

I felt warm fluid on my face and remembered the arrow that had whistled past me.

"'Tis . . . but . . . a . . . scratch," I announced boldly. The words felt thick and sticky in my mouth.

Julianne took the candle from me and shone it on my ear. "You've been hit by an arrow!"

My friends inspected my wound.

"Soooo sliiiiguuuuuush." My knees buckled and I felt Jeeves grab me. My eyelids were heavy. So, so, so, so, so, so, so, so, so, so, so, so, so, so heavy. So I let them drop

and

       collapsed

           into

              a

t
o
r
p
o
r

of

my

own.

An Error in the Chapter "Treacherous Traps!"

1. Unlike Carter, Ronald hadn't gone into torpor because of the cool water or lack of sunlight.

"The arrows must've been poisoned," Julianne said.

I tried to hold Ronald up, but there wasn't much that could be done. He was breathing, and, yet, just like the snake, he was completely unresponsive.

I washed the wound on his ear, splashed water across his face, but still he slept on.

A heavy mist gathered at the end of our tunnel.

"Try slapping him," Julianne said.

"What?" I scoffed. "Absolutely not."

She mimed a giant slap.

"You slap him," I said.

"You're his butler," she insisted. "It's your duty. Hurry!"

"You really think it'll work?"

"We have to try *something*!"

That much was true. So I pulled back my hand, hesitated, gritted my teeth and . . .

36
Liquid Death!

My eyes snapped open. Jeeves was holding me propped up against the wall. Julianne leaned in beside him with the candle.

"What happened?" I groaned.

"You were hit by a poison arrow," Jeeves explained. "We fanned you gently and suddenly you awoke. No one slapped you, if that's what you're wondering. Feeling better then?"

"Jeeves," I said, "didn't I tell you that **Ronald Zupan** is immune to poisons of all varieties?"

I tried to get to my feet but staggered and had to brace myself against the wall. Julianne snatched an arrow as it floated along with the current, inspecting the tip closely.

"I think the poison was weakened by all the moisture in the cave," she said. "You're lucky to be standing."

I fingered the notch in my earlobe where the arrow had clipped me—enough for an impressive scar, no doubt, but nothing more. As Helen Zupan says, "Though injuries may put us on our heels, eventually they're bound to heal."

I massaged my jaw. "My face stings too."

Julianne passed me the candle. "Oh, that's because—"

"*Of the poison*," Jeeves finished for her. "It's because of the poison. An unfortunate side effect, no doubt."

We started moving again, very slowly. The water was at my shoulders now, and we half drifted, half walked. Jeeves held Carter completely out of the river, but the snake showed no signs of life.

We didn't go far before coming upon three tightly bound bamboo shoots from our destroyed raft. They were wedged firmly into a small pocket in the tunnel wall and had cracked in the middle. Julianne dislodged the shoots and we draped our arms over them, cautiously allowing ourselves to drift along with the current.

Just before the end of our tunnel, we braced ourselves against a thick stalactite to make a plan. A few feet in front of us, the rivers met again in a wide cavern. There was a hole in the roof the shape and size of a manta ray. Streams of muddy water gushed down from above, thunder rumbled furiously, and each bolt of lightning lit up our grotto. Ghosts of steam swam away from the walls and collected in a thick gray cloud below the hole in the ceiling.

"No sign of Gunting," Jeeves said. "Which I think is a

good thing. He might not want to hurt us, but he hasn't done much to help us either."

He gripped the bamboo under one arm, braced against the stalactite with the other, and wrapped Carter around his neck. Julianne surveyed the wild, swirling water in front of us. I blew out the candle, tucked it inside the sailor's sack, and cinched the sack tightly around my torso.

Turning to her, I asked, "You ready, Sato?"

For a long moment, she didn't answer. The water rushed past us, splashing up on the tunnel walls.

"I don't know if I'd ever be ready," she said finally. "But since we don't have any choice . . ." She forced a weak smile. "The next time we go on an adventure, we're going to a desert, okay?"

"Next time," I said.

On the count of three, we let the current sweep us forward, holding the pieces of bamboo for dear life. We boomed downstream, tearing through the fog. The river carried us into the main part of the cavern, where the rapids spat and bubbled while muddy water poured in from above.

At the far end of the room, the river branched a third time. We swam for the wall between the split, each squeezing the bamboo under one arm and paddling with the other. Jeeves stretched his neck to keep Carter out of the water.

"Paddle!" Julianne yelled. "Paddle!"

Whirlpools sucked at our legs, doing their best to pull us below the surface, while we fought to stay afloat.

As we approached the wall, a rapid caught the bamboo and slammed all three of us roughly into the limestone. We'd ended up in a punchbowl eroded out of the cave. It was shallow enough to stand—a frothy mix of muddy foam and twigs swirled around us.

By the dim light we saw a third marking overhead:

Jeeves pressed his face against Carter's body, doing his best to warm the snake.

"Seeing as the last choice left us nearly crushed and skewered," he said, "anyone have any ideas?"

We all studied the wall.

"The first skull had one dot to the left and we went left," Julianne said, fighting to catch her breath. "Then the second one had two dots to the left and we went left again."

"But that was wrong," I said.

"Exactly. So with two dots, we were *supposed* to do the opposite, and with one dot, we go in the direction of the dot."

"Are you sure?" Jeeves asked her.

"Not in the least."

"I vote we go with it," I said over the noise of the river. "It's the best chance we've got."

We headed toward the right side of the fork. The tunnel immediately tightened; the low ceiling blocked out most of the light. It was pitch-black in a matter of seconds. I took the lead and waved my sword out ahead of me like the trunk of a drunken elephant.

The spiderwebs were thinner here, but the fear of trip wires was stronger than ever. Plus it seemed very possible that Gunting was in the tunnel waiting for us. I knew one part of him didn't want to hurt us, but the other part *clearly* didn't want us to reach Zeetan Z, and I wasn't excited to figure out which side of his personality would show up the next time we met.

Shhhhrklank! My blade scraped something solid. A wall.

The river drove us against the rock. I slid my sword through my belt and tried to read the limestone surface with my hands.

"It's a dead end," Julianne said. "Are we . . . ?"

I kicked off the wall against the current, grasping at the sides of the tunnel; they were smooth and slick. No handholds anywhere; no way to get back upstream. No light.

"There must be an escape," Julianne said, her voice swelling with fear. "Right? There *has* to be."

I reached for the last waterproof match and scraped it against the rock wall. Nothing. I tried again and again, but it was a dud. Now the darkness was yet another villain to be dealt with. I desperately searched the wall with my fingertips again—I felt for etchings, a clue, a skull chiseled into the stone, *anything*.

"I must have been wrong," Julianne said in a far-off voice. "It's my fault."

"Don't be silly," Jeeves told her. "It was the best guess we had."

I found a tiny crack in the wall and tried to pull it apart, imagining a hidden door that might suddenly spring open.

"And something else," Julianne added, "all that rain coming in . . . it's making the water rise."

FROM THE DESK OF
Thomas Halladay

A Note from the Chapter "Liquid Death!"

For all the danger we had been in and all the strange
foes we had faced, a simple rainstorm looked like it
would be the last straw. The monsoon aboveground was
filling up the whole system of caves. Rainwater
was coursing through the jungle and rushing into the
sinkholes across the island. The river had become a
wild surge, and the water was rising quickly.

How odd to think that we had survived a tongueless
giant, a crazed hermit, a clouded leopard, and all
sorts of other dangers, only to be doomed by a flood.

37
Masterful Deductions!

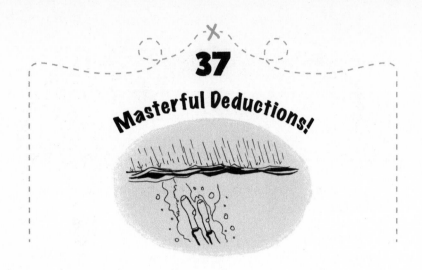

Our tunnel was flooding from above. I imagined every stream in the jungle turning into a torrent and breaching its banks. All that water was running toward us. We would drown. Each strike of thunder was a crack of doom; each droplet of water was a curse.

"What now?" Jeeves asked. "We've got to do something!"

Using the bamboo as a lever, we tried to fight upstream, but it was hopeless. Each time one of us made progress, another slipped and was ripped back to the wall by the current. I lifted my hand—there were only two feet left between the waterline and the ceiling.

Julianne took her violin off her back and bashed the case against the limestone. "No!" she cried. "*NO! NO! NO!*"

"Sato," I said, "we'll get out of this."

She kept pounding wildly.

"Julianne Sato, we will not drown," I promised. "It . . . it just isn't how this adventure ends. I'll swim right through the wall if I have to."

Julianne stopped beating the wall and broke down in heaving sobs.

"Occam's razor," Jeeves murmured distantly.

"Please," I said, "now really isn't the time."

"Occam's razor," he repeated. "*Occam's! Razor!*"

Julianne stopped crying. "What are you—"

"The easiest answer is the best!" Jeeves said. "Ronald told you that he'd swim through the wall, and he was right. This cave would be filling up a lot faster if none of the water was going anywhere. There must be an underwater tunnel!"

"Jeeves, you're brilliant," Julianne cheered. "Occam's razor!"

We both dove for him at once, hugging him from opposite sides. Hope had returned to the cave, and not a second too soon. Now it was time for us to make our great escape.

"Sato," I said, "if ever something was going to feel like drowning, this is it. We're each going to have to search blindly for whatever tunnel is down there."

The top of my head brushed the cool roof of the cave. There was less than a foot of air in the tunnel now.

"Well," Julianne said, "I didn't practice holding my breath in the backyard for nothing."

"Downward," I told my friends. "Hopefully the current will do most of the work."

We had to angle our necks just to draw our last gulps of air. Jeeves dove first. Julianne went next, a few seconds later. The water lapped against the ceiling, and I followed them— somersaulting and kicking off the rock.

The darkness swallowed me. This was truly the belly of the beast. My ears popped. I traced the wall deeper and deeper still. Finally, I found the tunnel and it sucked me in.

Once the current had me, there was nothing to do but trust it. I kept my hands stretched out, soaring through pure blackness. The air in my lungs aged and began to grow stale. Gradually, the water ahead of me turned to midnight blue. It was softening, shifting with every second. I thought of the shimmering sword that cuts through stone.

Light! I let out a silent, victorious cheer—only to feel my body wrenched back. I was snagged. I fought to shake free but couldn't. I flailed and kicked. The sailor's sack had gotten caught on a piece of limestone. I grabbed the sides of the tunnel and pulled forward with all my strength. My lungs screamed for air.

I tried to squirm out of the sailor's sack, but I couldn't. I reached for my sword to cut myself free, but there was no room to draw it. The darkness gripped me with its long, icy fingers, daring me to take a gulp of the cool water. White fireworks pulsed behind my eyes, then began to dim.

A single foggy thought formed in my head. "Mom, Dad, I failed you."

My body jerked forward, but I'd already given up. The second jolt was harder, too strong to ignore. I wrestled my eyes open.

My brilliant butler grabbed me by the armpits, pressed his feet against the wall, and fought to break me free. The snag in the sailor's sack pulled tight, stretched, and finally gave. I was loose.

We raced toward the light and burst out of the water. I gasped and choked as Jeeves dragged me to safety. We'd surfaced in a deep basin that was filled by water shooting out of the tunnel. To my right, the river plunged over a waterfall. I looked left and saw Julianne beaming at me. She was safe.

Jeeves's face was less than an inch from mine. In the faint light I could see his pupils reaching all the way out to the whites of his eyes.

"You came back for me," I said.

"*Fact*," he replied with a lopsided smile.

Julianne was holding Carter now, and I reached over to brush his cool skin. He was still deep in his torpor, but at least he was alive.

"Sato," I said, "that was close."

"But we made it," she said. "We didn't drown."

We peered out over the edge of our pool. Below us, the river spread into an enormous underground lagoon, wider than all of Zupan Hangar. At the far end of the lake, a giant wooden ship stood at anchor. The three of us gasped in unison.

This was it, Zeetan Z's lair.

Hazy light and trickles of water filtered down from above. The roof was at least a hundred feet overhead, with one lightning-shaped gash in the rock and dozens of small sinkholes. Up on land, the monsoon seemed to be weakening.

We climbed up on a rock shelf. Jeeves drew the spyglass from his pocket and handed it to me. I closed my left eye and pressed the cool brass to my cheek.

The stolen pirate ship sat twenty or so feet offshore, with a few smaller boats knocking up against its stern. The far left corner of the lake was wrapped in a sandy beach. Along the edge of the beach sat a collection of ramshackle huts made from wood and tin. Iron candleholders were set right into the stone, and massive candles dripped wax down the cave walls.

"Can you read the name of the ship?" Julianne asked.

The light was weak, but the words were made of big black letters painted against a yellow backdrop.

"The *Charming*—the charming something."

"The *Charming Yet Highly Dangerous Gentleman of Fortune*," Julianne finished. "That's Josh Brigand's ship all right."

I glanced at my friends. "The man knows how to name a ship, I'll give him that."

I suddenly remembered the lion and was hit by a wave of panic. I yanked off the sailor's sack. There was a tear in the fabric, where I'd been caught—hopefully it wasn't big

enough for the relic to slip out. I plunged my arm inside and released a sigh as my fingers found the grapefruit-sized candle.

A breeze blew upstream, and Jeeves's face contorted in disgust. "What is that *smell*?"

I wrinkled my nose. "Ammonia?"

Julianne pointed to the far, shadowy reaches of the cave, across the lake from the pirate camp, where more than a thousand bats clung to the ceiling, shifting and bickering. Below them rested a massive ash-colored mound in the shape of a pyramid.

"See that pile?" Julianne said. "It's bat guano. We're looking at an entire pyramid of poop."

She took a closer look with the spyglass and I faced Jeeves, who was busy wrapping my lethargic pet around his neck. I reached out, wishing that the cobra would strike me. My touch didn't even faze him.

"Hang on," I said, brushing my fingertips across the snake's clammy scales. "We'll be back in the sunlight soon."

Julianne gasped and pulled the spyglass away from her eye.

"Guys," she said, "someone's moving in the pirate camp."

Errors in the Chapter "Masterful Deductions!"

Errors? Yes, errors!

1. Ronald's claim of a thousand bats seems a tad off to me. Somehow I remember it closer to ten thousand. Maybe more.

2. That "pyramid" of guano? I remember it being the same size as the Great Pyramid of Khufu. Gigantic.

3. As for the pirate camp, I've never seen a more scurvy-ridden rat hole. Festering, horrid, putrid.

Surely you see what I'm getting at here. Is it possible? For the first time ever, I believe Ronald Zupan has managed to *under*exaggerate.

38

Final Battles!

Julianne pointed at the shacks lining the beach. "There are twelve of them, and two . . ."

The words seemed to catch in her throat. She handed the spyglass back to me. I saw two prisoners sitting up against a wall, with their hands tied behind them. Their faces were strained—but I knew exactly who I was looking at.

Jeeves set his hand on my shoulder. "Stay strong. They're alive."

FACT: A master adventurer never shows weakness. If my eyes were watering, it was because of the guano.

I splashed my face. Even without the spyglass I could make out a whole gang of pirates jerking my parents to their feet. They herded them into a skiff and paddled out to the ship.

Unlike the glass windows and blunt swords back in Pemburu's saloon, the ship was very real. It had two masts—main and mizzen—and there were sails tied up on the yardarm. At the back of the ship was a ten-foot-tall iron scaffold, built up on the quarterdeck. It had giant movie lights mounted to it and the biggest camera I'd ever seen.

Somewhere belowdecks, a generator rumbled to life. The lights began to hum and flooded the ship in a crisp white glow.

"I'm going closer," I told my friends. "The light on deck will make it hard for them to see." I leveled my eyes at Julianne first, then Jeeves. "You two could stay here, both of you, and sneak out of the cave at night. You've done so much already. It's not—"

"Stop," Julianne said. "I'm glad I came."

"Me too," Jeeves said. "I mean, I didn't really have a choice, but still . . . glad."

I drew a deep breath. "Once more unto the breach, dear friends."

We moved into the middle of the rock pool and let the current take us. It launched us over the waterfall, which felt like being shot from a cannon. I dove deep, surfaced, and began to swim in silence with my brave compatriots beside me.

Halfway to the ship, in the middle of the lake, a giant boulder rose up like the hump of a whale. We crawled up the back side and peered over the crest. The lights showed the action aboard the ship perfectly. I drew the spyglass again.

By now, the roughneck scalawags had forced my parents onto the deck, between the two masts. One of the sea devils was busy scampering up the ratlines, where he looped two ropes around the highest arm of the main mast. I watched in horror as the other crewmembers grabbed the ropes and hoisted my parents high up into the rigging, where they hung by their ankles.

The pirates tied the ropes off at the bottom of the mast and left my parents to swing. Francisco was about ten feet above Helen, probably so that they couldn't try to untie each other.

Next, one of the pirates stepped forward. "Hey you false-faced scupper rats, you've got some squawking to do!"

His yells ricocheted around the grotto—still loud enough to hear over the squeaks of bats and the crashing of the waterfall behind us.

"I'm going to get the captain now. You remember him? He's the man that was born in the seventh spleen of a tiger shark. Zeetan Z be the name. He's going to see if you mullet-headed scugs want to talk this time! Do you mullet-headed scugs want to talk?"

Jeeves furrowed his brow. "Mullet-headed scugs? Seventh spleen of a tiger shark?"

"I bet that guy stole those lines straight from the script of Josh Brigand's movie," Julianne said.

I gritted my teeth. "No one calls Francisco and Helen Zupan false-faced scupper rats and gets away with it."

We scrambled down the front side of the boulder and back into the water.

"Sato," I asked, "are you ready for the fencing match of your life?"

She gave me a solemn nod.

I patted Jeeves on the back. "And you still have the most venomous snake known to man?"

He sighed. "Nonvenomous. And I'm afraid he's in a torpor. He'll need some heat before he wakes up."

"What about your cricket arm?"

"I haven't felt this loose since I bowled one hundred wickets in the great test match at—"

"Take the lion," I told him. I fished inside the sack for the wax-encrusted relic and left all our other gear on the rock. "If I ask you to throw it, throw it."

Jeeves and Julianne both gaped at me.

"It's still just a statue," I said. "If it can help us survive, throw the thing."

We slipped back into the water. Swimming would be too loud, so we angled our bodies to let the current sweep us toward the ship. When we were just a stone's throw away, we dipped even lower—leaving only our noses and eyes above the surface. A hush came over the pirates.

A man stepped from the shadows and into the glow of the spotlights. He wore a red sailor's coat and a leather tricorn hat. His thin, oily hair fell from below the hat, and his stringy beard grew in uneven patches. His eyebrows were heavy, and his nose had been broken and rebroken.

The pirates began to clap and cheer and this new villain basked in their applause. He drew his sword and dramatically cut a "Z" in the thick cave air. The crew roared. Finally, the man held out his hand to speak. He glared up at my parents, dangling by their ankles above.

"I've tried to reason with you for days now," he shouted, "but this is where my patience ends!"

The voice was rough and cold. It didn't take any spectacular deductions to know that we'd finally found the nefarious Zeetan Z.

A Note on Our Enemies

Pemburu was a conniving rogue. I knew it from the
moment I saw him. Three-Fingered Jack was batty, but
not evil. Gunting could snap a man's arm like a
crisp carrot if he chose to—but as Ronald figured
out, he just wanted to scare us into abandoning our
mission.

   Then there was Zeetan Z. The villain was truly
heartless. It was right there in his cold, empty
eyes . . . and it terrified me half to death.

39

Counting Down!

We swam toward the front of the ship and found the anchor line. Julianne and Jeeves immediately began to shimmy up. I paused before following them, taking a second to edge out past the hull and peek skyward at my parents. In classic Zupanian form, they were both working on the ropes that bound their wrists.

I started climbing after my friends.

"*Whoagamush!*" A massive, bellowing yell came from the far end of the cave, followed by a mighty splash.

"What was *that*?" Zeetan Z's voice echoed.

Julianne stopped halfway up the anchor line and looked at me over her shoulder. "*Gunting,*" she mouthed.

I wondered if he knew we were still alive. What would he do once he saw us? Now that we'd made it to Zeetan Z, would he try to smash us like mealworms?

With the pirates distracted, Julianne, Jeeves, and I slipped over the rail near the front of the ship and dove behind a row of barrels.

Zeetan Z sheathed his sword. "Someone go check it out!"

Feet thudded across the decks. We peered over the edge of the barrels and saw three pirates climbing overboard. They clambered into a motorboat and buzzed off toward the falls.

"Now or never," I said to my friends.

Two crooked piles of crates towered beside the mainmast. They leaned dangerously and blocked our view. We could only get quick glimpses of Zeetan Z as he paced the decks— the flash of gray eyes, the glint of a silver tooth. On one pass I saw him lift his hand to touch a necklace made of small, odd-shaped pieces of bone.

"Wake up your tongues, you bloodstained layabouts," he bellowed up to my parents. "Or prepare to meet your doom!"

"You've already waited so long," Francisco called down, "you won't do anything until you find the Lion of Lyros."

"So says you!" Zeetan Z snarled. "The lion will turn up soon enough. I already sent some Liars' Club friends of ours called the FIB to search your house."

"FIB?" my father laughed. "They are kittens."

Zeetan Z frowned at this. "The lion will be found. I'll have the entire Liars' Club search for it if I have to. Till then, I believe I could be satisfied being the sea dog that got rid of Francisco and Helen Zupan for good." He spun to face his crew. "What say you, me hearties?"

"Aye!" his crew yelled.

Zeetan Z's voice softened. "Now perhaps, with the lion in hand, I might be swayed to show an ounce of mercy."

I heard movement on our side of the ship and turned my head to see Jeeves scuttling over to the opposite rail, where he ducked behind a lifeboat. There was an oar inside, and he silently removed it from its berth. I motioned him to stay crouched.

Zeetan Z crossed to the mainmast, drew his sword, and let the blade hover over the ropes that held my parents aloft. My throat tightened.

"So, you split-tongued dogs," he yelled up, "will you talk?"

"We've followed your dastardly deeds for years," Francisco called down. "So we know that even if we talk, you will not spare us."

Zeetan Z paused, then let out a murderous cackle. "You're right! You're so right!"

His pirates stomped and laughed. I looked up at my mother. Her hair hung down in a single golden sheet.

"I've told you over and over," she called down. "The lion lies in the light."

"*I don't know what that nonsense riddle means!*" Zeetan Z screamed. "Counting down. Ten . . . nine . . . eight . . ."

My parents were swaying slightly, and for a split second I glimpsed my mother's face. Hearing her repeat the clue sent the gears in my head whirring and clicking, but there was no time to think about it.

Julianne and I readied our swords. The buzzing of a motorboat drew closer.

"Seven . . . six . . . five . . ."

"Boss!" came a yell. "It's Gunting! He came in through the back passageway! Someone busted him up awful!"

Zeetan Z stopped counting.

"Bring him here!" the rogue snarled.

"He wants to write somethin'. Who's got a pen?"

The sour-faced captain waited as his crew scrambled to hoist Gunting up onto the quarterdeck. Four pirates wrestled him into a sitting position and leaned up against the scaffolding of the light tower. The men were all dressed in filthy costumes, with bright yellow scarves around their necks and dyed silks covering their matted hair.

Someone found a piece of charcoal, and Gunting frantically began scrawling words onto the deck of the ship. Zeetan Z read over his shoulder.

"What do you mean you couldn't catch them, you worthless bilge rat?" he snarled.

Gunting wrote something else, and Zeetan Z nodded. "Are you sure they didn't make it past the traps?"

The giant's face was blocked from view, but I saw Zeetan Z's arm draw back, then rocket forward with fury. The loud slap of skin on skin rang out across the deck. I shot a glance to Jeeves, who was watching with wide eyes.

"You colossal idiot," Zeetan Z yelled at Gunting. "You half-witted elephant. I asked, are you *sure* the children didn't make it past the traps?"

It was silent on deck while Gunting scribbled out his next answer. Zeetan Z studied him with hateful eyes.

"You'd better hope so, you squelching pile of miserable filth. I've already cut off your tongue—you don't want to see what happens next time you fail me."

Zeetan Z refocused on my parents, his voice full of daggers. Spittle flew from his lips. "Three people tried to rescue you. Two of them were children. It *didn't* work out so well."

My mother let out something between a gasp and a wail. My father's jaw clenched. My eyes burned with rage as my fingers found the hilt of my cutlass.

"There, there," Zeetan Z said. "They got pinned by boulders or shot by poison arrows. Gunting here saw it himself. Not so bad. Better than what you'll get."

"Ready, Sato?" I asked.

I signaled Jeeves and he gave me a brave nod.

"You go," Julianne whispered. Her eyes gleamed. "I'll stay back here. I think I have one last plan."

Zeetan Z started counting again. "Four . . . three . . . two . . ."

He sprang off the quarterdeck and stalked toward the mast, one hand on the pommel of his cutlass. I gripped my sword tight. The blood pulsed down the length of my arm.

"One!"

The muscles in Zeetan Z's neck flexed; his upper lip peeled away from his teeth. He drew back his sword to cut the ropes that held my parents just as Jeeves and I burst from our hiding places.

"Stand back, you treacherous villain!" I yelled.

The Fine Art of Butlering

As I said before, a butler needs to be needed.
Usually that means answering the door and welcoming
guests. In my time with the Zupans, I've done
everything from ironing Francisco's shirts to
cataloguing eighth-century relics.

As I looked up at Francisco and Helen, then over
at Ronald, I thought, "This is probably a more
dangerous task than any butler has ever had . . .
but the Zupans need me now more than ever."

I gritted my teeth, tightened my grip on the oar
in my hands, and got ready for the fight of my life.

40

Sato's Scheme!

We were out in the open now, just a few feet from Zeetan Z and his crew. We stood side by side, blocking the pirate captain from the mainmast so he couldn't cut the ropes that held my parents.

The spotlights shining down from the scaffolding burned hot and bright. At first, I had to squint to see anything. Jeeves peeled Carter from his neck and set the serpent on the deck of the ship. Immediately, the cobra began to stretch and pulse, basking in the warmth of the glowing lamps.

"I said back off!" I repeated.

The pirate captain's eyes were like storm clouds without a silver lining. His skin was pale and as clammy-looking as the belly of a long-toed salamander. Suddenly, Zeetan Z tipped back his head and roared with laughter. His entire crew fell into hysterics too, pointing and holding their ribs.

I heard my mother's voice above us: "He's alive."

"And he's here to rescue us," my father whispered.

"Hi, Mom; hi, Dad," I said with a glance skyward. My father's fingers were sunk deep into the tangle of ropes behind his back. I made a quick count of the pirates. "There are only eight of them," I called up. "You'll be down before you know it."

Two more rogues stepped into the light.

"Ten," I corrected.

Another two pirates, each with knives clamped between their jaws, slithered over the railing and stood near their captain.

"Twelve plus Gunting makes a baker's dozen," I said. "All the devils are here."

"*You're* the Zupan boy?" Zeetan Z scoffed. The muscles of his arms were thick; when he lowered them, they jutted away from his body. His voice came out low and cold and cruel. "What a scurvy scupper shrimp!"

> FACT: If the pirate captain thought he was the only person who could come up with cutting insults, he was dead wrong.

"Yes, you pig-faced buffoon," I said, "you base-souled herring. *I* am **Ronald Zupan**, the only son of Francisco and Helen Zupan, and I demand that you let my parents go!"

I drew my sword and sliced it through the air so fast that it whistled.

"Oh, you *demand* it, do you?" Zeetan Z spat. "I love demands. So easy to ignore. But you've got me curious: What makes you think you can demand anything from me?"

I took a step closer. The Liars' Club leader gave a black-toothed smile, reached a hand up to his collar, and fingered the bone necklace.

"Because," I said, trying to slow down my racing heart, "I know where the Lion of Lyros is."

Zeetan Z's gray eyes widened. He tipped back his tricorn hat and pointed his cutlass at me. It gleamed under the spotlights. His men leaped down from the quarterdeck and crowded tight behind their captain.

Zeetan Z tugged on his scraggly beard. "*You* know where the lion is?"

I forced myself to look directly into those soulless eyes. "Yes."

"Where?"

I turned to Jeeves; he lifted the crimson candle for the pirates to see.

"That is a ball of wax," Zeetan Z spat. "What do you take me for? A fool?"

"Indeed," I said, "because the Lion of Lyros is *inside* this ball of wax. It's a candle, and the 'lion lies in the light.' Who could possibly miss that clue?"

Jeeves held the candle steady, and I pressed my sword against it until the wax started to split and crumble away. Inside, it was easy to see the shape of the lion, kneeling upright.

"Oh, yes. There it is." Zeetan Z looked around at his crew with a menacing smile. "We've got the lion. Now cut them all to shreds."

There was a collective *sheenk* of pirate swords being yanked from their scabbards. The blades shone under the hot movie lights, looking every bit as sharp as our own.

"Not. So. Fast!" I boomed.

Zeetan Z held up his left hand and the pirates froze.

I rolled my shoulders back, glaring fiercely at the sea dogs. "You see, the lion is in the care of my beloved butler—who happens to be a highly skilled cricket player. A cricketeer, if you will."

"Cricketeer, eh?" Zeetan Z said, looking at Jeeves. "Test cricket? The English side? My father played for—"

"The point is," I interrupted, "he's an expert, and he's ready to throw the Lion of Lyros at the walls of this cave and shatter it into a million pieces."

Zeetan Z pondered this new wrinkle, twisting a scraggly strand of beard. "So," he said, glowering at me with those hateful eyes. "We have ourselves a good old-fashioned standoff?"

My cutlass blade danced in front of me, ready for battle. "Until you lower my parents down from the mast and agree to let us go in exchange for the lion, yes, we have a standoff."

Jeeves was ready to throw the statue at a mighty stalactite, jutting down near the port side of the ship . . . a stalactite that seemed to be a few feet farther away than it had been just seconds before.

Julianne cut the anchor cable, I thought. *We're headed downriver. If we make it out of the cave, Three-Fingered Jack and his orangutans might help us again.*

Zeetan Z didn't seem to notice that the ship was moving. He took another step toward me. "How old are you, youngster? About ten, I'd guess."

"Eleven."

"A little on the short side for your age, looks like. Skinny too. Isn't that right?"

"Not skinny," I snapped. "Wiry, like a jungle cat."

Zeetan Z sheathed his sword. "I stand corrected. *Wiry* . . . like a jungle cat."

The smell of bat guano hung thick all around him. Jeeves and I backed up. My spine rubbed against the two lines that were tied to the mast. They were all that was keeping my parents from plummeting to the deck.

"Well, Jungle Cat," Zeetan Z said. "I appreciate your offer of the lion, but I'd also like you to surrender." For the moment, he'd stopped using the strange insults from the movie script. His voice dripped with danger. "Besides, we don't *really* have a standoff, do we? Not when I've got this."

Zeetan Z plunged a hand inside his heavy red sailor's coat. His arms were so muscle-bound that he had to shift and squirm to find the breast pocket. I saw my opening and lunged for him.

CLIIIICCTCHK. Zeetan Z's hand reappeared, holding a chrome pistol. I stopped in my tracks.

"What *is* it with all the guns?" Jeeves groaned.

"No master adventurer would ever carry one," I said.

"Shut up." Zeetan Z leveled the pistol at me. "Just hand over the lion."

I glared at the sea dog, then slowly turned to face Jeeves. Zeetan Z might have been done dishing out pirate insults, but I still had a few good ones up my sleeve. "You heard the snot-bellied scalawag," I said, "give him the lion."

"Gladly," Jeeves replied.

He reared back and hurled the Lion of Lyros at Zeetan Z's hand, knocking the gun high into the air. The pirate stumbled—cursing and squeezing his eyes shut in pain.

Like a rabid lemur, I dove toward him, but I was blocked by a skinny rogue with yellow eyes. The man swung his sword with both hands, and I dodged under it, then barreled into his side, toppling him headlong over the railing.

"One down, twelve to go!" I yelled up to my parents.

I turned back to the battle to find two more pirates charging toward me from opposite sides. One had a plaster parrot attached to his shoulder; another wore a black eye patch. I fought them off at the same time, moving my sword faster than I ever had before.

Attack. Glissade. Attack-parry-riposte. Glissade. Lunge.

I pushed them back to the mast just in time for Julianne

Sato's grand entrance. She'd appeared atop a tower of crates, holding another crate high over her head. She heaved it down and it crashed across the shoulders of the man with the plaster parrot. Tin plates, goblets, and gold doubloons— all props from the movie—scattered across the decks.

"Don't touch my friends!" she yelled.

FROM THE DESK OF
Thomas Halladay

A Note on Julianne Sato

Since the moment Ronald and I arrived at 107 Oak Street, Julianne had proven herself over and over. She was a deductive genius and a kind friend. But of all the interesting ideas that young Sato had, none ended up helping us more than when she sliced the anchor cable. Now, every time we knocked a pirate overboard, they'd have to swim after us before they could try to climb back onto the ship.

   And here's a fortunate fact that Julianne probably knew from watching Josh Brigand movies: pirates are terrible swimmers.

41

Daring Rescues!

Before the pirates could figure out where Julianne had appeared from, she lifted another crate and smashed it over the shoulders of the yellow-eyed ruffian. It broke open, showering the rapscallion in fake beards and wigs.

One of Zeetan Z's tallest henchmen saw what was happening and yanked the bottom crate out from the stack Julianne was standing on.

"Sato, look out!" I yelled.

Julianne sprang to safety, just as hundreds of movie props spilled out of the crates and scattered across the decks. She held her sword in one hand and her violin case in the other, battling three pirates at once.

Attack. Glissade. Attack-parry-riposte. Attack. Attack. Attack.

After pushing another sea devil over the rail, I spun to look for Jeeves. He was chasing Zeetan Z around the mast, slicing his oar through the air. My first thought was to help him, but there were two things I had to do first.

I scanned the deck and saw both the gun and the lion. I sprinted to the gun, picked it up, and flung it into the river. When I turned back to find the lion, I came face-to-face with a woman who could have been Gunting's sister. She gritted her teeth and swung a broadsword at me with both hands. The sword whistled as the giantess thudded across the deck. It was impossible to parry the blows; my only chance was to dodge backward.

My heel hit something and I looked down to see the lion skidding into the shadow of an upturned crate.

"Ronald!" my father yelled from above. "Trip them!"

I looked up to see that he'd untied himself, and his hands were now free. He dropped his rope down to me, and I dodged toward Jeeves and Zeetan Z.

"Here," I called, tossing one end of the rope to Jeeves.

We pulled the rope tight to make a trip wire, held it at ankle height, and charged forward to upend any pirate in our path.

> FACT: The scalawags stepped over it with ease.

"I hoped that was going to be far more dazzling," I said. "I really thought that was going to work."

"Seemed like it might," Jeeves panted.

Julianne had four pirates advancing on her. They cursed and spit as they drove her back. The crew that Jeeves and

I had tried tripping approached steadily too—herding us toward the mainmast. Zeetan Z rubbed his bone necklace again as he closed in.

The ship drifted at an angle through the lagoon, toward the pyramid of bat guano.

I glanced behind us and saw another tower of movie props tottering, ready to collapse. A single plump honeybee flitted out of a gap between two boards in a crate. It flew in a series of spiraling loops and landed on my arm.

"Where is the statue?" Zeetan Z demanded.

Over his shoulder, I saw Gunting pulling himself in our direction, his broken leg dragging behind him limply.

"Where. Is. The. Statue?"

My eyes flicked toward the lion, hidden in the shadow of an upturned crate. Zeetan Z caught the look.

"There you are," he said.

He crossed the deck in big strides and quickly found it. He held the lion in one hand and his sword in the other, then stalked toward us again. We were cornered and outnumbered. I felt a prick on my arm and realized that the bee had stung me.

> **FACT: A bee sting hardly mattered now.**

"Ye tried yer luck, ye half-witted hogfish," Zeetan Z said. He was celebrating his victory by quoting lines from *Buccaneers of the South Seas* again. "Methinks this noose ends here, in agony. By truth, I might just make you cut your parents' ropes. Gentlemen o' fortune, if you be in favor say 'Aye!'"

Screams of "*Aye!*" rattled through the cave, sending the bats into a screeching frenzy. I glanced behind me. The two ropes—one attached to Helen's feet, the other to Francisco's—were tied off to a wooden cleat.

Up above us, my mother finished untying herself. She let the rope that had bound her hands fall to the deck. It landed beside Julianne, who immediately stooped to pick it up.

Jeeves was in fighting stance, keeping the crowd of pirates at bay. Julianne was staring at one of the crates; I could hear faint humming coming from inside.

"Untying your hands changes nothing," Zeetan Z called up to my mother. He let out a loud, braying laugh. "Except that now you'll be able to wave at us as you fall to the decks."

The pirates closed in, inches at a time. I looked back at the ropes and had a truly spectacular idea . . . which was also possibly fatal.

"Oh this is all so *tragic*," Zeetan Z cooed. "So wonderful."

He was only a few feet from me now. Our sword blades danced.

"Time to cut the cord," he said. "Everyone clear a landing space for the great Helen and Francisco Zupan! Mingo, roll film!"

The pirates sucked back to the rails in a wide semicircle. It took three of them to drag Gunting away. As they did, I took the chance to look at his face. His bottom lip was trembling.

One of the pirates scrambled to the top of the light tower and began working a giant movie camera. Zeetan Z took another menacing step toward us.

"It'll make a great newsreel," he said with a lopsided grin. "Master adventurers fall to their doom at the hands of devilish pirate."

I focused on the ropes. I was trying to work out my most dazzling plan ever.

"Mom, Dad," I called up, "are you ready to trust me?"

They looked at each other, then back down to me.

"Yes," they both shouted.

Zeetan Z had his sword out. "Cut them down, boy."

I leveled my eyes at the rogue. "You asked for it."

In one swift movement, I spun toward the mast, twisted the rope tied to my dad's ankles around my free wrist and held tight. Then I slashed my sword and chopped the rope, just below where I was holding it. Instantly, I was launched off my feet and went soaring into the rigging—sending my father plummeting toward the decks.

"Mom, grab my rope!" I yelled midflight.

She arched her back and swung out, gripping the rope just above where I held it. In the same second, I stretched as far as I could to slice the line tied to her ankles. Her legs kicked out and her feet swung down below her head. Now we hung side by side on Francisco's rope.

I risked a look below. Our weight had stopped my father's fall mere inches before he crashed into the deck. The rope

started sliding in our direction, not so fast this time. My father was headed back up as my mother and I came down gently. We touched the decks just as he wrapped the yardarm in a bear hug.

The pirates were too stunned to speak.

I let go of the rope. Zeetan Z's jaw dropped. For a long second, his men stood motionless behind him. My eyes darted left. Julianne was silently shimmying up the mast with the rope that my mother had dropped. She threaded it between two slats of the buzzing crate and tied it off.

The cave was eerily quiet. Then, all at once, the air went electric and the battle began again. My mother dove for the first pirate she saw and disarmed him with her bare hands.

Zeetan Z came at me, his cutlass in one fist and the Lion of Lyros in the other. I dodged backward between the scattered crates. My feet slid on fake-looking doubloons and ridiculous hairpieces.

I turned and caught sight of Julianne and Jeeves. Julianne's sword sung through the dense air. Her violin case had been shredded to pieces, but she still held the violin in her free hand, waving it like a second sword to distract the pirates, clacking them on the head every chance she got. Jeeves used his oar to block sword blows and smash the fingers of any villain who tried to climb back on the ship.

Zeetan Z came at me from the right, and I parried to the left. He swung at my head in a wide arc, and I ducked under his deadly blade. I had to get off my heels. I thrust my sword right at the pirate's ribs, and he jumped backward.

"Aha!" I yelled.

I lunged toward him. *Thrust, parry, riposte. Attack!*

He beat a retreat, and I followed him toward the stern of the ship. Just when I thought I had him cornered, Zeetan Z swung his sword at my shoulder, missing by mere inches. The blade smashed a metal camera post and sparks rained down between us. I jumped back and tumbled off the quarterdeck—staring up into the bright lights.

My sword clanged to the ground and skidded out of reach. Even worse, I'd landed just inches from Gunting. The giant looked down at me, and for a split second our eyes locked.

"Crush him, you imbecile!" Zeetan Z screamed.

All Gunting had to do was reach out one massive arm and throttle me. He could finish me in a second. But I could see that his heart wasn't in it. Instead, he just sat there, blinking under the lights.

I rolled for my cutlass, but by the time my fingertips touched the handle, Zeetan Z was already standing above me. He caressed the lion with one hand and raised his sword with the other. His cold eyes widened as he started to bring the sword down.

"Noooooooo!" Julianne screamed.

She threw her violin end over end across the ship. It

smashed into the side of Zeetan Z's head and the back panel cracked completely off, spraying torn hunks of airplane seat cushion everywhere. The villain wobbled backward but didn't fall.

His upper lip was split, and blood ran across his hideous teeth. He wiped his mouth with the back of his hand, then faced Julianne.

"I'll finish your friend," he bellowed, "then you're next!"

I snatched up my sword and crab-walked backward, getting as far as I could from Zeetan Z. Two pirates charged Julianne, but Francisco was there to help. He swung on a thick rope from high in the rigging, gathered her up in one arm, and dropped her safely on the quarterdeck.

Julianne handed my father her sword and he stepped into fencing stance. Then she did handsprings across the deck, landing right below the mast. She picked up the rope that she'd tied to the buzzing crate and gave it a single tug.

The crate lurched forward and was dashed to pieces against the deck. Thousands of angry bees burst forth in a droning swarm.

"BEES!" Francisco yelled. He picked up a tangled dread-lock wig to shield his face but never stopped battling.

The bees flocked to the brightly colored clothes and ripe smells of the pirates. The scalawags shrieked wildly. In seconds, the insects quickly attracted hordes of disoriented bats swirling overhead, squeaking when they collided midflight.

I rose to my feet and leaped onto an upturned barrel; I finally had the upper hand on Zeetan Z. But at that moment, the ship washed ashore against the mountain of bat guano. The decks rolled hard to the starboard.

The *Charming Yet Highly Dangerous Gentleman of Fortune* had run aground. Zeetan Z and I were both thrown overboard, landing midway up the enormous pyramid of guano. Between the two of us, in a soft puddle of light, sat the Lion of Lyros.

More Details from the Chapter "Daring Rescues!"

At one point in this wild melee, a shovel-faced wretch popped up right in front of me. I swung at him with my oar, but the skunk snuck his cutlass under my guard and pierced my hip. It was slight, but I was bleeding. The pirate drove me back against the port rail.

"Death to cricketeers," my enemy said, drawing back his sword.

Suddenly, a horrible shriek rang out. "I'M SNAKEBIT!"

The ruffian's weapon clanged on the deck. I looked beside me and there, clamped to the villain's leg, was a king cobra. It seems the spotlights had warmed Carter up from his torpor (just as I'd hoped!), and the serpent was feeling a tad hostile.

The attack gave me an opening to knock the pirate overboard and grab his sword for myself. So yes, I must admit, sometimes a snake *is* incredibly useful on an adventure.

42

Splendid Friends!

I choked. The smell of guano made my head spin. The mountain we'd landed on felt spongy and moist. It moved and shifted underneath my weight. I looked down and discovered a carpet of cave beetles writhing in the guano. They clicked and wriggled through my toes.

I wobbled to my feet and picked up my fallen sword. Zeetan Z was already standing, holding the high ground. Above us, bats screeched, jostling for space on the ceiling.

"This is the end of you," the pirate said. "Say good-bye."

"You keep saying that," I answered. "And you haven't been right yet."

"Third time's a charm."

The sea devil paced closer, hate burning in his eyes. Each step brought him shin-deep in the guano and sent ripples of the dreck sliding toward me. I stood strong, feet wide.

"You kidnapped the wrong two master adventurers," I said.

Our blades crashed together, and the fight was on again. We battled up and down the pyramid with millions of beetles hissing underfoot. I circled the top of the pile, but Zeetan Z held his position. The guano was like quicksand—soon I was panting, unable to catch my breath. I swung wildly and my enemy knocked my blade back. I tried again with the same result.

A horrid smile cracked across the pirate's lips. "Child's play."

He took two long strides downhill toward me. I could feel myself weakening. His sword came level with my chest.

"Your parents were smart not to bring you here," he said. "You get in the way."

His eyes longed for blood. He lunged, thrusting his blade at me. Before the cutlass could pierce my skin, I blocked him, but just barely. My arms were jelly.

Zeetan Z thrust from the left. I toppled backward and the guano slid out from under me. I skidded downhill and the sea devil approached, sneering.

"All alone, boy," he said. "Just you, me, and fate."

He lifted his sword high over his head. Had I come all the way here only to fail? Was this the end of **Ronald Zupan**? Zeetan Z sneered down at me, ready to strike, but something distracted him. He was scowling, and I turned to follow his gaze. The pirate ship leaned at an angle and my family and friends had the advantage. They fought as a unit, swinging on ropes and picking off the pirates one by one.

"Where were we?" Zeetan Z snarled, refocusing on me. "Oh yes, your last words!"

He raised his sword even higher.

"Get away from my son!" my mother threatened from the rail of the ship, kicking another pirate overboard.

The words made Zeetan Z waver again. It was only a spilt second, but a split second was all I needed. Before he could bring his sword down, I rolled out of his reach, and felt a pulse of energy ripple through my entire body. I rose to my feet, legs quivering, and thrust at Zeetan Z's chest. He parried the blow, but when he shifted, the guano swallowed him up to his knees.

"Use Bonetti's Spiral!" my father called from the ship.

I began to lift my sword over my head. Then stopped. It wouldn't work. It was too wild; my feet would sink.

"Bonetti's Spi—"

"I've got this," I called, waving him off. "I'm using Occam's razor."

I'd do exactly what Jeeves and Julianne had talked about—simple moves; the easiest answers were the best. I'd stay light on my feet and push Zeetan Z back on his heels. He'd sink, like he was being swallowed by quicksand.

Attack, riposte, attack, riposte!

Again and again I swung my sword with brand-new force. Each parry pulled Zeetan Z deeper into the loamy muck.

"You were wrong, what you said," I said. My skin rippled with goose bumps.

"What are you on about now?" Zeetan Z grunted.

"You said I was alone . . . but I wasn't. Not for a second."

I felt the pyramid shift underfoot and danced around Zeetan Z, then scampered to the top of the pile. I had the advantage now. I lunged at him once! Twice!

"*This is for kidnapping my parents!*" I yelled, thrusting my cutlass a third time.

The sea dog leaned too far back and toppled over, his thick arms flailing. The guano pyramid started sliding on top of him in waves. Half the mountain sheared off, swallowing the pirate completely.

I skidded downhill, fighting to keep my feet.

As the guano settled, Zeetan Z's head burst clear of the muck with a gasp. He was up to his neck in the ash-colored foulness—beetles scurried across his face and into his mouth.

"Ronald," Julianne yelled, "the ship is drifting!"

The avalanche of putrid gunk had pressed against the side of the *Charming Yet Highly Dangerous Gentleman of Fortune*, forcing it upright again. Free from the guano, it started to float through the cave, downriver, out of the lagoon. On top of the movie scaffold, my dad drove the last pirate, Mingo the cameraman, overboard.

I moved toward Zeetan Z, holding my nose with one hand.

"You're finished," I said.

FACT: The words didn't come out sounding very heroic with my nose plugged.

I pointed my sword straight at the dastardly dog.

"Surrender!"

"Finish me quick," Zeetan Z sobbed.

I smiled. "**Ronald Zupan** is a master adventurer, a brave swashbuckler, an exemplar of derring-do—but he's not a killer. Let cowards die a thousand deaths!"

I stepped close to the pirate and tore off his necklace of bones, then jumped over his head and ran into the shallows. Julianne and Jeeves scrambled up on the yardarm of the ship.

"Catch!" Julianne called through cupped hands.

Jeeves launched a long rope with a metal hook on the end across the distance between us. As it unfurled, its coils caught in a shaft of sunlight streaming in from a hole in the cave roof. I grabbed the hook in my free hand and held tight.

"Adventure ho!" My voice boomed through the cave.

Julianne looped the rope twice over the top yardarm of the mainmast. Next she and Jeeves gripped and dropped toward the decks. They sank slowly and I began lifting up into the air. Even Zeetan Z's crew, bloodied and bruised, scattered along the banks of the river, gasped in amazement as I soared across the cave.

When Julianne and Jeeves landed on the deck, my mother helped them reel me in. My father waited at the rail to pull me aboard.

"Son," he said, grabbing me in a hug. "You saved us."

"Naturally," I replied.

"**Ronald Zupan** is a spectacular adventurer of the highest—" I stopped midsentence. "Dad?"

"Yes?"

"I want to go on your next trip."

My father squeezed me tighter than ever. "I swear it."

I stepped back. "But not just me. I travel with a team now. And you should know, I don't leave them behind for anything. Not even in a case of mutiny."

"So you read the letter?"

"Yes," I said, "but when Jeeves and I got in a fight, I still went back for him."

My father smiled. "You trusted your heart. That's the most adventurous thing anyone can do."

"We're so proud of you," my mom added, stepping in to kiss my forehead.

Julianne crossed to the helm and took over the ship's wheel, navigating a path out of the cave. I didn't say anything, but it seemed like maybe steering her favorite movie star's ship downriver was the last step in forgetting her fear of open water for good.

Behind us, we could hear Zeetan Z screaming at his men to pull him out of the guano. I hoped that Gunting would sneak away during all the chaos and never have to deal with the terrible captain ever again.

As the voices echoed, I spun to face my friends with a saucy grin. "Hoist the mainsail!"

"We're in a cave," Julianne said, "there's no wind."

"I know . . . But just imagine—it will look extraordinary!"

We unfurled the sails, and Julianne set a course downstream. Carter snuck up behind me and bit my ankle.

"Carter, great to have you back in top form!" I said, petting his head.

Jeeves stood beside us, smiling down at the serpent. "And he saved my life in the end."

"I knew you two would be friends!" I said.

My dad stepped toward Jeeves. "Tom, I am indebted to you. You have brought my son here safely and helped rescue Helen and myself from that dastardly dog Zeetan Z."

"Only doing my duty as your butler, sir," Jeeves said. He hesitated. "But I would like to know one thing."

"Of course," my father said.

"Well . . . I've been with you for so long, why didn't you tell *me* about the Liars' Club or the FIB or your secret office? Elexander Davidson knew all sorts of things that I had no clue about."

I could see that Jeeves was hurt. My father passed a scarred hand through his thick beard. "It's true, Elexander is trusted with things connected to our work—which is important."

"But you're trusted with our sun and moon," my mother finished. "Ronald is our greatest treasure, not the Lion of Lyros."

Jeeves's face shifted. "Oh . . . I never thought of it like that. I see. Yes." He stood up straight as an arrow. "It's an important duty. Thank you."

"And may I just say," my mother went on, "I'm bowled over by that bold mustache."

Jeeves turned the color of a tomato frog. I picked up the fragments of Julianne's violin and brought them to her at the wheel of the ship.

"Mom, Dad, this is Julianne Sato. She's my . . ." I hesitated, with everyone looking at me. "*Partner* in dazzling adventures and grand schemes," I finished.

They faced her, beaming.

"I thought it might grow on you," Julianne said to me, grinning slyly. Then, she frowned. "But with Carter and Jeeves, we need a title for our whole team."

I was just about to say that we could find the perfect name on the trip home when Jeeves spoke up.

"Remember what Pemburu kept saying?" he asked. "'*You're in danger, gang.*' But we *were* the danger, in the end, weren't we?"

"The Danger Gang," Julianne mouthed slowly.

I smiled. "Jeeves, only a true master adventurer could come up with a name like that."

"It certainly does have a ring to it," my mother said.

"Perfection," my father agreed.

The diesel generator sputtered, then died. The lights snapped off overhead, but we could already see sunlight filtering in through the end of the tunnel. It was a wide arch, with a massive curtain of vines and ivy hanging down in front of it.

Julianne glanced behind us.

"Troubled, Sato?" I asked.

"What if the pirates chase us?"

We all peered back toward the underground lake. The frantic screams and the calls of screeching bats were fading into the distance.

"I think they'll have something else to worry about," I said.

"What could possibly be more important than not letting us escape?" Jeeves wondered. "Zeetan Z seems to truly hate it when people slip out of his clutches."

"Somewhere in the pile of bat guano is the Lion of Lyros."

Jeeves looked dumbstruck. Even Julianne was shocked.

"But . . . it's the most valuable artifact known to man," she said.

"Not if my last deduction is correct."

My mother looked at me and raised her eyebrows.

"What?" Jeeves asked. "What is it?"

My parents started to giggle.

"Tell us," Julianne pressed.

I grinned at my parents. "When I heard the words 'the lion lies in the light' coming from my mom, I wondered about the lion hiding in the candle. A few minutes later, when I cut the wax with my sword and saw the figurine posed upright, I was certain."

Jeeves shook his head. "I'm not sure I follow just yet."

"I think I've got it," Julianne said. She pulled the wheel to the right to trace the curve of the river. "If the lion was standing up inside the candle, then the clue that 'the lion lies in the light' would be wrong. It wasn't lying down."

"Exactly," I said. "So if the lion wasn't lying in the light, it must have been *lying* in the light. Meaning that the Lion of Lyros inside the candle is a fake."

"Dazzling deduction," my mother said. "We knew it might be stolen, so we made a copy."

At that exact moment, hundreds of leafy vines draped across the sails of the ship. We glided out of the darkness and into the warm sunlight. The monsoon had passed. The birds were out and called joyfully through the jungle.

We blinked like newborn wallabies, but as our eyes adjusted, the whole crew felt overjoyed to be away from the cave. No one was happier than Carter. He slid forward to bask at the bow.

The afternoon sun blazed red as it set over the wild jungle. From the decks of the ship it was hard to tell one tree from the next, let alone decipher any of Borneo's many secrets. Somewhere in that wilderness there were clouded leopards, leeches, and ravenous mosquitoes. Somewhere there was a papaya farmer—whose eyebrows I hoped were growing back—and a strange hermit with an army of orangutans.

The jungle held more excitement than even **Ronald Zupan** knew what to do with. There were trees to climb, sinkholes to dive into, and vines to swing on. But for one perfect moment, our adventures were finished.

Soon there would be more swashbuckling and derring-do, but for now, I was happy right where I was: leaning comfortably against the quarterdeck, with my father jotting notes in his adventure journal and my mother singing softly nearby, surrounded by two friends and one excellent snake, watching the sun disappear below the hills.

With pink streaks spreading across the horizon and wisps of fog tangled in the treetops, a hornbill honked in the distance as if to ask, "Isn't this spectacular?"

"Indeed," I said.

THE END!

Farewell

Quite a fine way to finish, if you ask me. End on a
high note. Of course, knowing Ronald, he'll want to
write an epilogue. He'll insist on trying to tie up
loose strings. But as his butler and confidant, I'd
recommend against it. Why ruin a good ending? Less
is more, am I right?

Right?

Oh, fine!

Brilliant Epilogues!

Once we'd left the cave behind, my parents revealed that the real lion was also hidden in the atlas—in a second secret compartment cut out from the book's binding.

"It's time we find some new hiding places," my father said, laughing.

"Or maybe a museum?" Jeeves suggested.

"So we have to find Three-Fingered Jack again," Julianne said.

"You *found* Three-Fingered Jack?" my mother asked, her voice filled with surprise.

We anchored the *Charming Yet Highly Dangerous Gentleman of Fortune* in a sluggish backwater where the pirates wouldn't find it and began our inland trek. For hours, we beat back vines and spiny ferns with our swords, telling and retelling the many mysteries of the past four days as we plunged deeper into the jungle.

When darkness fell, we still hadn't found Three-Fingered Jack, but we *had* managed to stumble upon the tree with flamingo-shaped fungus five different times. The mosquitoes were growing ornery, and we were just about to set camp for the night when Jeeves's foot caught on a snare, catapulting our entire party into the treetops.

Which is exactly where Three-Fingered Jack found us. He offered us a place to rest and as much of his famous stew as we wanted.

> FACT: Everyone was so hungry that we ate two bowls each.

The next morning, as we got ready to go back to the ship, I set the necklace with three knobby bone pieces in Three-Fingered Jack's hand. "I think these belong to you."

"Aha! Those must be the phalanges from my index finger!" he gasped. "They'll be good luck for me and my orangutan army, I'd bet!"

"You're still going after Zeetan Z?" Julianne asked.

Three-Fingered Jack nodded excitedly, rubbing his hands together. "It will have to be soon, though. This jungle is too filled with odd happenings for my taste! Just yesterday a giant blimp soared over my tree house."

My parents locked eyes.

"A blimp?" my dad asked. "What color?"

"Silver," Three-Fingered Jack said. "It flew in wide circles all day."

"That's no blimp," my mother said, "that's the Zupan zeppelin, *Zuppelin*. Elexander must have come to rescue us."

Three-Fingered Jack tied the necklace around his neck. "In that case, I still have a few flares for my flare gun if you want to signal them!"

Soon, the fruit-throwing orangutan army began to beat on the roof of the tree house. After quick good-byes—and thanking the primates for helping us with Gunting—we cut a path out of the undergrowth and onto the dirt road, headed toward the river. Every half mile, Jeeves shot the flare gun into the air.

An hour into our hike, we came upon the wreck of the Rome.

"You landed this plane?" my father asked.

I gulped, eyeing the long smear of scorched iron.

He whistled and turned to my mother. "Landing in a jungle! My love, I *told* you we should have taken him with us."

My dad clapped me on the back, and my mouth dropped open.

FACT: All this time it had been Helen rejecting my adventure applications.

She knelt down beside me, her blue eyes glistening. "I'm sorry . . . I only wanted to protect you."

"I wanted to protect you too," I replied. "That's why I came."

"Well then," she said, squeezing me close, "from now on we'll just have to protect each other."

Jeeves was loading another flare when a giant shadow loomed above us. We craned our necks to see *Zuppelin* hovering overhead. Mr. Sato leaned out of one of the windows and waved.

"*That's* why Elexander came," I said. "Your grandfather must have rushed to the hangar the second he heard that we left. It probably took them this whole time to get here."

No sooner had the words left my mouth than a rope unfurled to the ground. In no time we were all aboard *Zuppelin*, sharing the story of our adventure once again. I noticed Julianne studying something out the window, and she waved me over.

"Look," she whispered.

We huddled together and she pointed down to the ground where the road had crumbled and left a red scar in the jungle.

"Stop the zeppelin!" we cried.

Without offering an explanation, Julianne and I harnessed ourselves to the ends of two thick cables and had the others lower us down to the jungle floor. Once we hit the ground, we scrambled across the silt and debris until we found Jeeves's buried motorcycle. We quickly fastened the cables to the undercarriage of the motorbike and climbed on top.

"Now lift!" we yelled up.

The zeppelin angled skyward and the trusty motorbike lifted out of the mud with a tremendous *slurp*. As the *Zuppelin* flew higher, Julianne and I soared above the jungle canopy—standing on the underbelly of Jeeves's motorbike—until we reached the river. We could see the pirate ship from above, her loose sails flapping in the breeze.

My parents called down to me, "Ronald, come with us! We'll sail home!"

No sooner had they said it than they executed two perfect swan dives, splashing down into the river below. As I readied myself to dive after them, Julianne gave her grandfather a signal to hoist her back aboard the zeppelin.

"I'll fly back," she said. "Maybe by the time we land, my

grandfather will be done yelling at me." She leaned close and wrapped me in a hug. "I'll also have time to write the whole story in my adventure journal."

"Be sure to use India ink," I said with a smile.

She gave me a wink and I leaped off the motorbike and down into the cool water. I swam to the *Charming Yet Highly Dangerous Gentleman of Fortune* and climbed aboard to meet my parents as the zeppelin turned toward home.

And so ended our adventures in Borneo, but there's one last moment worth sharing. Three weeks later, the three Zupans sailed into our local harbor. We were greeted at the docks by Julianne, Jeeves, Mr. Sato, Elexander, and, of course, my dear snake, Carter.

They brought me a birthday cake for the one I'd missed, and even though the party was simple, it just so happened to be the most extraordinary celebration I've ever had.

In the midst of this perfect evening, a rugged-looking fellow dashed down the gangplank and rushed toward the ship.

"It's in one piece!" he yelled. He kissed the bow, then bounded aboard in just a few long strides.

"You must be Ronald Zupan," he said to me, swallowing my hand in both of his.

"In the flesh," I said, tightening my grip.

"Yes! Yes, and I'm Josh Brigand! You've seen my movies?"

I shook my head and kept my hold on his hand.

"But you've heard of me? And you and your friends have rescued my ship! Julianne told me everything—I can't thank you enough!"

I released his hand. "Good, because I have two requests."

"Name them."

"First," I began, stroking the spot where my mustache would soon be reglued, "I'm planning to embark on a journey with my partner in grand adventures, Julianne Sato, to search for some underwater artifacts that are very important to her. We'll need a ship."

"Any time you like and for as long as you want," Brigand said. "As long as the timing doesn't interfere with *Buccaneers of the South Seas*. We're still trying to figure out how to finish the movie without those trained bees."

"Have you considered using trained *orangutans*?" Julianne asked.

The actor's eyes lit up.

"But first there's the matter of my butler, Jeeves," I went on. "He had a letter, accepting a job with you."

Jeeves coughed. "Ronald, if I may—"

I waved him off. "No, Jeeves, let me finish. Mr. Brigand, I promise you will never find a more loyal, kind, and brave man in all the world. I want you to promise to treat him well."

"Alas," the movie star said with another gleaming smile, "this second favor I cannot do."

I scowled. "Why not, Bridgeman?"

"Because," he began, "and, by the way, it's *Brigand*— anyway, the gentleman called me a few days ago and said he decided to keep his old job."

My eyes flashed to Jeeves. He stroked his new mustache and gave me a sly smile.

"It seems that there's more of an adventurer in me than I once thought," Jeeves said. "Besides, the FIB stole my lucky cricket bat from the house. I'll need your help to get it back."

"Never did understand that game," Josh Brigand muttered.

"It's really quite simple," I told him. "It all starts with the wickets, which are . . ."

A breeze fluttered in the sails, promising a cool night.

"Should we move this party indoors?" Mr. Sato asked. "I have ice cream in the freezer."

With the Zupan home still in disarray, we headed to 107 Oak Street. **Julianne Sato**, **Ronald Zupan**, and **Jeeves** boarded the motorbike where **Carter** waited, coiled in the sidecar. And even though we never went faster than a Siberian walrus climbing a volcano, we were smiling the entire ride.

THE END!

FROM THE DESK OF
Thomas Halladay

One Last *Last* Thing . . .

As we headed to the motorbike, Ronald handed me
a gift he'd found aboard the ship during the
homeward sail. It was a hat—a prop from the pirate
movie. Inside, on the lining, he had stitched the
words, **"To Thomas Halladay, aka Jeeves—adventurer,
cricketeer, friend."**

    I set it on my head. "Nice hat," Ronald and
Julianne said at the same time, smiling at me. And I
like to think they're right.

FACT: Ronald Zupan is a master at getting the last word!

THE END!

FROM THE DESK OF
Thomas Halladay

Correction: "The End" is two words.

Fine . . .

END!

Acknowledgments!

Just like Ronald Zupan, I'd love to think that I was the solo leader of this expedition, but that's far from the truth.

First, big love to VCFA—the warmest incubator for creative people on the planet. Alan Cumyn, Betsy Partridge, An Na, Tom Birdseye, Uma Krishnaswami, and Tim Wynne-Jones: you made me a better writer at every turn.

The children's book community is a progressive, supportive, and kind-hearted collective. Shouts to Aaron Hartzler, Ben Esch, Estelle Laure, Cassie Beasley, Mac Barnett, and M.T. Anderson.

To Sheryl Scarborough, Ingrid Sundberg, Jeff Schill, Caroline Carlson, Nicole Valentine, Erin Barker, the Bev Shores crew, the Dystropians, and everyone who read this book in its infancy: I'd wrestle crocodiles for you. Matt de la

Peña and Varian Johnson: I'm eternally grateful for your advice and friendship.

Brian Jacoby and Sam Mehan: you pick the jungle and I'll be there. Rachel Hylton and Mary Winn Heider are my trekking mates—endlessly patient and fiercely brave. To the extended Parker familia and the Portland crew: our tales of derring-do inspire me daily.

Sara Crowe is a superagent who believes in the work of her clients down to her bones. Mary Kate Castellani is a dream editor—razor sharp, encouraging, and insightful. To the whole Bloomsbury team: it's been a true joy.

Miles of gratitude to my personal Danger Gang: my sisters, Gina and Anna, who have a deeply inspiring passion for the natural world; my mom, who gifted me a love of stories spun by moonlight; and my dad, who taught me that the most dazzling schemes are the ones where everything goes haywire. Lastly, thank you to my sweet Nikta—for endless patience and spot-on advice. I love you immensely.

++Steve

When the movie star Josh Brigand is kidnapped from his latest film premiere by the FIB, a branch of the dreaded Liars' Club, the Danger Gang races to the rescue. Will they be able to survive a poisoning poet, a band of Roman candle–wielding thugs, and thousands of feral foxes to save their friend?

When we arrived at the theater, we saw a red carpet lined with a crowd of photographers, autograph hounds, and rabid fans.

"I'll be across the road at Ridgemont Hall," Jeeves said. "See you after."

He disappeared into the surging crowd and I swung to face Julianne. "Sato, the masses await."

I offered her my arm and she took it with a smile. Side by side we glided into the glow of floodlights and flashbulbs.

"Those are the kids who brought Brigand's ship back from Borneo!" someone yelled.

"You two," a photographer cried, "turn here!"

Julianne and I spun around, both smiling wide. All eyes were on us. It was too bad my parents couldn't be there to see it.

"What are your thoughts on *Buccaneers of the South Seas*?" a reporter called.

"Well," I said, striking another bold pose, "clearly there would be no movie if the Danger Gang hadn't—"

Halfway through my sentence, the whole crowd turned away to watch a stretch limousine glide up to the curb. Light from the popping flashbulbs bounced off its tinted windows.

"It's *him*!" someone yelled.

The door swung open and a man with a stubbly chin and aviator sunglasses exited the car. The crowd went wild— failing to realize that Sato and I were the *real* adventurers and the man they were gawking over was nothing more than a handsome, charming, internationally beloved actor.

"Josh, who designed your tuxedo?" one reporter yelled.

"Where's Isabella Montoya?" another called. "A little bird told me she didn't like the final movie!"

Julianne cupped her hands around her mouth. "Josh, we're down here!"

Brigand looked in our direction and his face lit up. "Julianne! Ronald!"

He strode toward us—scribbling autographs, hardly looking at what he was signing—then scooped Julianne up in a hug.

"Ronald," he said, clasping my hand and raising it high for the cameras, "so happy to see you! Why haven't you been coming for tea and cake at my estate with Julianne and Old Sato?"

Before I could answer, he was dragged off for more questions. I scowled at Julianne. "You and your grandfather go to tea and cake with Jimmy Blockhead?"

She leaned close. "It's *Josh. Brigand.* And yes, every Friday. He's been inviting you, too."

I frowned. "Then why is this the first I've heard of it?"

"Because you always say his name wrong," she said, "and you don't *like* him."

She had a solid point, but that didn't make it sting any less.

"I like *cake*, though!" I snapped.

Moments later, Brigand returned and whisked us inside. The noise of the crowd faded as we stepped through the glass doors. In the lobby, a concession girl carrying a tray loaded with candy, soda, and striped popcorn boxes rushed toward us.

"Popcorn? Cola? Peppermint Patties?" she asked.

"Thanks," Julianne said reaching for one of each.

The concession girl turned to me. I narrowed my eyes and gazed straight into the windows of her soul.

"Let me ask you a question. Who do you think is more impressive: an actor who *pretends* to be an adventurer, or a boy who defeats a wretched pirate while sword fighting on a pile of bat dung?"

Her only response was a confused stare.

"Let me phrase it another way," I said. "Imagine you were going to ask someone for an autograph—"

Julianne elbowed me in the ribs—a technique for getting my attention that she relies on a little *too* often.

"Ronald," she said, dragging me away, "you're acting *particularly* weird tonight."

"I was just making small talk," I replied. "I wanted to see if we had similar interests."

"No," Julianne said as we followed the buzzing crowd down the theater aisle, "you wanted her to say that you're more adventurous than Josh."

I shrugged. "Well . . . *that* would be a similar interest."

Brigand sat down in the middle seat of the middle row. There was a spot reserved for Julianne on his left and one for me on his right.

"This is so exciting!" Julianne gushed as we sidestepped to our seats. "Josh, you must be thrilled!"

"And a pinch nervous," the movie star confessed, rubbing his hands together. "I put everything into this film. What if the crowd doesn't laugh in the funny parts or cry in the sad parts, or fall in love with the brave hero?"

"Very possible," I said, only half listening. "They could hate it . . . or worse yet, ignore it all together."

Julianne shot me a look. "Don't listen to him, Josh. I'm sure it's great. And I'm so flattered you added my idea about the fruit-throwing orangutans!"

The actor chewed his lip silently. A few seconds later, the lights dimmed and the red velvet curtains pulled back to reveal a wide shot of a jungle.

Everyone in the theater clapped as giant letters flashed across the screen:

CAPSTONE PICTURES PRESENTS
BUCCANEERS OF THE SOUTH SEAS

Written by . . . JOSH BRIGAND
Directed by . . . JOSH BRIGAND
Starring . . . JOSH BRIGAND

The jungle slowly dissolved into a man standing at the helm of a ship.

"So we meet again, Cannonball Island," said the man on-screen (who was also the man sitting beside me).

The camera pulled back to reveal a parrot pacing on a nearby perch. The captain rubbed his chin and gazed into the distance.

"The last time I saw your shores I left a piece of my heart behind."

The parrot squawked. "*Akkk*—Princess Esmeralda—*Gaaak.*"

"It's *Queen* Esmeralda now," the man corrected. "The rose of my heart's garden. The diamond of my eye."

"Sounds painful," I muttered.

"*Shhhhhh,*" Julianne hissed.

Brigand sat with his fingers gripping his knees, leaning forward, mouthing every word. I could pretty quickly deduce that I'd need sustenance to power through this drivel. I reached across the actor for some popcorn, but Julianne swatted my hand away.

"How long is this movie?" I asked.

"Capstone wanted me to cut it," Brigand said in a hushed voice. "But I stayed true to my creative vision."

"Meaning?"

"It's three and a half hours."

I sunk in my seat. On-screen, the swashbuckler and his parrot recited a love poem together.

FACT: It was going to be a long night.

Mistaken Identity!

Before Ronald even gets into his thoughts on *Buccaneers of the South Seas*, let me just come right out and say: it could have been better.

Okay, fine. It stunk.

Watching Josh talk to a parrot for the first hour was . . . slow. Then there were chase scenes and swordfights, but it was all just sort of a blur.

I'd been excited to see the actress playing Queen Esmeralda, because I read in a newspaper that she did her own stunts, but all those parts must have been cut. Instead, she just sort of *appeared* at the very end and I hate it when characters just show up like that.

For Josh's sake, I hoped other people would love his movie, but by the time the credits rolled, the theater was half-empty. I jumped up to give a standing ovation as the lights hummed to life.

Julianne's clapping jolted me awake. I shook out my stiff legs and looked at the movie star seated beside me. His skin was slightly green, and his teeth didn't gleam quite as white as usual.

"What's the matter, Brickman?" I asked.

"They hated it," the actor cried. "My heart and soul are in every frame of that movie, and they *hated* it!"

I gave him the sort of skeptical look Jeeves gave me, back when I tried to dig a secret tunnel under his bedroom.

"Your heart and soul are in *every* frame?" I asked. "Even the scene where the drunken buccaneer confused a sea cow with a mermaid?"

"It was supposed to be funny! Didn't you think it was funny?"

I was saved by a skinny teenager in a crimson uniform at the end of our row.

"Excuse me," he called, "can I ask a favor?"

Brigand's face softened a little. "What can I get you, young fellow? An autograph for your favorite chum? A publicity photo signed to your sweetheart?"

The theater employee looked away, scuffing his toe against the carpet. "Oh . . . I was just going to . . . I have to sweep this row."

The actor's whole body sagged and he started trudging up the aisle and out of the theater. The crowd of photographers was long gone. So were the fans and the studio executives.

We neared the glass doors of the theater, when a voice came from behind.

"MISTER BRIGAND! MISTER BRIG*AND*!" It was the chirpy candy girl we'd seen before the show. She was holding a silver platter and rushing toward us. "I was supposed to give you this when the movie let out!"

We all looked down at the platter:

BEST ACTOR, WRITER, *and* **DIRECTOR AWARD**

Presented by
the Guild of Actors and Show People

"Look!" Julianne said. "An award from GASP! That should cheer you up!"

The actor hung his head, running a finger across the engraved lettering. "I . . . I sort of . . . *invented* the Guild of Actors and Show People. To build buzz."

FACT: Creating a fake organization just to impress people sounded like my type of idea.

"Well done," I said, stroking my upper lip. "Maybe I should start a club and name myself *Adventurer of the Year*. Or better yet, *Adventurer of the Decade!*"

Julianne rolled her eyes and spun away. "Let's just get some ice cream."

Josh trudged toward the street holding his platter. I could see that the concert hall across the street had closed up already, but there was a light on in the tea shop two doors down.

I started toward it. "I'll get Jeeves!"

"Wait, I want to talk to you again really quick," Julianne said. "Josh, you okay?"

Brigand had plopped down in the middle of the red carpet and was using the silver award to inspect the lines around his eyes. Julianne pulled me back inside the theater lobby.

"Ronald," my adventure partner said, "could you be a little nicer to Josh? He's had a rough night."

I glanced sideways at her.

"And call him by his *real* name?"

"Fine," I said. "But you have to admit that movie was absolute—"

"LET GO OF ME, YOU BRUTE!"

It was Brigand's voice, echoing behind us. We turned to see him being dragged, kicking and screaming, off the curb by a gang of thugs in bandit masks. They shoved him into the back seat of a black sedan.

"STOP!" the actor yelled. *"HELP!"*

Julianne raced toward him, and I bounded after her. The driver's side window of the sedan rolled down, revealing a familiar-looking man with a square jaw and overgrown eyebrows. He held up a stun gun, crackling with electric pulses.

"Not another step, kiddos."

We skidded to a stop in the middle of the street.

"Sorry, Ronald Zupan," he said in a flat, thudding voice, "we're kidnapping your beloved butler."

"That's not my beloved butler!" I yelled back. "That's just some world-famous movie star!"

"LET HIM GO!" Julianne yelled. *"JOSH!"*

The driver of the car glanced into the back seat. "Of course it's your butler. He has a tuxedo! And he's carrying a platter—probably for holding cocktails and appetizers!"

"My butler is British! . . . And *bald*!"

The villain glowered right at me, then sneered. I recognized those teeth immediately.

"I know you!" I said. "You're the FIB rogue with the terrible breath!"

"Breath? *What?*" the man said. "No! I'm Deadly Dirk Grimple—the one with the cool sunglasses!"

"The breath was more memorable," I said.

Dirk Grimple squeezed the stun gun again, and the blue electric pulses crackled with energy.

"See you later, Zupan," he said, "*if* you can find us!"

With that, he rolled up the tinted window and jammed on the gas. The car's wheels smoked and screeched as the devilish fiends raced away.

STEPHEN BRAMUCCI fell in love with stories and adventure at a young age. In the years since, he's braved a flash flood in the Ecuadoran Amazon, hiked for days without food in the Australian outback, and rowed down the Mekong River in a Vietnamese boat (called a sampan). Steve loves connecting with wild animals during his travels, and a percentage of his proceeds from this book have been donated to the Borneo Orangutan Rescue. He lives in Laguna Beach, California.

www.StephenBramucci.com

@stevebram

ARREE CHUNG is the author and illustrator of *Mixed*, *Ninja!* and *Ninja! Attack of the Clan*, as well as an entrepreneur. That means he's a full-time dreamer who thinks of ideas and makes them happen! When he's not working on ideas for stories or businesses, you can find him playing basketball or riding his bike around the San Francisco Bay area.

www.arree.com

@arreechung